'Jackie Morris and Tamsin Abbott are spell-makers. These are sonorous tales, iridescent with enchantment and power. Stories of transformation, loss and defiance, exploring that much-forgotten border between the natural and supernatural worlds. The illustrations, made on glass, are luminous, remarkable things'
KERRY ANDREW, author of *We Are Together Because*

'*Wild Folk* is a wondrous weaving of story and image, glass and ink, dream and song, created together by two makers at the height of their huge powers, who also happen to be dear friends with one another. Born of love and collaboration, the art here holds light that spills and fills, and spaces in which to breathe and swim'
ROBERT MACFARLANE, author of *Is a River Alive?*

'A glorious and unforgettable book told masterfully through the perfect combination of words and images. Exquisitely beautiful, it will sing to your very soul'
LIZ HYDER, author of *The Twelve*

WILD FOLK

ALSO AVAILABLE BY JACKIE MORRIS

The Unwinding and Other Dreamings
Feather, Leaf, Bark & Stone
The Wild Swans
East of the Sun, West of the Moon
Song of the Golden Hare

ACCORDION BOOKS

Fox
Otter

WILD FOLK

Tales from the Stones
Jackie Morris & Tamsin Abbott

Jackie Morris & *Tamsin Abbott*

First published in 2025

Unbound
An imprint of Boundless Publishing Group
c/o Ketton Suite, The King Centre, Main Road, Barleythorpe, Rutland, LE15 7WD
www.unbound.com

All rights reserved

Text © Jackie Morris, 2025
Illustrations © Tamsin Abbott, 2025

The right of Jackie Morris and Tamsin Abbott to be identified as the authors of this work has been asserted in accordance with Section 77 of the Copyright, Designs and Patents Act, 1988. No part of this publication may be copied, reproduced, stored in a retrieval system, or transmitted, in any form or by any means without the prior permission of the publisher, nor be otherwise circulated in any form of binding or cover other than that in which it is published and without a similar condition being imposed on the subsequent purchaser.

Design by Daniel Streat, Visual Fields

A CIP record for this book is available from the British Library

ISBN 978-1-78965-210-9 (limited edition)
ISBN 978-1-78965-230-7 (trade hardback)

Printed in Türkiye by Özlem Print

1 3 5 7 9 8 6 4 2

For Love, Land and Story
To Jeremy and Mary for beginnings
To Susan Cooper and Alan Garner always
To Mike, Nettie and Dougal for ever

TAMSIN ABBOTT

*Old stones
stand in wait
chalk streams
myth's gate*

The Smith's Tale

The Black Fox's Tale

The Owl's Tale

The Selkie's Tale

The White Hare's Tale

The Silver Trout's Tale

The Ravens' Tale

FRAGMENT I	13
FRAGMENT II	43
FRAGMENT III	67
FRAGMENT IV	87
FRAGMENT V	133
FRAGMENT VI	161
FRAGMENT VII	185
Finding the Words	209
The Glass	213
Supporters	217
Notes on the Authors	236
Acknowledgements	239

THE SMITH'S TALE

FOR ISABELLA DAY,
WHO WORKS MAGIC WITH METALS

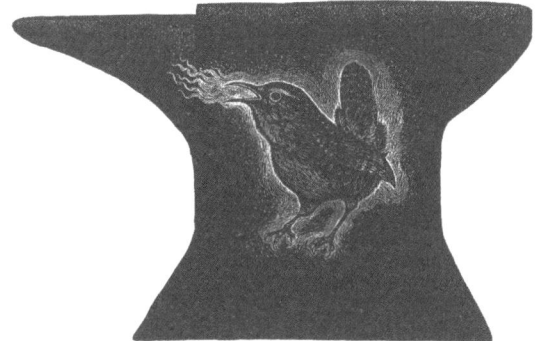

The sound.
A soft whistle of air against feathers.
A soul song.

He heard it as he came to the lake's edge at the setting of the sun. Low light painting the water into a golden mirror, and not a breath of wind to wrinkle the surface.

At the lake's edge reeds blushed, emerald-silver in the fading light. Above the reeds small insects danced like smoke. All the world silent, except for the whistle of white swans' wings.

He had come to the lake to find peace and cool after a long day in the forge. Late summer, the air so hot, the forge fire hotter still. All day working the metal with hammer and anvil and muscle and heat. So he had come to the lake to wash away the toil of the day.

Still as stone, crouched in the reeds, he watched the swans circle. Curious to find swans here in summer. They were winter visitors.

A harrier flapped a low hunting dance to his left. No threat to the swans. A bittern boomed, small birds hopped through reed stems, finding pathways in the ever-moving maze.

Down flew the swans, almost touching the water, white bodies mirrored in the gold, clear surface, then at a movement beside him, they lifted. His brothers had joined him, stealthy and silent, bows notched with short arrows. Silently they watched together.

The Smith's Tale

They saw the three birds land. Wayland pushed his brother's arm down as he raised his bow. They saw the three birds land, and in that moment when day tips over into night, by the setting of the sun, by the rising of the full moon, they saw three swans swim to shore and shake their aching wings and stand, dropping heavy, feathered cloaks of white and rising from the water. Three women, naked, beautiful.

The brothers watched as the women waded into the darkening water, moving sinuous as fish, languid. Then, one by one, the brothers crept through the spaces in the reeds, stealthy as foxes, and each reached out and took a feathered cloak.

Still, they watched as the women swam, and now bats and moths danced above them.

When the women returned to the shore, they found the three brothers. Wayland held out his cloak first and, with a wild shyness, Alwyse stepped towards it. He draped feathers around skin. As the feathers fell, clinging around her smooth body, she looked into the smith's dark eyes and her swan skin became a white dress that hung heavy around her body.

His brothers drew back; both feared the beauty of these wild creatures, both longed to take one for a wife. Both knew that if they offered the feathered cloaks, the women might choose to flee to the skies. Neither wished to take that chance. So they folded and folded the feathered cloaks and as they did so, the two women cried, as if each fold caused them pain.

Wayland turned away and beside him walked his swan bride, her hand in his. Behind them his brothers, struggling under the weight of their feather bundles, and behind them the swan sisters, for they could do nothing now but follow.

The brothers hid the swan cloaks deep in the hollow bole of a wych elm in the heart of the dark forest, as far from any water as possible, and so the swan maidens were forced to stay with them. Alwyse wore her cloak as a dress that glowed with a sheen of freshly preened feathers. Wayland loved her. And she loved him.

*

The Smith's Tale

Before her arrival, Wayland had always made beautiful things. Now his work took on a new heart. He worked the metals, melding together and forging and shaping. His true language was in the working of metal, and what had been beautiful before, now took on a wild magic. All day he worked the metal and it would sing to his touch. People came from far and wide to see and to learn and to buy.

He made teething rings and rattles, cold metal, smooth that could pacify the most fractious of babies. He made wedding rings and torcs of such beauty that only those with the truest bond were brave enough to purchase and to wear them. He made axes so light and so sharp a skilled woodsman could fell a tree with three blows. He made weapons, but only if he felt that the man or woman who would wield them would do so with courage and grace, weapons so fine the owner would always be cautious to mar their beauty with spilled blood, would look for other ways to resolve conflict.

He made brooches that carried heart and soul, armlets that brought subtle protection to the wearer. His fame spread. If a king could have an army with weapons forged by Wayland, it was said they would be invincible, and he would be a great king indeed. But Wayland had more interest in ornament than armament, was more content with village life than court life. So he stayed with his bride in his forge in the village, and each piece he made was a step towards making a perfect gift for his swan bride. But each piece he made was never good enough for Wayland, nor, in his mind, for her.

And every evening after work they would walk together at the setting of the sun to the lake's edge and there they would happily wash away the heat and the dirt and the dust of the day. Together they would turn and spin and twine in cool water.

Together they would lie on the banks and watch the moths dance, wild things come down to the water to drink, and the world turn and the stars make patterns and pictures in the sky.

Sometimes, at dusk, Alwyse would shake out her feathered dress, stretch wide her arms and fly, restless in spirit and bone, high over the wildness as he watched, earthbound. Always she came back to her love. He would stand as she lifted on great wings into the air. Each time she flew, a small piece of his heart would go with her.

And this was how she found her sisters' feather cloaks. A small glint of white, like a star in the fresh green of the wild wood, deep in the bole of an old wych elm. The new spring leaves were still sparse on the trees. She marked in her mind the place as she circled low, and the next day she went to her sisters. She told them the way through the wood, and then she went back to Wayland.

It was early spring. The sisters bided their time. The sisters told their husbands they needed to go into the wild wood to gather wild strawberries. Deep in the wood they searched for the wych elm and as they neared the centre, a wild white swan called from above the green leaves.

The sisters came to a clearing. At its heart was the wych elm. They climbed together through its branches, reached down inside the dark bole and pulled out the two heavy feathered cloaks. Spiders and moths had made their nests among feathers. Fallen leaves snagged like gold brooches on feather barbs. Each woman shed her clothes and wrapped the feathers skin-tight around, preening and smoothing and stroking the beloved feathers. Cloaks became wings, women became swans. They leaped up into the sky, calling, calling, joining their sister, rejoicing in flight, and far away in the village the three brothers heard the wild swans calling, rejoicing in flight, and knew what had happened.

The Smith's Tale

Across the forest they flew, circling high, so high. But Alwyse flew down to land beside the forge. She did not need to say anything to Wayland. He knew that she wanted to go, needed to go. Each year he had felt her soul grow restless. He knew that only the entrapment of her sisters had kept her beside him through many years. And love. Always love.

She kissed him.

'I will return,' she said, 'with the curlew, next winter. For now, we will go east where my sisters can be free.'

His brothers had seen the circling swans. They too had come to love their beautiful swan brides. Their shame at having hidden the feather cloaks, keeping the women as prisoners, land-bound, made them angry. They ran towards Wayland screaming, 'Hold her, chain her, the others will not leave without her.'

Wayland wrapped his strong arms around his swan wife, holding her tight, even as her wings began to open. He whispered, 'I love you,' then lifted her high into the air and threw her with all his strength, up and up, and fingers became feathers, arms became wings as she rose into the sky, circled three times and headed east.

*

All summer long, Wayland worked at his forge. He learned more every day. He learned how to build the fire so that the heat would be perfect, how to temper the metal, to mould and to fold – into his work he put his love and his trust, his longing and loneliness, his skill and his courage, and each piece he made was finer, purer and more perfect, apart from one small flaw, the dark part of his heart and his mind, the small nagging doubt that whispered that she would not return. Always this held him back from beautiful perfection. Though no one but him would ever see this flaw.

His brothers packed up their belongings and set off to follow the swans' flight, with ropes and nets and bows. As they walked past the forge, they had only dark looks to offer to Wayland. They knew their beautiful swan wives would never return willingly. Angry with Alwyse, the brothers set off to hunt the swans, to bring them home. But Wayland waited. He would wait by his forge, throw himself into work, until she returned with the first snows.

People came to buy, marvelled at his work. He had no interest in it once it was made. It was the making of it that he loved, not the thing itself. Once made, it was out of his mind as he moved on to the next piece.

*

The King of Sweden sent ambassadors to visit Wayland. He had heard great tales of the smith's artistry. They took home swords, spears, brooches and rings, shields, axes, all that he had.

The King of Sweden sent his general-in-chief to request that Wayland come to the royal palace and become the king's own smith.

Wayland said no.

He worked for no man and for all men, but mostly for himself. He loved his home and there he would stay, he said. He was waiting. For someone.

The King of Sweden sent soldiers.

They came in the night while Wayland was sleeping. They

bound him in chains and carried him to the court in a cage made of iron.

Again, the King of Sweden offered Wayland the position of King's Smith. Again, Wayland refused. He knew he would never willingly make a weapon for this man's hand.

So the king ordered the smith be taken to an island. Soldiers carried him again in a cage made of strong iron. Here Wayland found all his tools had been brought, all his ore, all his wood. Five soldiers held him down while another sliced through his hamstrings, leaving him in agony, no longer able to walk. The king watched. They used a sword forged by the smith's own skill. It was a clean cut.

'Now,' said the King of Sweden to the smith, 'work for me, or die.'

They left him, trapped on the island in a sea of agony and despair, shattered, broken.

*

One day in late autumn a wild white swan was seen high over the village. She landed by Wayland's smithy.

The fires were cold.
No sound of metal on metal.
Tools all gone.
Silence.

A child watched as the swan preened her white feathers then took to the air. She said later that it looked as if the bird was crying.

The girl watched until the swan became a pale flake of white in the distance, against a sky dark as a bruise. Then more and more specks appeared, a great flock, hundreds, thousands, falling down from the sky, feather flakes, and the child realised the first snows of winter had come, drawn by the feathered strength of the swan.

*

Alone on the island Wayland was lost, adrift in a sea of pain. The wounds in his legs were clean but deep. They healed fast. The wound in his heart grew. He could not walk, would never walk again.

Every morning a boat came, bringing him enough wood to stoke the forge, some food, fresh water. It took away whatever work the smith had completed. Only through work could he find refuge from the pain of his broken heart, his shattered mind.

Every day he crafted work so beautiful, arm cuffs twisting with birds, torcs elegant as a swan's neck, rings that glowed. But he would not make swords. He would not make spears. He would not make arrowheads.

The Smith's Tale

The King of Sweden was not happy. He came again to the island. He threatened to break Wayland's hands on the anvil if he refused to make weapons. Wayland stared back at him. He handed the king a hammer and offered up his hands.

But the king knew that even if Wayland wouldn't make swords, he could sell the beautiful ornaments for high prices and buy weapons, so he threw the hammer down and walked away, leaving Wayland to continue with his work.

Wayland grew accustomed to his loneliness. There was a peace of mind to be found in the absence of people, to be found in the sounds of the island. Every evening he would sit beside the dying fire of the forge and watch the skies and listen for the sound of the wind in a swan's wings. He would watch the patterns of the stars making pictures in his mind's eye, new designs, beautiful jewels. He would sleep and dream of swimming again in the cool water of the lake with his love. Every morning, he would wake again, alone.

And then one day, as he was seated beside his anvil winding and twisting the finest metal to make an armlet, a feather fell from the sky and drifted, in a slow, rocking movement, down, down, landing in the palm of his outstretched hand. A single feather, dove-grey, delicate.

The hammer went still, silent. Wayland looked up. Overhead a small flock of gulls. He listened. All around him, birdsong. He had not noticed before. Now the air was thick with song, the trill of small linnets, the rise and fall of a curlew's call, screaming, distant gulls, piping oystercatchers, buzzards, raven, stonechat, chough, skylarks, high and distant swallow call, sparrow chitter, plovers and doves.

He held the feather between his finger and thumb, studying the delicate shape of its curve, the soft down, the strong shaft of it. As he moved his hand, he felt the feather catch at the smallest breeze, as if it wished to lift from his fingers and fly again. An idea began to grow in his mind.

*

The Smith's Tale

From the bars of the cage that had carried him over to the island, he forged himself strong wheels mounted on a low platform, a curious structure. He kept it hidden from the eyes of the king's men. With this he could move more easily around the island, propelled by his strong arms. And he could crawl. Wayland began to explore his island prison and everywhere he went, he searched for feathers.

On the beaches he found salt-stained feathers abandoned by seabirds, sometimes the dark feathers of a raven, black as night. In the woods he found blue flashing feathers of jays, soft grey pigeon and dove feathers, pheasant feathers like fire, and long striped tail feathers. He found soft serrated owl feathers, great wide buzzard feathers, eagle feathers as wide as his hand, and red-tailed hawk feathers that scooped the air beneath them as they were lifted, desperate to be back in the air.

Beside a small pool fed by a waterfall at the island's heart, he found the jewel feathers of a bright kingfisher. He swam in the pool, loving the feeling of easy movement, of feeling whole again, weightless, fearing the memories it brought to the surface of his tattered mind. When he crawled from the water, he found a tiny pile of merganser feathers, the wrappings from the meal of a fox or a mink. He took them to add to his growing hoard.

He did just enough work each day to keep the king's men happy.

As the collection of feathers began to grow, Wayland recognised the futility of his task. So many feathers, colours, sizes, shapes. He sat and watched birds, observing how they flew, looking at their wing shapes, from the great scooped fan of buzzard wings to the arrow dart of a swift. Each wing shape, each body shape was different.

One morning, waking early, crawling to the door of the forge to watch the sun rise, he found the still-warm body of a young wren. He thought it must have been left there by a hunter, a weasel perhaps or a stoat. Such a fragile and tiny creature. He marvelled that such a huge song could rise from so small a bird. He pressed the wings between finger and thumb, fanning them out, careful not to break the feathers. The bird's tail feathers were like splinters of copper wood. He studied the fashion and form of the wing, trying to see how muscle attached to bone, feather to flesh. He thanked the gods for the tiny, feathered gift, spurned by the stoat, no more than a mouthful for a hungry animal, then he clipped its wings and added the feathers to his collection.

The Smith's Tale

An osprey came to the island for a while. Beautiful killer. He watched it rise on heavy wings over the water and lower itself with deadly accuracy to pluck a silver sewin from the sea, then lift into the air, wings pushing upwards to carry the weight of the bird and the weight of the fish. He wondered if his arms could ever lift him up. Doubt. His biggest enemy. And still he picked up every fallen feather.

*

Now he began to beat out a fine golden thread. Slowly, in secret, by firelight, by moonlight, he began to draw together the gathered feathers, binding them with a golden thread so fine, so light, into a huge pair of wings.

All through the short nights of summer, the long nights of winter, he hammered and threaded and wove metal and feather until in his hands there grew the most marvellous wings, made from feathers cast aside by all the birds in the land.

As Wayland worked, watched only by mice and wayward woodland creatures, he looked like the strangest of land-bound fallen angels.

Finally on Midwinter's Day, just before dawn, he finished. His wings were huge. Heavy. Beautiful. By the rising of the sun, he wheeled his chair to the top of a small cliff. He shrugged his way into the bright metal harness that fit tight and snug against his strong body. He strapped light cuffs around his wrists.

It was not a long drop. High enough to give him some lift. High enough to kill him should he fall.

Wayland sat on the low cliff edge, wings strapped to his back, and closed his eyes. He thought about the metal, the scent of the forge fire, the sound of the anvil. He remembered the soft touch of his swan wife's hands, the feel of her feathers, the brush of a wing. He smiled. With his eyes tight closed to the world, he thought he could hear above him the soft whistle of the wind through a swan's wings.

He leaned over the edge, spread wide his arms to scoop the air and fell,

      down,

            down,

                  down,

and he could feel the wind in the feathers, for that was all that they were, not wings, just a tattered collection of cast-offs, a hope tied in metal bonds, the weight dragging him,

      down,

            down,

                  down.

And then he heard again the sound of whistling wings, air through feathers, opened wide his eyes and saw, above him as he tumbled, a wild white swan circle down, and at the same time he felt small claws catch at his back, and the wind came beneath his outspread cape of wings and lifted Wayland up, up, up towards the light and the swan and love.

The Smith's Tale

They circled the island once, wingbeats matching in harmony, then flew out across the sea, west towards Albion. Here they flew over the land until they came to a place where a great white horse was carved onto the hillside – chalk horse, charger, dragon horse.

When they landed, Wayland shrugged off his winged harness and his wife knelt beside him, arms wrapped around him. On his back they found the smallest of wrens, tiny copper bird, clinging with thorn feet. She had thrown her strength to him, given her will to help lift him. Why, he did not know, until later, much later, he remembered the small body he had found, whose feathers he had added to his wings. But now, gently, the smith's great hands held the bird, felt its small heart pound, then steady, then stop, all strength gone.

*

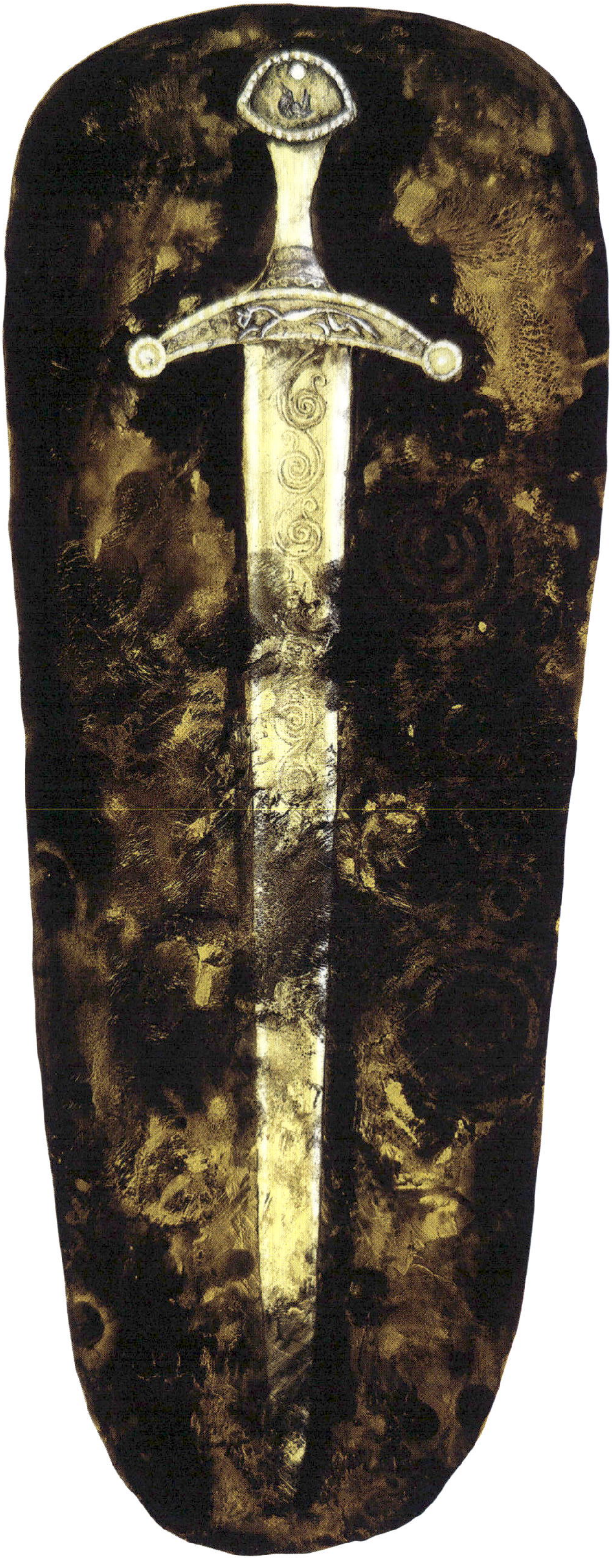

The Smith's Tale

Here, on this ridgeway, Wayland and his swan bride made a new home and here Wayland again worked metal and flame to fashion one last weapon. He made a sword, tempered with flame, metal and magic, beautiful, sharp, smooth, elegant. Into the forge's fire he placed the small body of the dead wren. Its courage formed part of the weapon, its strength and the heart of the bird gave the sword its voice, made the sword sing. A sword with a soul. A sword to end war and bring justice. A weapon that could be wielded only by one who was brave, true and just. A wise sword to bring people together, to end war. Unadorned, except for a small wren, carved into the pommel. He named the sword Excalibur.

*

Together Wayland and his swan bride lived in love and peace. He made little now, but when he did craft something, his skill shone through in the making. He spent his days shoeing horses, great gentle creatures.

In summer, the forge was silent. Every spring, when the swans began to trace feathered paths across the sky, Wayland would take down and shake the feather cape that hung on the wall. Together they would preen and shape his wings, and then his wife would lift them over his broad, strong back. Together they would leap into the sky and together they would follow the ancient pathways east towards the furnace of the rising sun.

Dragon hill
morning wren
chalk horse
nightingale

*Moon rise
swan rests
night falls
bird's nest*

Full moon
cloud shadow drift
stars bleached
shapeshift

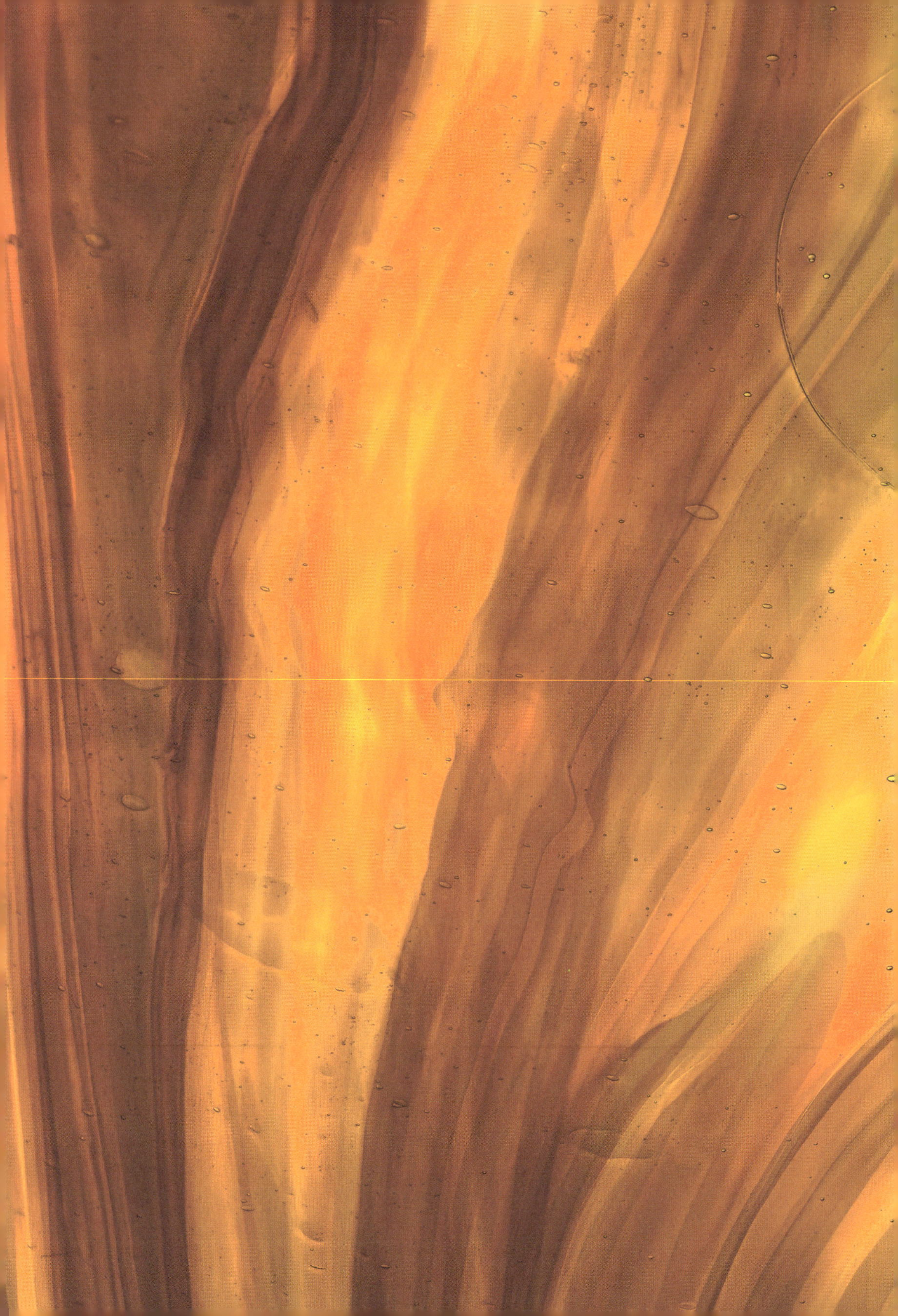

THE BLACK FOX'S TALE

FOR TAMSIN,

WHO ILLUMINATES THE WORLD

The black fox lived in the place of deep greens in summer,
leaf-light, air textured with birdsong. So many small voices,
and waves of song that rose and fell like a tide with the light.
She shifted into shape
formed from smoke.
Wild spirit
out of ashes
into the heart of
the wild wood –
shadow
shade
guardian.

She remembered: sunshine on skin, wind in her long dark hair.
The time before flames.

If she became a symbol of courage, resistance, it was despite
him, not because of him.

The Black Fox's Tale

Born in the wood, she grew with the wild things. Their home, a small clearing, a cottage built against a stone so ancient its original purpose was lost to the memory of humans, even as the birds remembered. And, if you listened long and hard enough, the stone could tell you its stories, written on its skin with lichen and moss. All around the house, trees spoke of green life above and below the ground.

Her lullabies were birdsong,
her guardians the wild wood foxes
and woodcats.

She never learned to read books but was wise in many ways.
She could read the trees,
knew when rain would fall by the turn of a leaf.
Birdsong was a familiar language.

She loved the various songs of the small wren, dunnock and the dippers who sang with the stream that tumbled over river-stone and root. She measured time in the coming and going of birds, the seasons of trees, the flowering carpet of woodland floor, the fruiting berry, moss and fungus.

At heart she was wild.

There were other folk who made their homes in the woods: charcoal burners, coppicers, greenwood chair and bowl makers, fishermen and miners who mined for ochre, iron or coal. She had few friends among the humans, preferring the company of the small, wild lives.

For the most part she was left to live in peace, unless someone required a remedy – for fertility, or to help a restless soul sleep, for a cough or a fever, or the burning aches in joints brought on by hard work or old age.

She had grown wise in herb-lore, so some thought her to be a witch, but if she had any magic about her it was the simple wisdom of holding a seed in her hand and knowing if it would thrive or if it would fail.

Under her quiet stewardship the woodlands grew, as she planted acorns, cobnuts, ash keys, willow wands, sweet chestnuts, crab apples and wild raspberries, stretching forest into field, keeping saplings strong, weaving honeysuckle and dog rose into hedges, warding them from grazing sheep and wild deer.

The Black Fox's Tale

Some questioned why she lived alone. She was young. Long dark hair, dark skin, amber-eyed like a wild hare. Uncanny eyes, some thought. The forest folk filled the silence around her with stories, some kinder than others. Her father, they said, had been a highwayman, robbing travellers who foolishly entered the woodland pathways. This, they said, was how he had bought the land on which the woodland grew around the cottage.

Truth was, her father was a freed slave from far across the world. Her mother was a highwaywoman, who dressed as a man to pursue her trade. Of her mother's origins nothing was known.

She remembered the stories her father told her – desert-born, he described the shifting sands, treeless lands, landscape shaped by the wind's hands and how the winds were given names, had their own seasons. He spoke of how you could see for miles, not like the woods, where the trees kept the focus close. He told her how the wind moving through trees sounded to him like the roar of the ocean over which he had travelled, held in chains, prisoner, property, until he won his freedom. He taught her the names of the stars, their patterns and stories, in his language and her mother's, two worlds colliding. Although he loved her, he left, like a swallow in autumn. She missed him.

She hoped, at one time, to go and search for him, but she knew her soul was bound and rooted to this small refuge of wild wood.

The Black Fox's Tale

    Buzzard mew
      raven cry
       fox bark
        green dark

        wind in the trees and the sound of rainfall,

      stream flow
     otter holt
      kingfisher flash
     heron roost
    hare's form
   home.

When the fire came and took the little house in the woods, the wild folk who lived in the bounds of the trees had their suspicions. Words were whispered, rumours grew. A few, but only a few, said she had brought the flames down upon herself.

The woodland haven was encircled by lands belonging to the estate of the Great Hall. Built over generations, the hall rose out of grounds tamed to impress, rich with statues and fountains, gardens clipped and shaped, glasshouses filled with exotic plants taken from lands owned by the family around the world. The house itself reflected light from its many windows and wealth from its walls. They owned plantations in India, the West Indies, and each year saw their wealth grow, from cotton and sugar, built on the backs of exploitation and slavery.

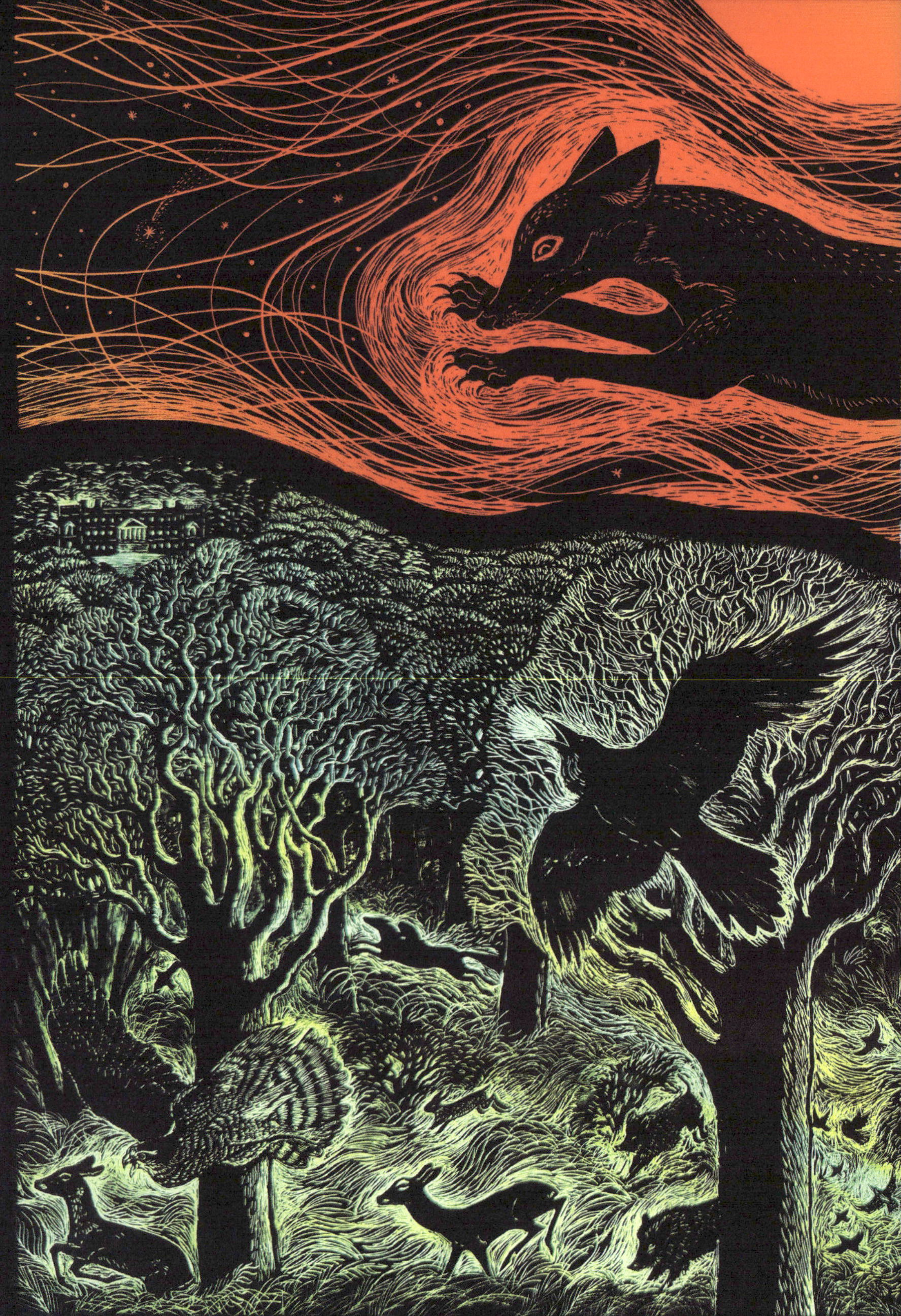

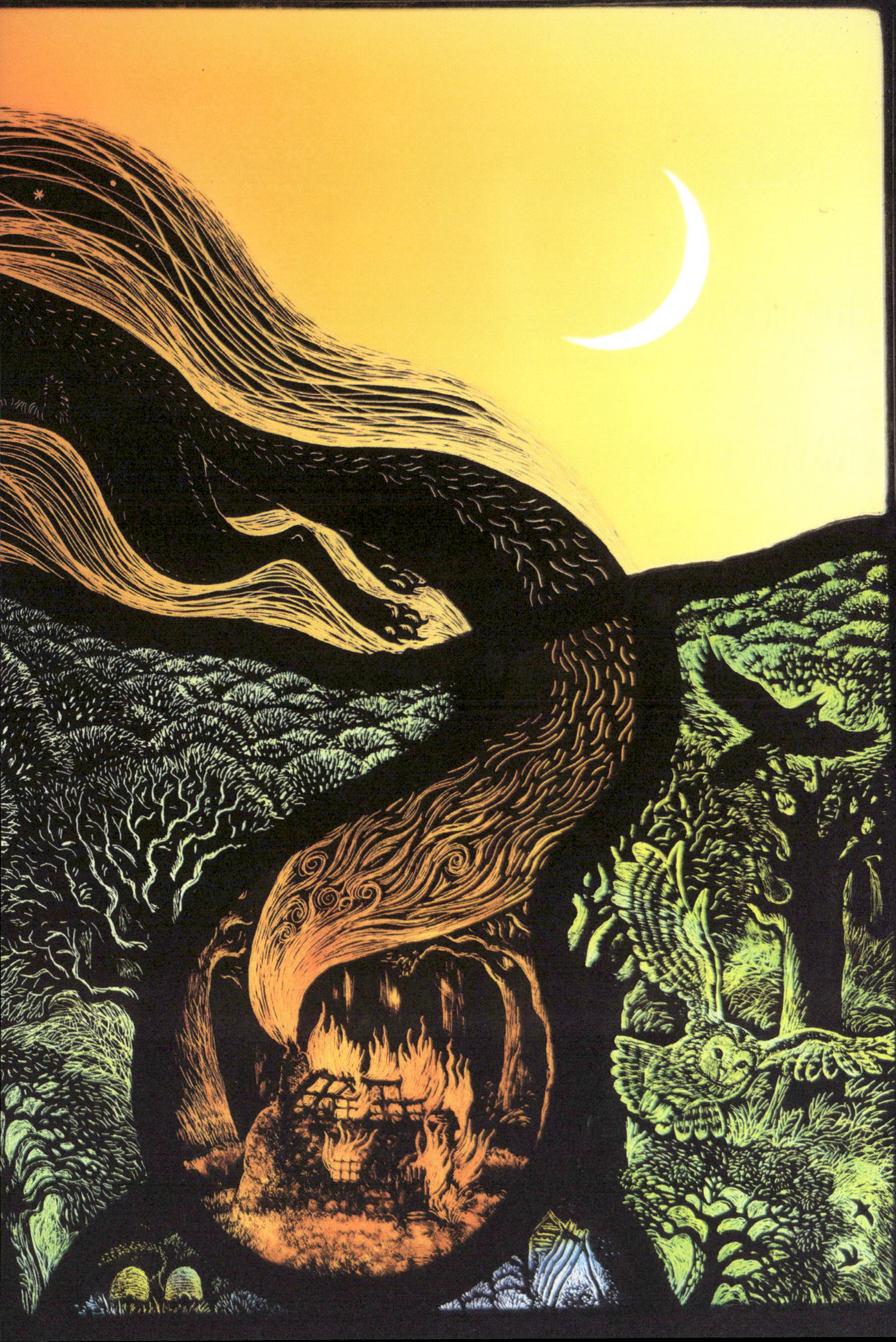

In this house the young master grew up.

When he was young he heard of the child growing in the woods. He would steal away to find her, and for a while they became playmates, until his parents discovered his secret. She was beneath him, they said, little more than a beggar, a gypsy, and he was forbidden to enter the woods again.

So he grew, tutored to accept his rank and his privilege, unquestioning. He accepted his place in the feudal society. If he wanted something, he took it. His family owned land, ships and people, and everything was there for him to exploit. This was his right, by birth. His family, even the Church told him so. Lord and master, dominion over all. When sent away across the ocean, to learn more of the management of the estate, he took to the cruelty of life on a plantation with vigour.

On his return home he took to drinking, waiting for his father to die, so he could step up to his place. He spent money on fine wines, fine horses, gambling. He loved to hunt, deer and hare, fox and pheasant, with horse and dog and hawk, and was often frustrated when his quarry took refuge in the dense and tangled wild wood.

And sometimes, he would go deep into the wild wood, hide in the shadows and watch the woman who lived there. Somewhere, deep inside the man, his child self remembered the friendship, the love he had felt in her company, perhaps the only real love he had known in his life. He loathed how this made him feel as she was so far beneath him, and yet he felt she drew him to her, like a moth to a flame.

When his father died he became the lord of all the estate. When, shortly after, his mother also died, he decided the time had come to take a wife. He rode into the wood, took the finest

The Black Fox's Tale

necklace he could find from his mother's jewel box, rich with emeralds that echoed the green of the forest, gold, diamonds. High above the leaf canopy the red kites wheeled and marked his progress through the woodland track.

She welcomed him with an offer of tea, declined his offer of marriage. She saw in his face the echo of the young man who had been her friend, but recognised the cruelty that lived behind the eyes and the smile that travelled only as far as the mouth.

He took her rejection, wrapped it in anger.

When he could not buy the woman he tried to buy the land, but again she turned him away. He wanted to clear-cut the wood to make a park. The trees blocked his view. And he wanted her to go. For weeks he neglected his work, hiding in green shadows, watching her, haunting the clearing at night while she slept, watching her bathe in the clear-water pools, dark skin, dark hair. She reminded him of his slaves. And he knew that she knew he was there. That she was aware of his presence, but refused to feel fear. She hoped he would grow tired of his games, even as his eyes hunted her and his longing grew more intense.

Night-time
moon dark
deep green
owl hoot
fox bark
spark
flame
fire.

The Black Fox's Tale

It was the day after the fire that the black fox first appeared. Almost as large as a wolf she was, with stars in her amber eyes and a tail like a crescent of the dying moon, they said. She soon became a creature of omen.

One by one the black fox picked off all the hens in the Great Hall's farm. He would see her at twilight in his garden, set the hounds to run her down, but always she eluded them.

He began to suffer ill fortune. One by one his ships sank and his investments failed. His servants began to slip away as his mood grew darker. They feared his cruelty; they feared he was cursed. At night the black fox would call from his garden, a challenging shriek, like the ghosts of the dead calling from hell, troubling his dreams, even if he managed to sleep.

Things fell apart and he slipped towards madness. He vowed to kill the black fox. The look in her eye reminded him of someone, but he would not say who it was. So he vowed to kill her.

He bought, with the tattered remnants of his fortune, the swiftest hunter that money could buy, he unleashed what was left of his pack of hounds and at dawn they rode out.

They say the black fox came to meet him, goading his hounds with her fearful cry. They say she ran the hounds ragged until their paws were bloody and their bodies broken. By dusk light they could still be heard baying to the rising moon. All night he rode, as fast as the horse would carry him, but no matter how fast they galloped, the black fox always ran faster.

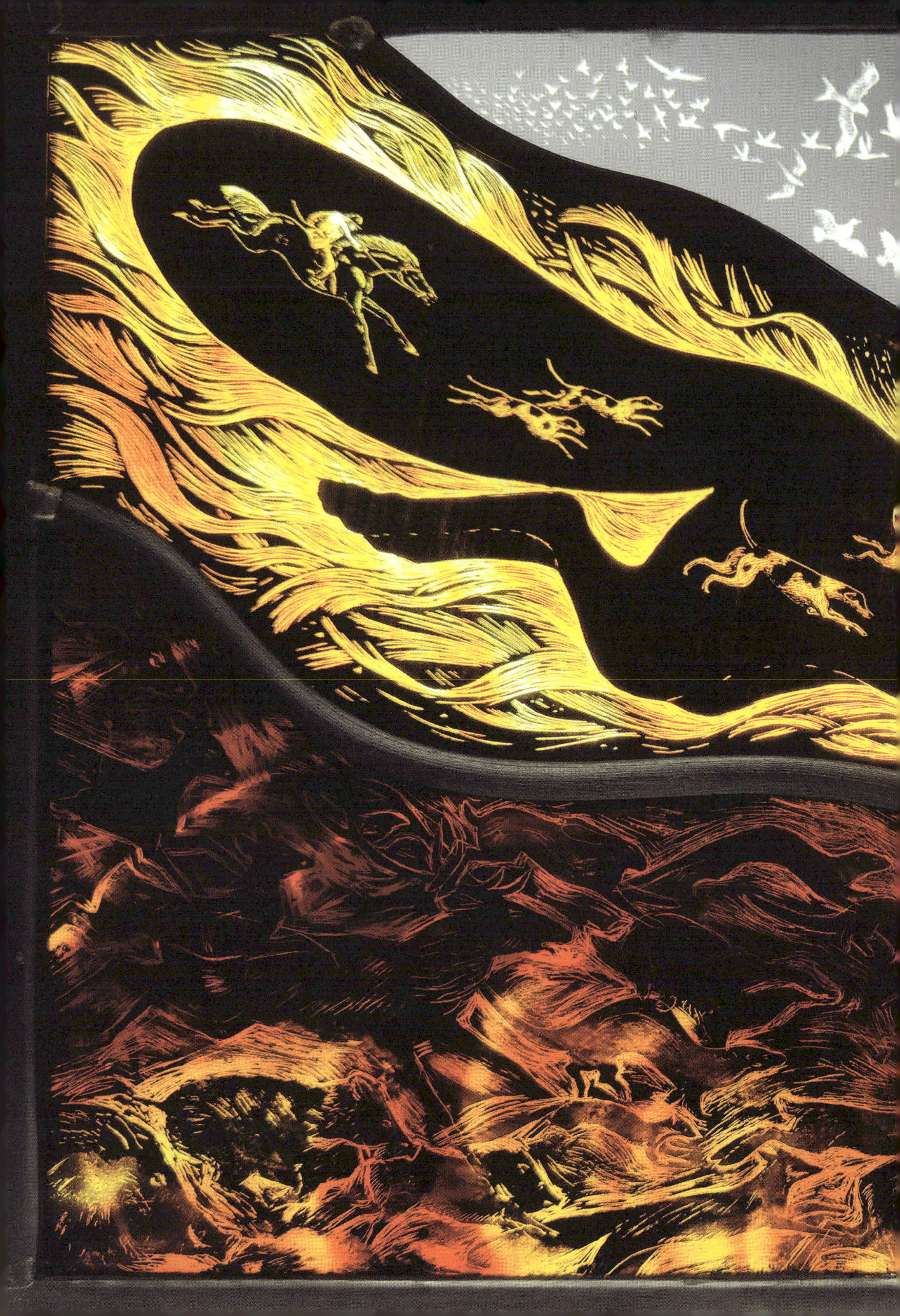

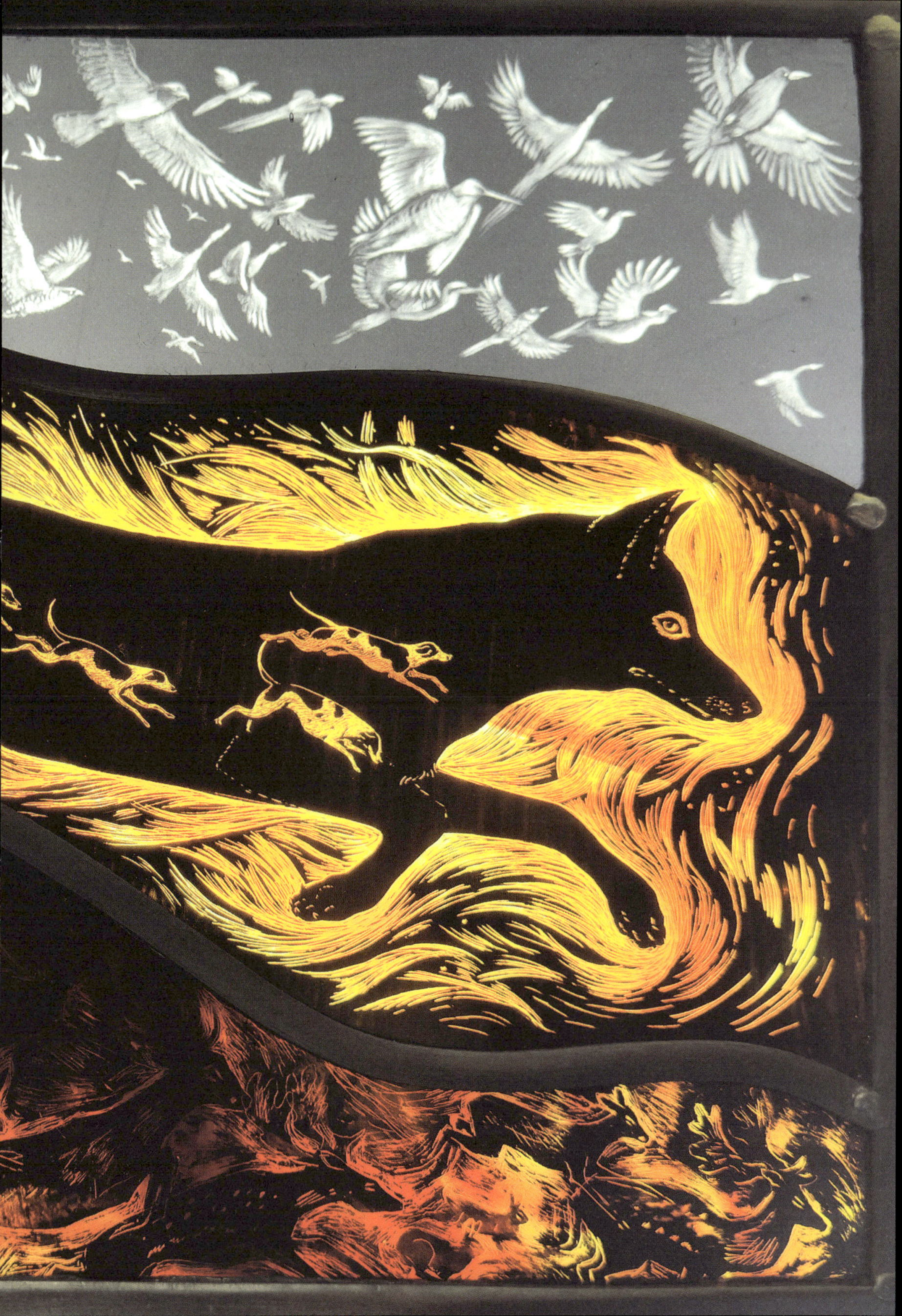

By first light the next day he was gone, his horse was gone, his hounds were gone. Some say he rode so fast he crossed over the river that runs between this world and the next. Others say the devil took him.

The black fox still wanders through the gardens of the manor house, but now the wild wood trees have taken it for their own, seeding the lawns with sapling oaks, climbing ivy over the statues and fountains. The Great Hall's windows are blind now, the stone walls tumbled in ruin.

Men fear sighting the black fox. They think her a creature of ill omen, the devil's familiar.

Women know better.

No one could say exactly when it began, but women began to wear a black fox, hidden, stitched into their clothing, on a chain around their neck, a brooch pinned beneath a scarf, inside a hat. They drew the shape of her in dark charcoal, in hidden places in their homes, above a girl-child's crib, to protect the home, to protect the heart, to protect the life, against the cruelty of some men.

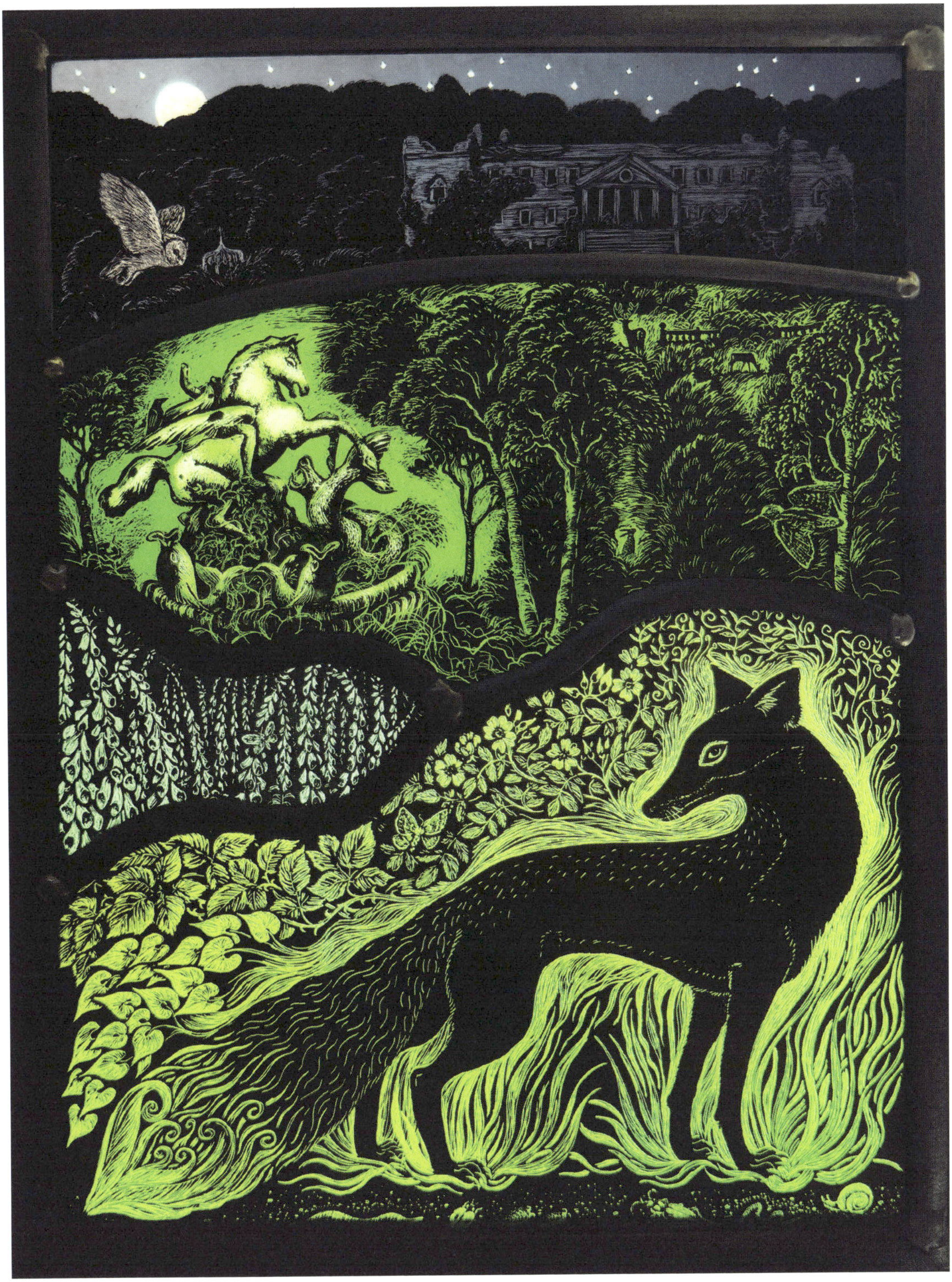

*Catkins
collar dove
snowdrop spears
foxglove*

*Bramble scratch
tear of briar
sting of nettle
fox fire*

Winter crackles
branch creaks
lichen patterns
stone speaks

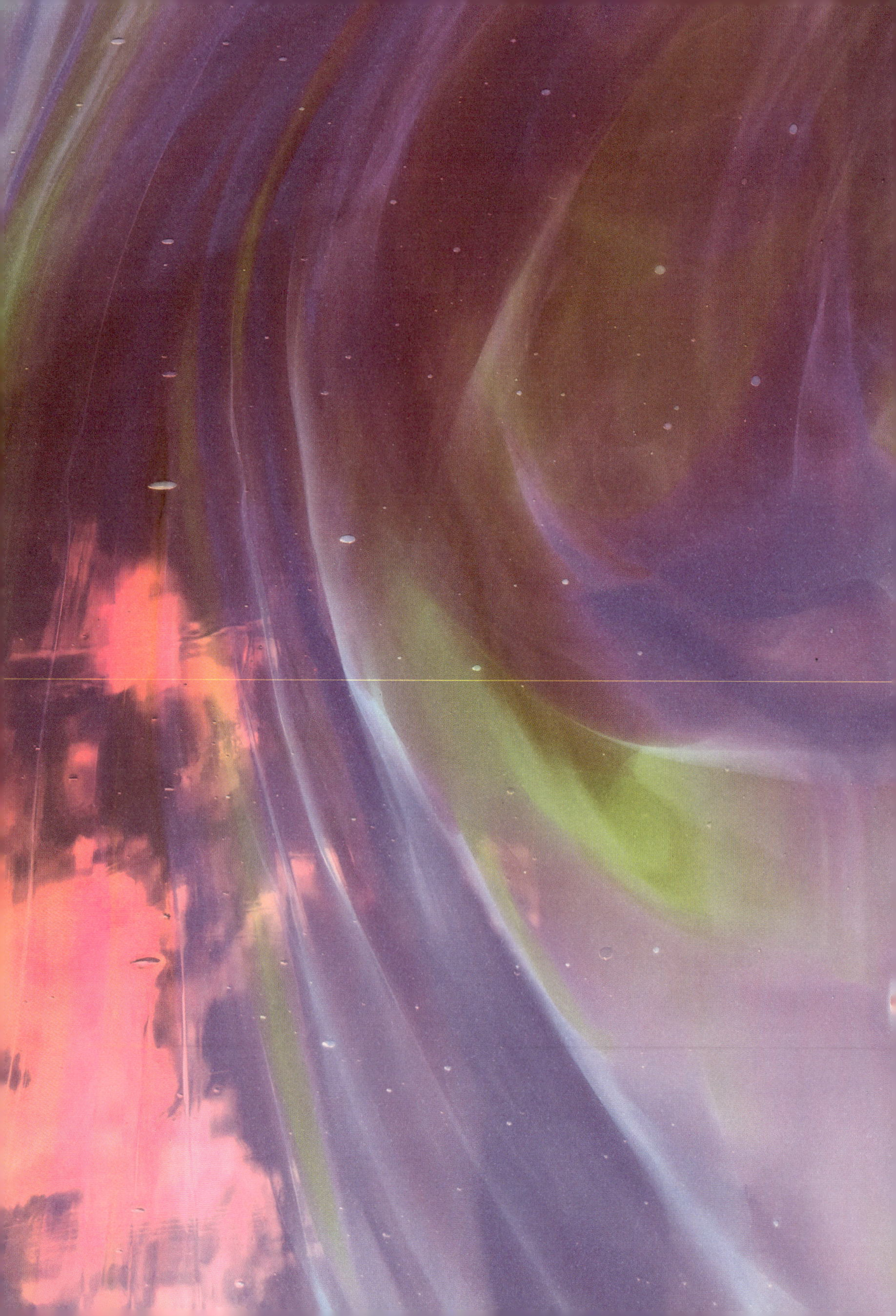

THE OWL'S TALE

FOR ALAN GARNER,

ALWAYS

He did not ask permission, either of my selves, nor of the wild gods, when Math tore me from the mountain's side and wove his spells to bind broom and meadowsweet and the flowers of oak and shaped them into woman.

He knew nothing of how ancient I was, nor how beneath the earth we connected, spoke, in a slow chemical language of green, connected in ways he could not begin to imagine.

He neither understood nor cared that I left behind me so many of my children.

He made me woman, skin meadowsweet cream, pale, hair gold as broomflower, eyes green as leaves and heart of oak. I felt now the sun on my skin as once I had taken its sweetness into my leaves. The light bit into my eyes.

Lleu took me as his wife. He fell in love with the woman who rose fully formed from the land, fashioned by magic to be perfect for him in every way. Every way. In his way he loved me. I loved the scent of the soil, the feel of rain on my flesh, on my tongue, the touch of the wind.

He took me to a castle with walls of stone, uprooted from the earth, like me, shaped, like me, into a new unnatural form. Like me. I was given as a gift to this man as some would give a bunch of flowers.

People said when I entered a room a honey-sweet scent would fill the air.

I missed the taste of earth, minerals, feeding on sunshine, the kiss of moonlight. I learned the names of colours.

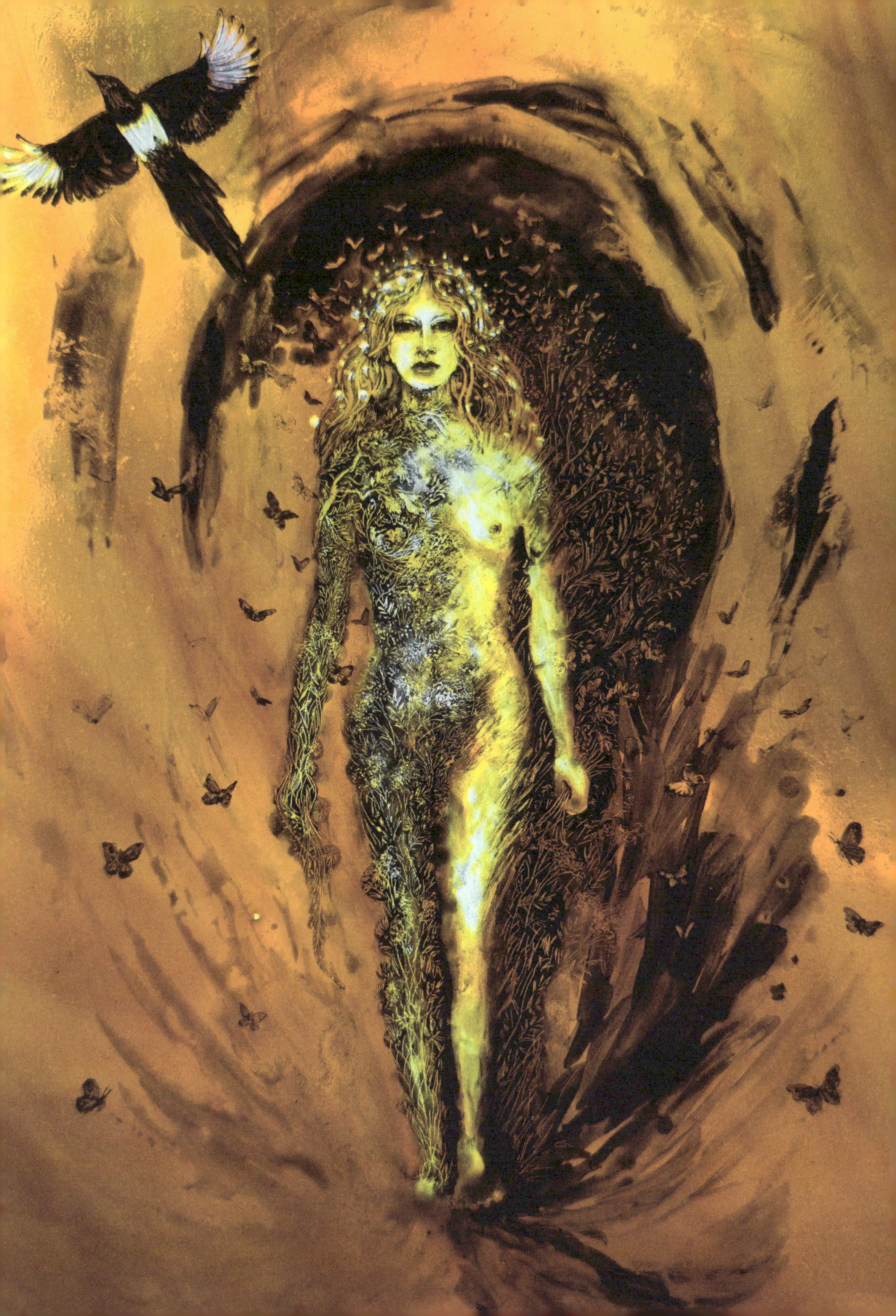

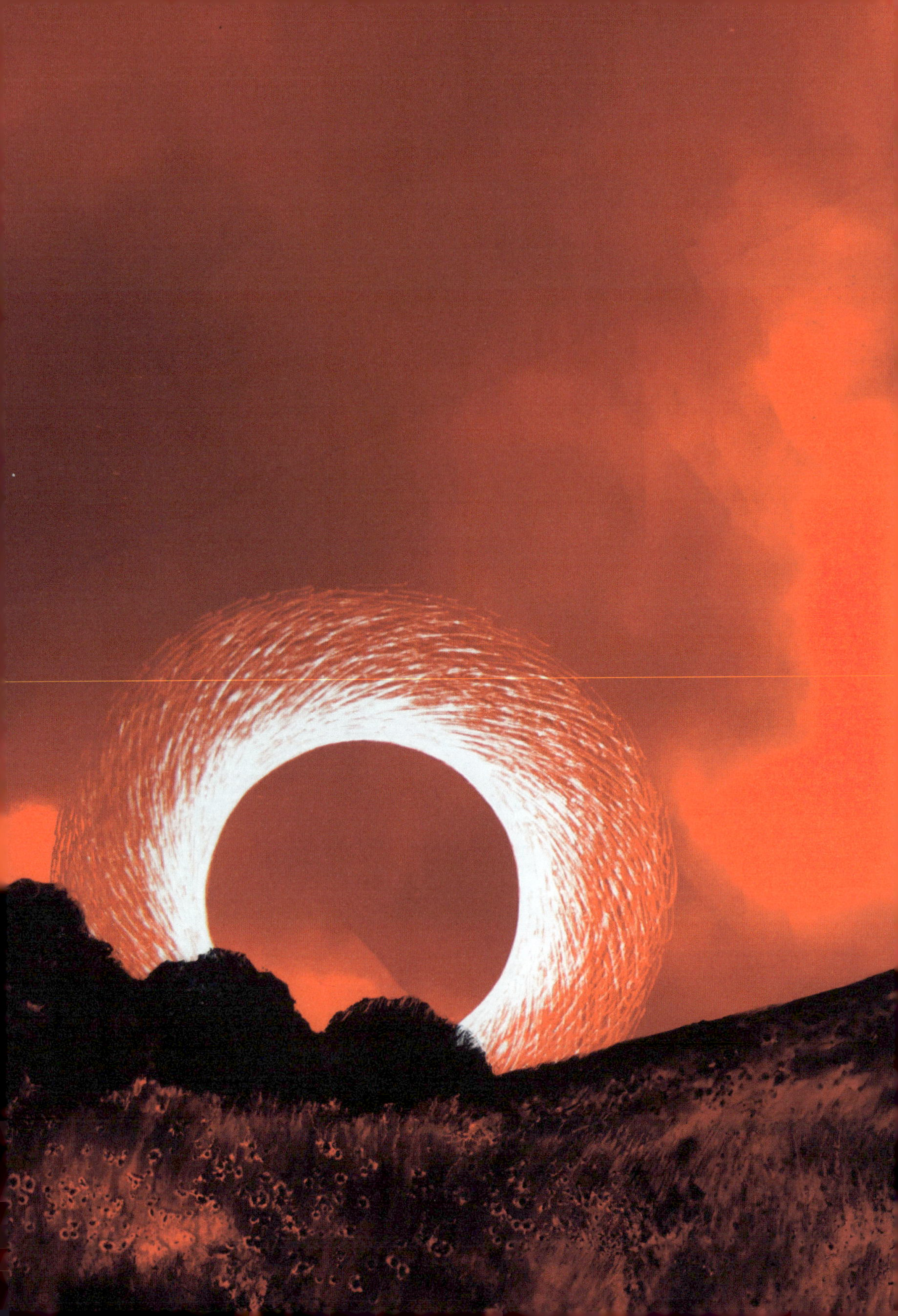

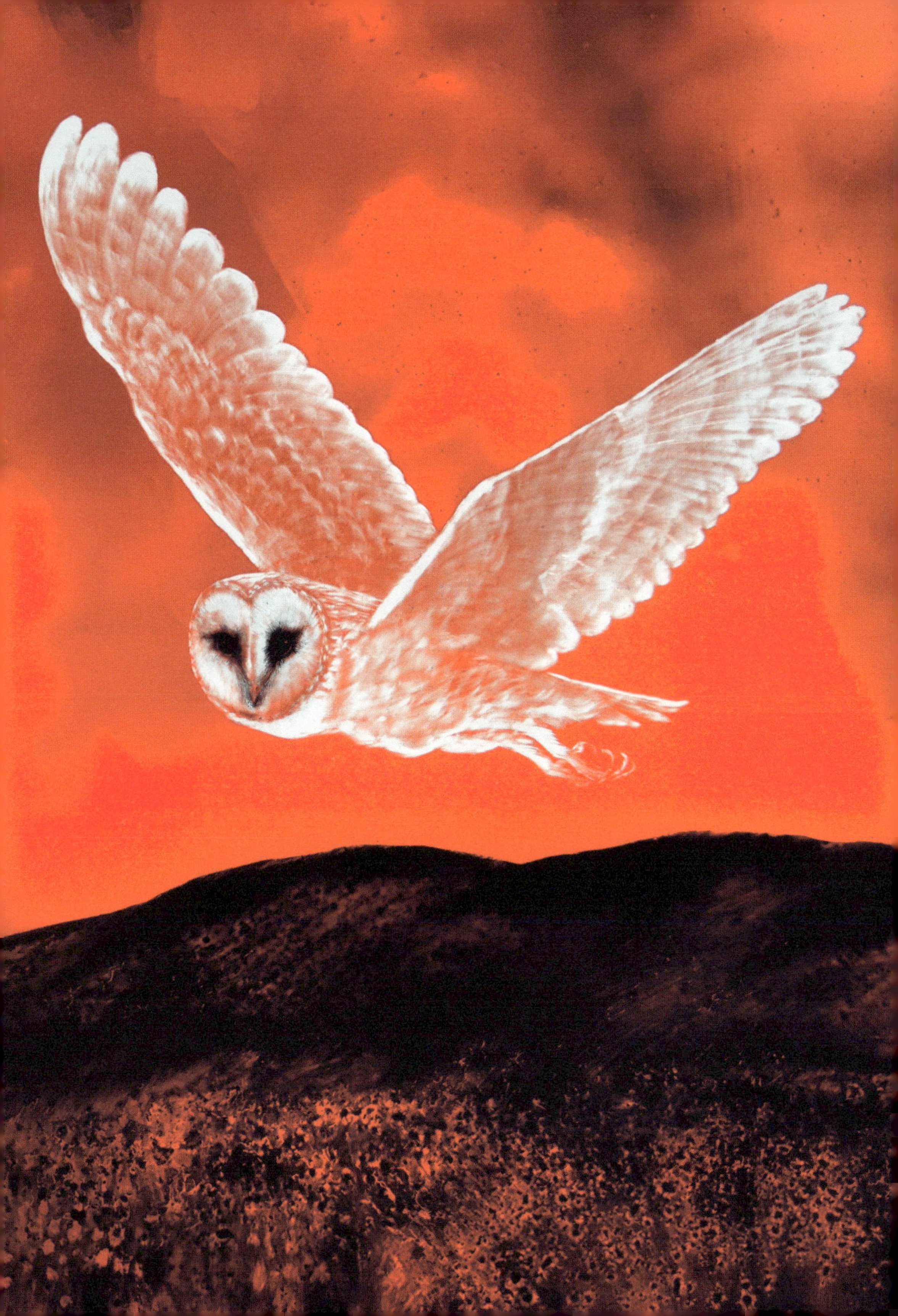

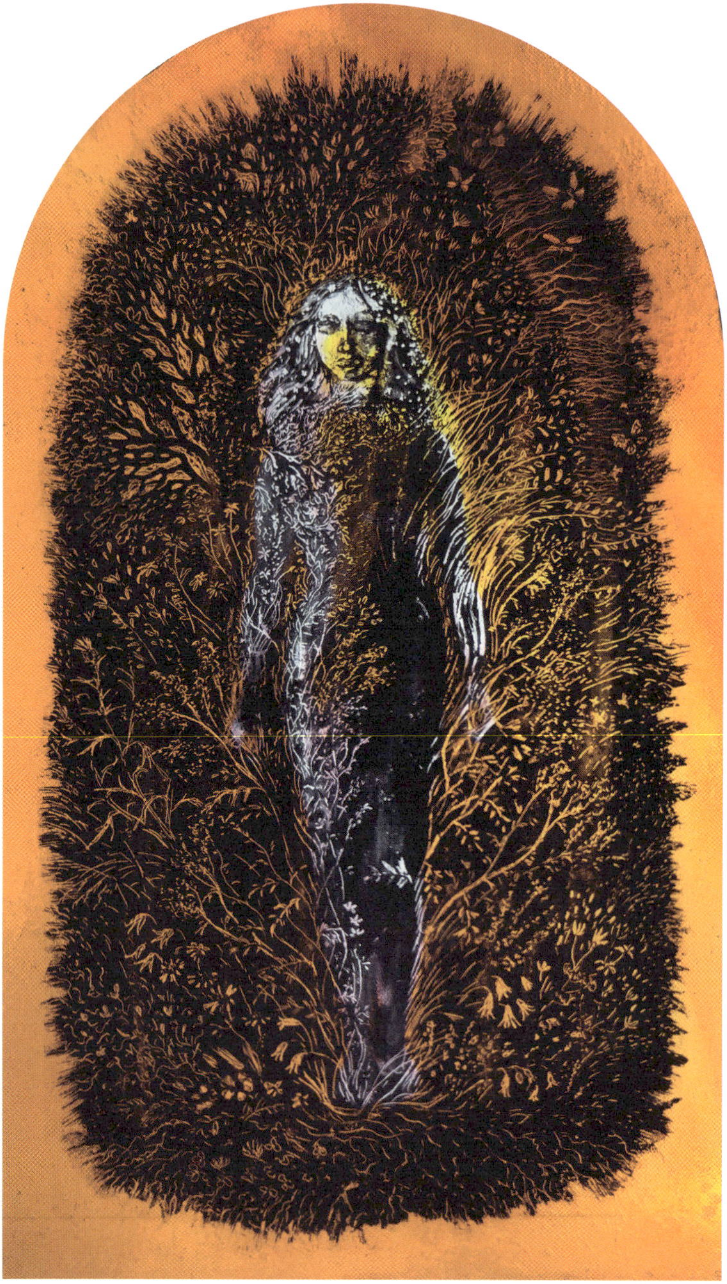

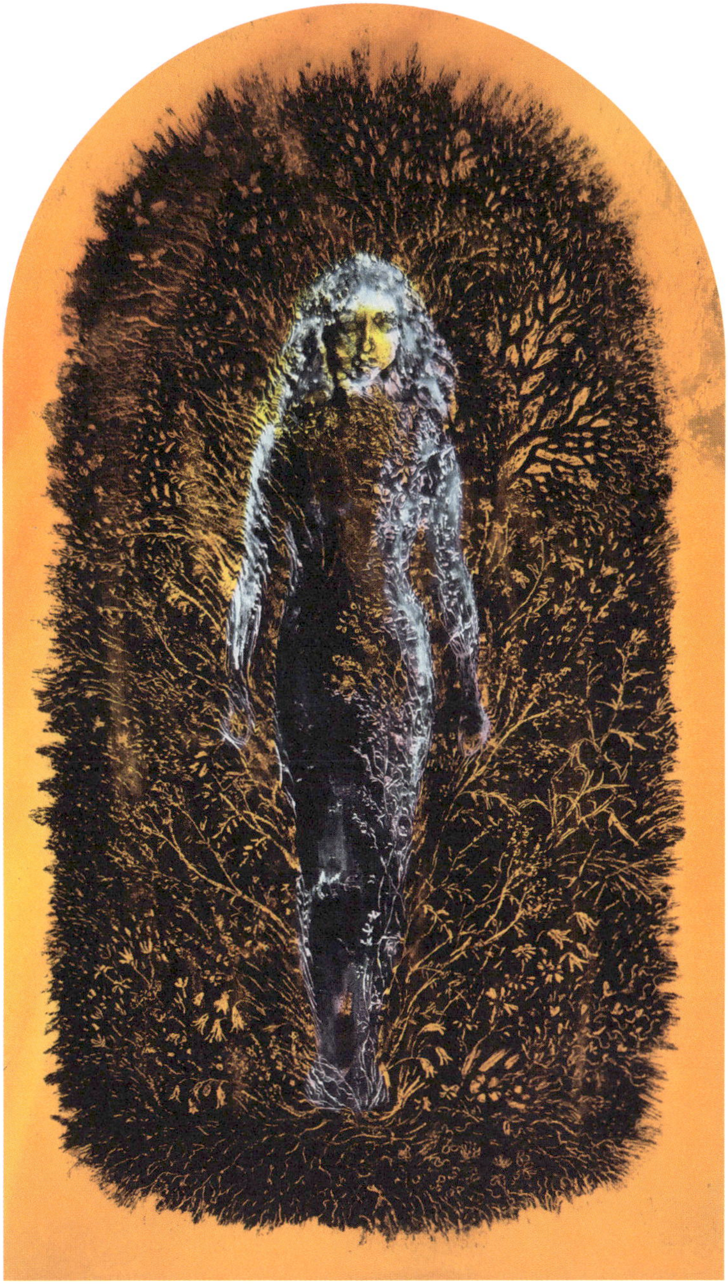

I missed the many moths and bees, butterflies and insects who brushed my stamen, pollinated my flowers, fed from the nectar.

I tried to understand the ways of men.

But human ways of love seemed harsh. I missed the voices of the plants, the song of the earth that would thrill my roots.

Lleu would not take me with him when he hunted.

And so it was that one day when he hunted, and I, alone in the stone walls, dreamed of the touch of bees, the hunter rode by.

The stag he chased was almost spent.

The Owl's Tale

Lonely.

I sent a servant out to discover who this was who hunted so close to our castle. I asked if he would come, rest, eat.

It was only when I saw this man that I understood what Lleu meant when he said he loved me. I gave my heart to Gronw Pebr. He saw the wildness trapped inside my green eyes. His touch made my human self whole for the first time. Wild and human united in my form and I gloried in being made flesh for the first time.

For though I was made to be the perfect wife for Lleu, he was not made for me. All night I learned the ways of love, and now I no longer desired the touch of bees and blessed the day Math took me from the mountain's side.

I killed my husband to be with Gronw.

If Math thought he had punished me when he ripped away my human form and made me owl, then he was wrong. I have been changed so many times, been so many things: seed, to plant, to flower and tree, to flesh and bone.

Now I hunt the twilight times, the blue hour, on hushed wings, breast white as meadowsweet, pale gold back like broom, claws like thorns and heart of oak, wedded to the air, to the night.

Flight gives me freedom.

And I would always rather be owl than flowers, for now I can still hear the wild song of the night, and I have wings for flight, and I have eyes to look upon the beauty of wild things.

And I can hunt.

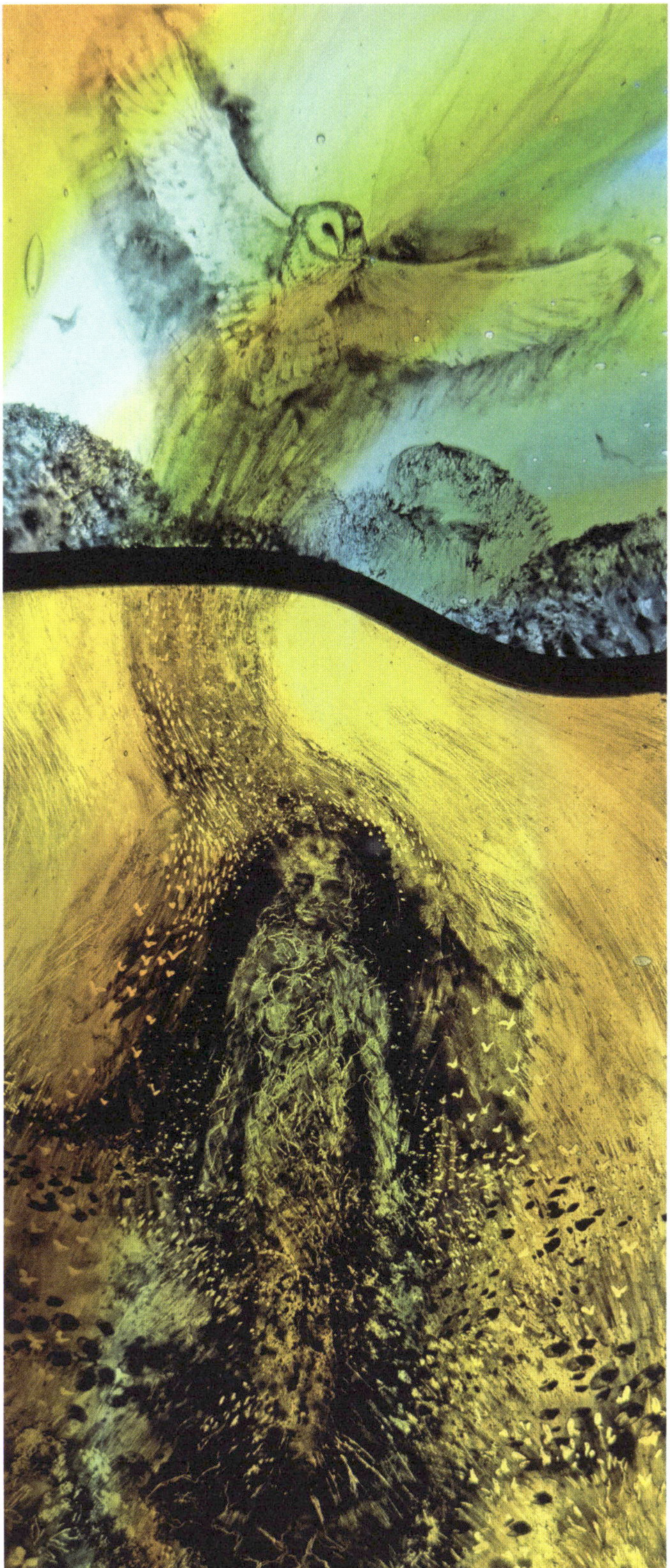

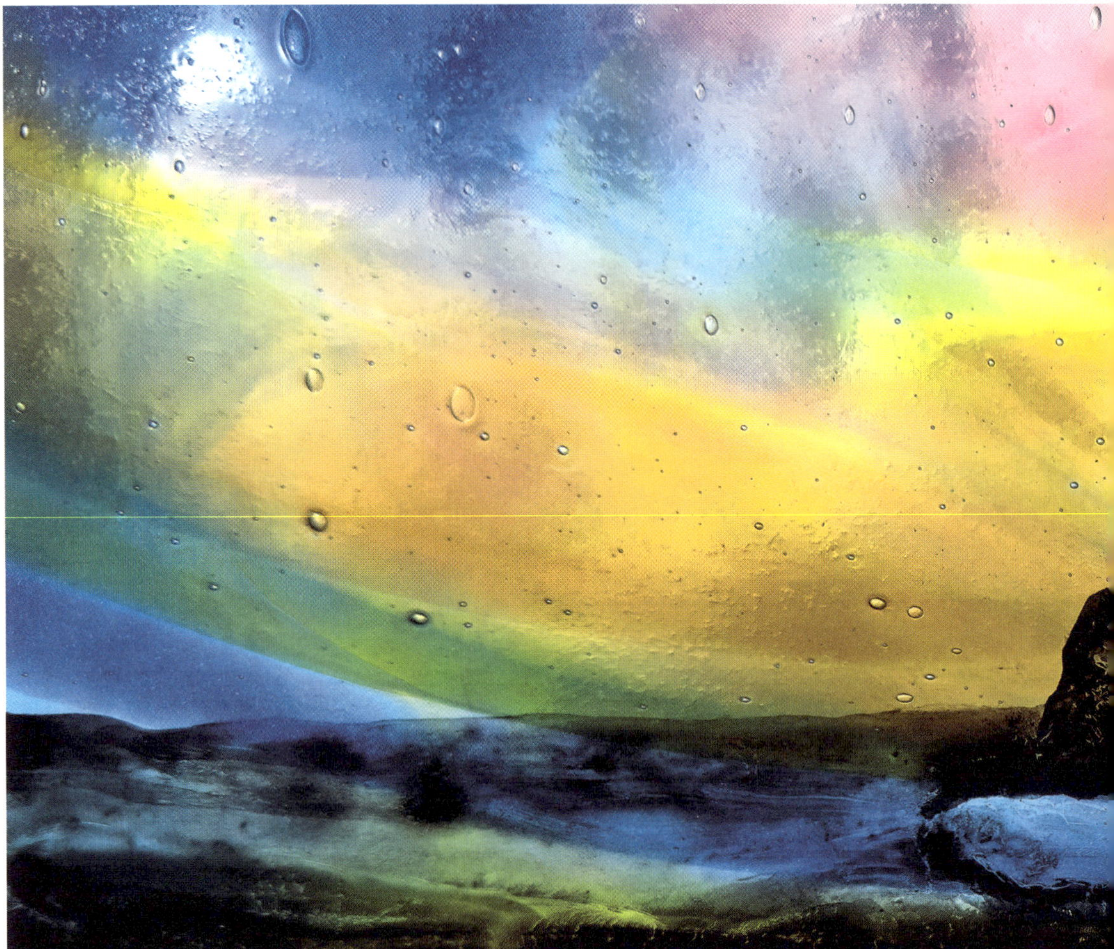

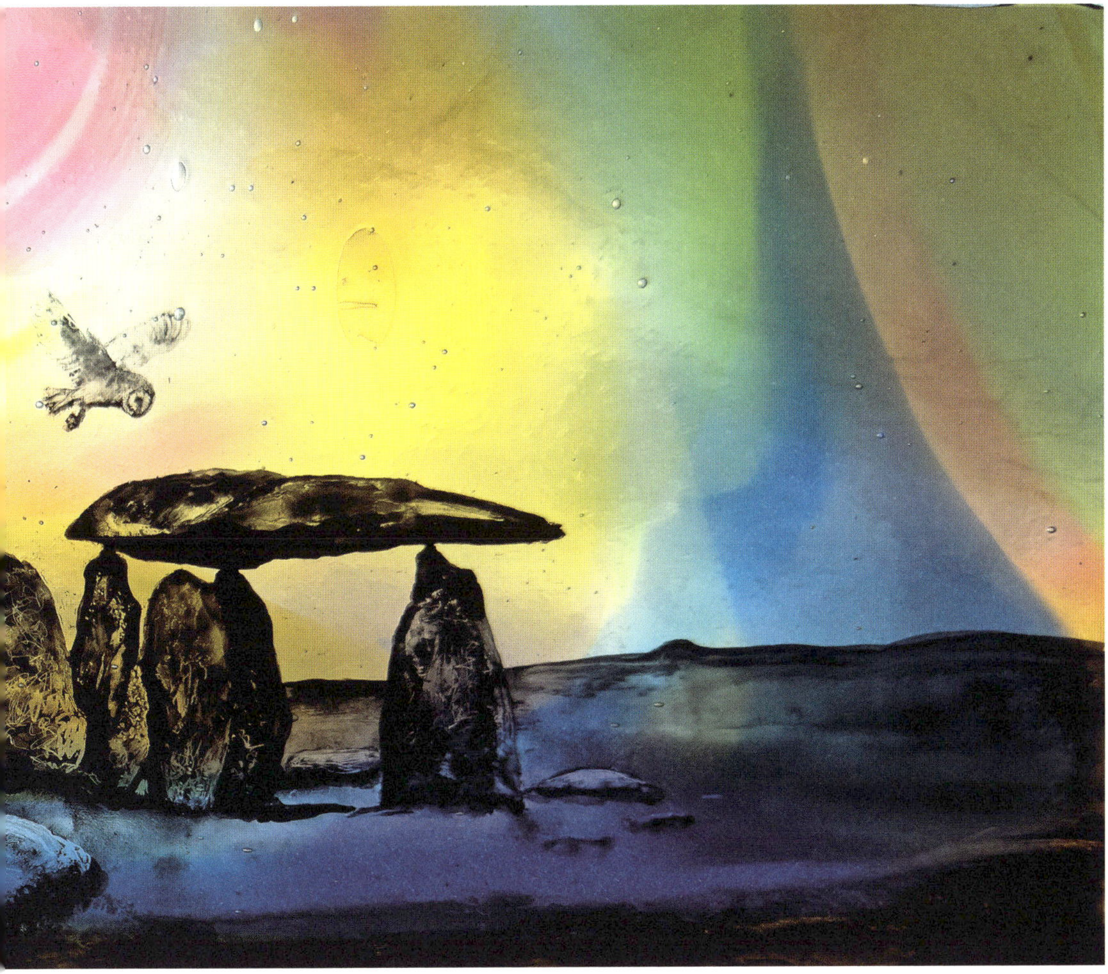

Owl call
fox bark
night falls
ink dark

*Star pattern
darkest night
moon hides
owl's flight*

*Eagle soars
on thermal lift
wren song
shapeshift*

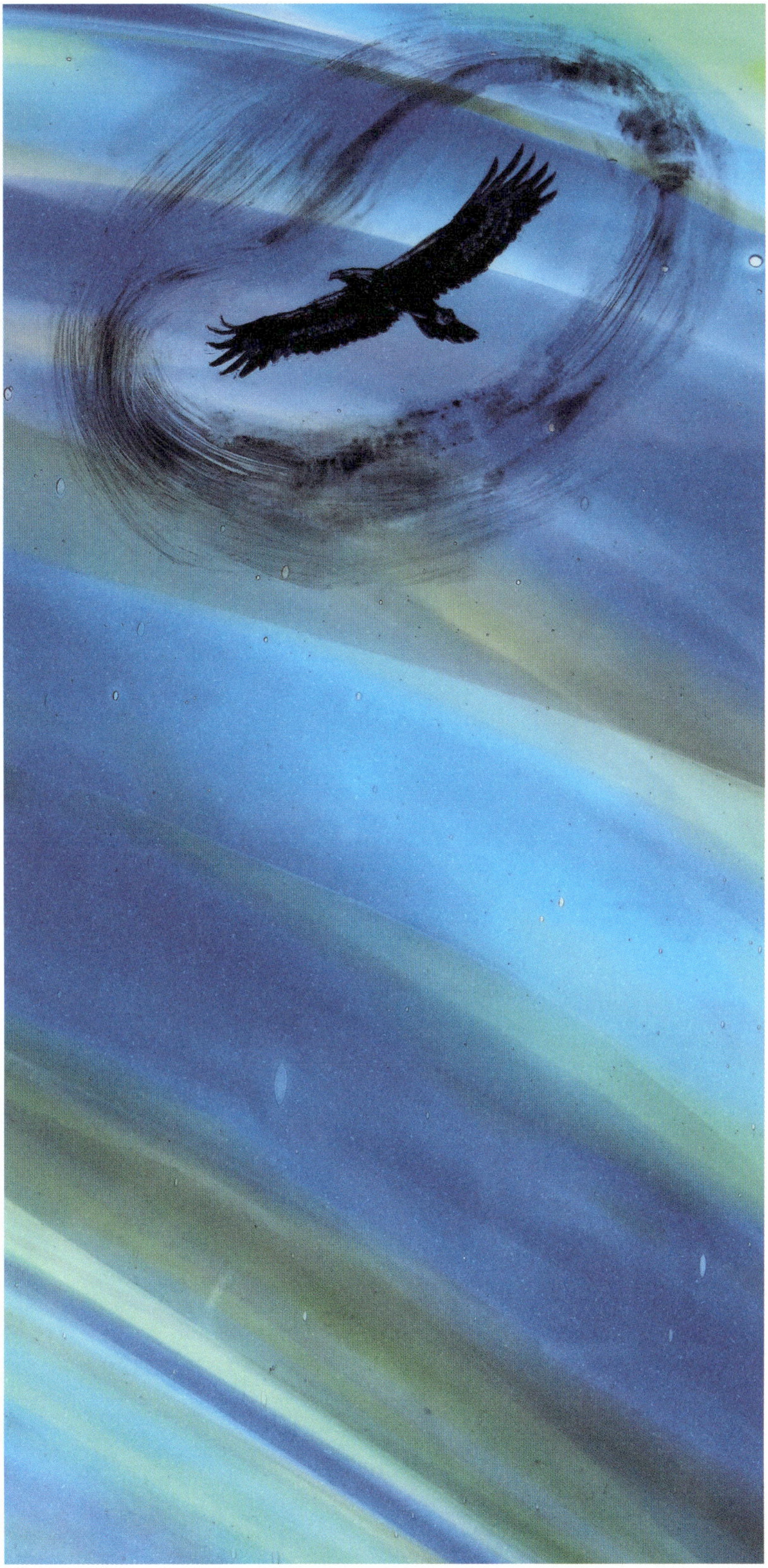

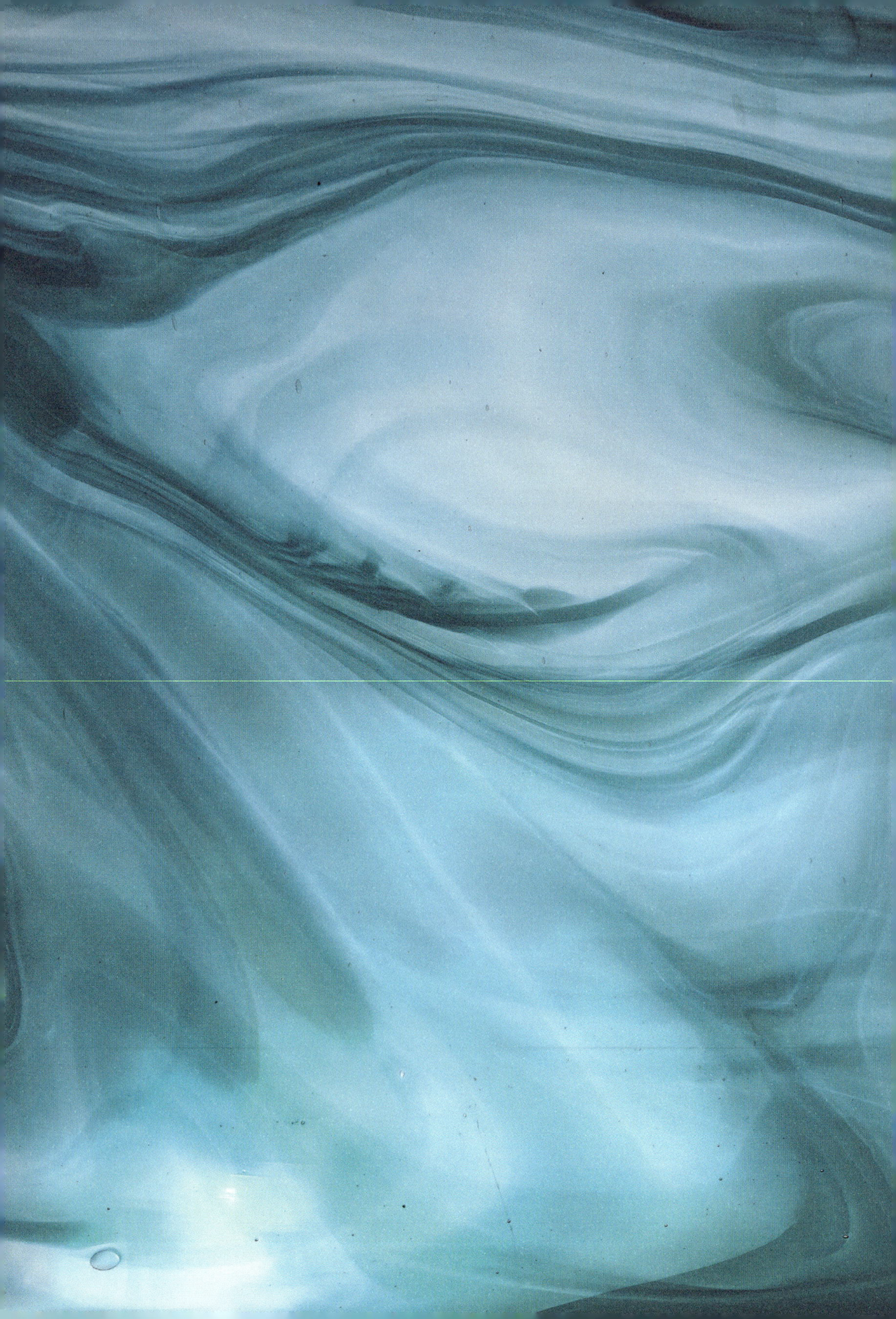

THE SELKIE'S TALE

FOR SAM LEE,
WHO SINGS THE LAND

*Oystercatcher
raven cry
pale moon
clear sky*

*Kelp sway
salt spray
wave spell
sea shell*

*Seal song
spindrift
curlew cry
shapeshift*

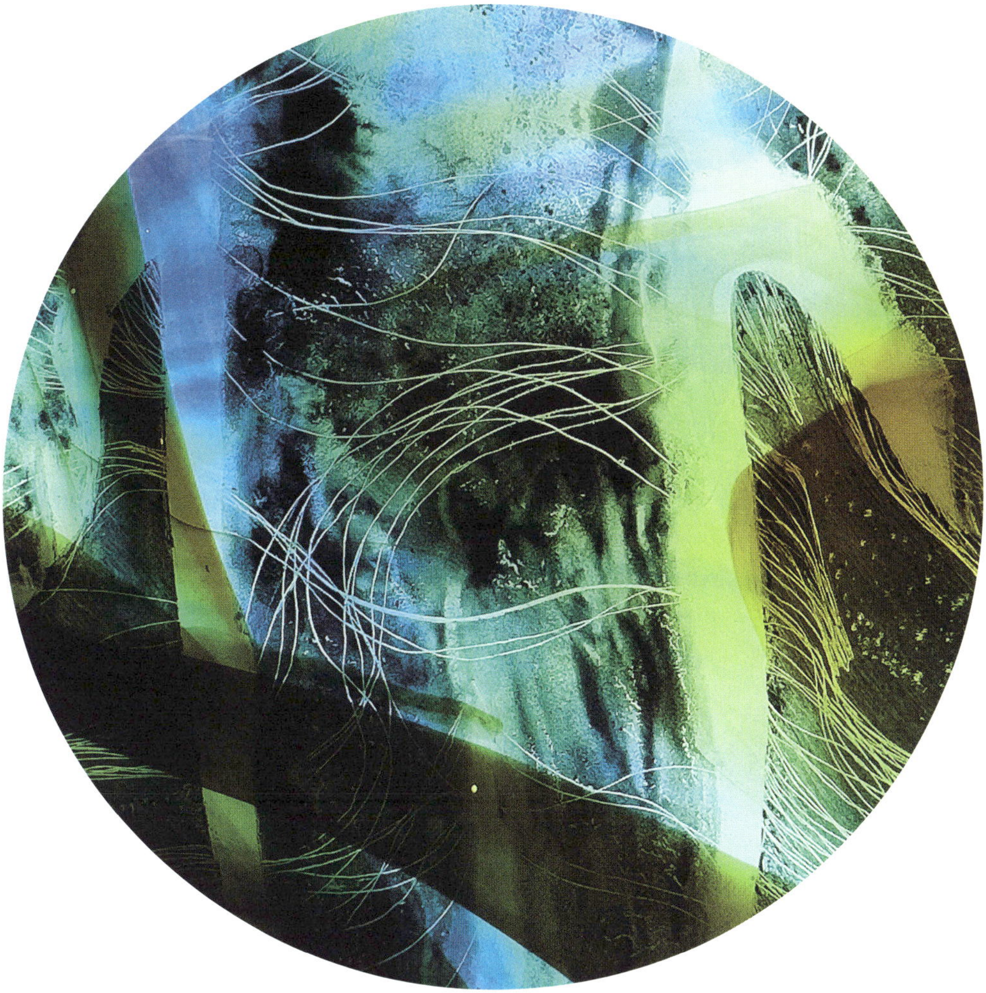

PART I

One lived by the shore, land-bound, but sure of her need to be beside the waves.

One lived in the deep ocean, far from land's edge, yearning for learning, fascinated by patterns, of weather, of wild, weaving her stories of the people of the sea.

One lived in a city, where buildings rose to the sky and the music of birds was drowned by the clatter and chatter of humans, where street lights blinded the stars and ate the shadows of the moon.

As streams flow to become rivers, to become sea, so these three lives flowed, woven together in a beautiful pattern of life…

Was it a day like this when first they met? Perhaps. A day of blue sky reflecting the distant country of clouds, and the lazy sea lifting and shifting smooth stones with gentle hands. A lullaby sea, a lilt of melody, a lazy weaving of wind in and out across the skin of the sea.

The creature of the sea swam closer, lifting her head above and below, hearing the song through air, through salt water.

All of the focus of the woman on the rock was on the small sticks, the thread held in her hands as she wove the song, the sea air, the wave-sound in between the stitches of the fabric that grew with each movement. Spellbinding.

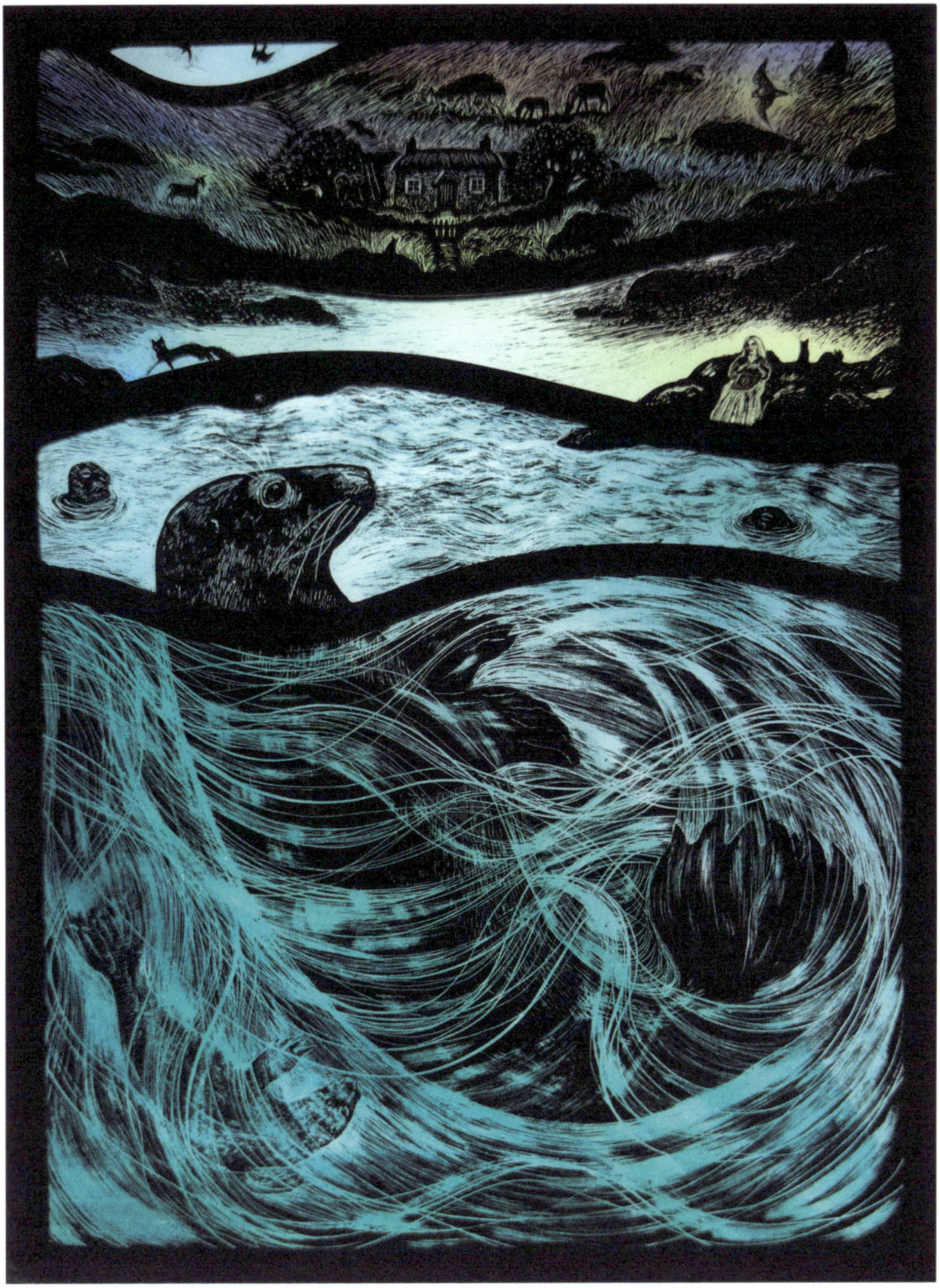

As the tide came in, pulled by the full moon, which rose over the sea in the daylight hours, the swimmer drew closer, closer, like moth to a flame.

The song ended. The woman on the rock lowered hands into lap, looked the seal in the eyes.

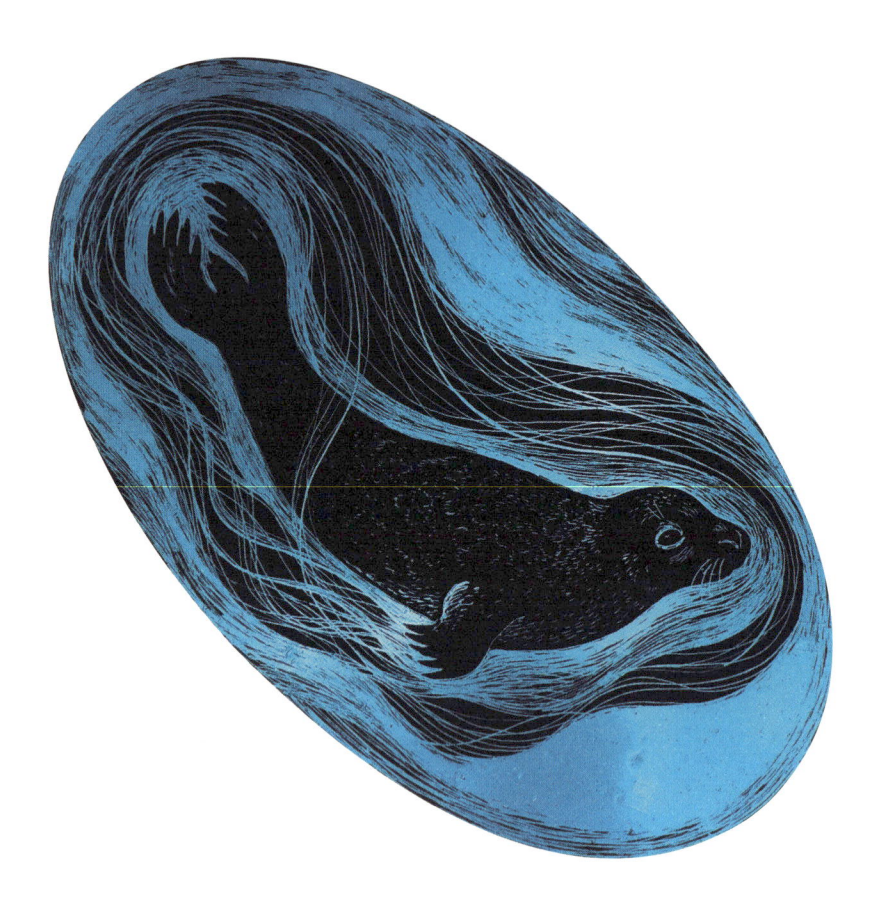

'I know you,' she said.

'I know who you are, what you are, and what you desire most in the world.

'If you can trust me, I will teach you.'

Closer still the seal-child swam. Seawater lapped at the woman's feet.

'But,' said the woman, 'there's a price to pay, Sea-Child. So consider carefully.'

The child of the sea felt the lift and the sway of her element, cradling her body, tasted the scent of the seaweed and brine, heard the wild messages through whiskers' tips, looked at the shape of the woman on the rock.

What was it about this woman that drew her closer to land each day?

The song she sang?

How her hands moved? Old hands, but sure of their craft.

How she seemed to wind the music into the fabric that formed from the thread?

The peace that seemed to live around her?

The Sea's Child swam to the shore, felt the sea-smooth stones beneath fur pelt, felt the shift of weight as water became air, felt the cool of the air stroking a different skin as she shed her selkie's pelt for the first time in her life. As her form shifted, she stood, tall on the edge of land and sea, green-eyed, marvelling at the fingers, hands stretched before her, feeling the subtle weight of myth and magic in flesh, in bone.

She stooped to scoop the skin, rolled it close, turned landwards and followed the woman on the rock as she gathered her needles, wool, into a basket that she carried on her back, up the beach towards a small cottage sheltered by a crag, and a new life.

Seven years she learned.

Seven summers of spinning and stitching.

She learned to shape a spindle, to whittle needles from driftwood. She learned to weave in the patterns of myth, of lore, of land, sea and sky, and all the while she kept her skin safe and the woman who taught her guarded her secret also.

Seven summers, winters, autumns, springs, and all the many small seasons in between; seasons of May blossom, berry brightness, damsel and dragonfly, of nesting, hatching and fledging, of migration and fruiting and harvests.

And she did feel the turning of time, sense it.
Seven years of learning.

In exchange for the teaching, freely given by her elder, she would cook, gathering land herbs and sea fruits. Each evening, as the sun slipped beyond the edge of the sea, she would take her sealskin, preen and oil her pelt, slip from the land to the water, become again the sea's daughter, and bring back a catch of silver beauty.

Between these two, on an island famed for its fabrics, a legend grew, like a ring-ripple of bright water, about a couple of women who made such garments of great beauty that they seemed to be woven of spells. She wove the patterns of stories through garments as small island birds hunted for food around them: oystercatchers, turnstones and knots, while gannets plunge-dived in the waves. And sometimes an otter would leave the water and curl beneath the knitting, the fabric and the fur seeming to form something mythic, from a story of saints and angels. Now and again a black fox would wander the wrack line, searching for sea scraps, undisturbed by the women, as if somehow they knew each other.

The sea's daughter grew a reputation for making small boots for babes, that when worn would ease even the most fretful child into sleep and peaceful dreams. She made mittens that eased the pain of arthritic hands.

She made sweaters with intricate patterns that moved and twisted and echoed the sea, and it was said that if fisherfolk wore them, they would never drown. There was even a tale of how one young man, pulled overboard when setting a line of lobster pots, tangled in the ropes, dragged deep beneath, was rescued by a seal. He had been wearing one of the creations of the quiet woman. But fisherfolk are full of stories.

And so, the ripples of their fame spread. And far away, in a city on a river, a young man heard tell of two women with skills to spin songs into thread, combine textiles and stories, weave legends and make magic.

He was a singer with a love for story. There was much about him that was beautiful, gentle. He was a listener, so people shared with him the old songs, and he became a collector.

The Selkie's Tale

The harshness of the city had begun to grate at his soul. The cacophony of dreaming of thousands of souls drained him. And so, one morning he packed a small bag with the intention of taking a walk. He headed north towards the city edge where the world was greener, navigating by trees.

As he walked, he thought about the rumours he had heard of the women by the sea. He knew the songs and the stories of selkies. He knew the fame of the knitting folk, some of the songs of the fisherfolk. And he kept walking, as the movement soothed his raged soul, away from the city, towards the north.

He wondered if this was how birds felt when they began their long journeys of migration. A quiet compulsion of movement. He'd had no plans that day to leave, and not much money, but he did have his voice and his charm. So he trusted to his skills, sang for his supper, moved gently over the land on a curious pilgrimage in search of new songs.

PART 2

In the north the women prospered quietly, sitting by the sea, learning and teaching, teaching and learning, often in silence, listening to the quiet music of the turning world.

For seasons now the sea's daughter had been teaching her teacher. She knew from her life as a seal how, deep beneath the sea, mussels grew. She had watched them weather storms, currents, tethered to the rocks by fine filament threads. She had found that she could harvest this, trimming the mussels, but leaving them to grow, a sustainable harvest. She could spin the sea silk of the mussels into fine thread, a thread that held all the colours of the sea in its fibres, reflecting the light like water.

With this she could knit the most beautiful garments that seemed to steal the breath away. In their stitches was
- sunlight,
- warmth,
- the song of the wind on water,
- herringbone-light ripple of wind-wrinkled water,
- the seabirds' cries,
- the patterns of tides
- the lace edge where sea meets land
- the language of seals
- moon on the water,
- secrets,
- protection.

She harvested the filaments, spun and stitched in the secrets of navigation, wound in the beauty of oceans and the deep secrets of the sea.

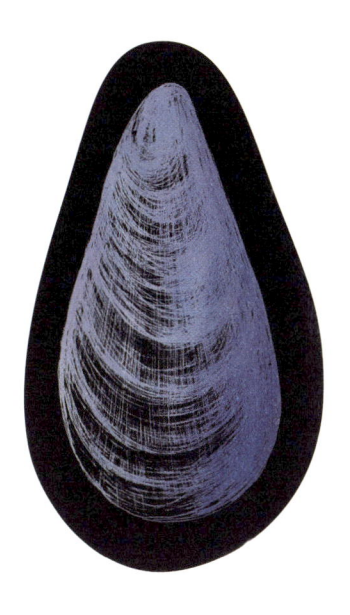

The first thing she knitted with the mussel-thread fibre was a pair of tiny socks. She gave these to a woman who had lost her first child, born frail, from hunger, from poverty. The socks were small, golden, perfect. From the moment she pulled them over the tiny feet of her newborn, the child thrived. The seal-woman also gave them fish for their table, showed them where the samphire grew and how to read the tides to reach it safely, where the sweetest seaweed could be found, how to harvest the seabeet, where beds of wild strawberries grew, and how to care for these wild gifts so they could prosper together.

Quiet friendships grew. The islanders knew that she was different, not like them. It wasn't that they accepted her as one of their own, rather that they acknowledged her different ways, her strangeness, her 'otherworldliness', and welcomed her into their community they knew was enriched by her being a part of it.

And if some were jealous, that is no surprise. And if people who travelled from far away to purchase the works of the younger were frustrated to discover they were not for sale, that too was unsurprising. She had, she said, no need for money. And she continued to make exquisite boots for babies, island-born to poor crofters, who would find them as an offering on their doorsteps just after a child's birth. And sometimes, when young folk set foot in their family boats to begin their fishing lives, they would find, wrapped in fine fabric, their first sea-shirt.

On a day of soft light and distant cloud, the sea's daughter asked her companion, 'When first we met, you told me you knew me. Somehow you recognised me. You also said you knew what I most desired. How?'

The Selkie's Tale

The old woman lowered her work, looked out to sea at the gathering storm front. Emotions moved across the lines of time etched into her beautiful face, like cloud shadow over land, over sea. For a long while, silence. Then:

Listen.
  I will tell you a story.
    Long ago I came to these islands from far away.
      I met a woman here, where we are now.
        She offered to teach me all that she knew.
          And so I too shed my skin, kept it safe, hidden,
            moved between the land and the water,
              never far from the sound of surf on shore.
                Then one day a young man came.
                  Oh, and in his eyes he held
                    all the colours of the sea.
                  Strong hands, dark hair,
                a builder of boats, skilled in his craft.
              In love, I told him of my true nature,
            showed him where I kept my skin.
          Oh, and we were happy in that summer.
        I gave him my skin to keep safe.
      An act of love.
    An act of trust.
  Seven children we had,
    and I the seventh of seven.
      All girls, each with sea salt rich
        in bone, in blood.
          Each took a piece of my heart
            as they left to explore the world,
              from sea to sea.

Torn between the love for the man,
the love for my children.
He watched my sorrows grow,
and with my sorrow his jealousy took root.
Jealousy is a form of twisted love.
It breeds on fear.
So when I asked if I could have my skin,
he said, Yes, tomorrow.
Each day I longed for the touch of waves,
the scent of world through whiskers,
the cradling of salt water, holding my old bones.
Each day he said, Tomorrow.
Until the day when the moon was full,
the tides high, the sea so still.
I begged.
We fought.
He left the house in a storm of rage.
When he returned he stank of smoke
and storms of darkness filled his eyes.
I asked him,
one more time,
Give me my skin.

Silence, broken by the piping call of the oystercatchers rising as the black fox nosed along the wrack line.

I burned it,
he said.

He knew he had done a great wrong.
Such a violent ache.

The Selkie's Tale

Such pain.
And so I am land-bound,
a lost soul.
I never thought to be happy again,
but you make me so.

The horror of the tale cut deep into the sea woman's heart.

'What happened to him?'

'It doesn't matter. We never spoke again. Too high a price to pay, and no going back from there. He left. Driven from the land by his shame. I never think to miss him, but I miss my skin, that part of my soul, with every ounce of my being. I could never understand why I failed to feel it at the time, that act of violence. Why I did not know until he told me.'

The sea's daughter thought of her own skin, safe in the wooden box, longed to wear it now, but stayed by her friend's side and grieved for her loss.

PART 3

It was a day of soft, calm air. She had risen with the light, taken her spindle down to the shore and was standing, feet in the sea at the edge of the land, spinning. The older woman was resting. Each day she moved with a little more stiffness in her bones, joints inflamed by arthritis, pain aflame in the bones.

As the day dawned, the black fox wandered the wrack line searching for sea scraps.

The sea's daughter watched as a great grey heron slow-flapped across the bay to land on the golden, barnacle-textured rocks and hunt in the rock pools.

Far out at sea a string of bright white terns, like pearls, decorated the wave's edge with their beauty.

Oystercatchers rose with calls of alarm as the black fox neared.

She brought her focus back to the fine thread of mussel fibre, damping the thread with fingers dipped in seawater, to smooth it – so fixed on this was her attention that she did not see the young man, also hunting the wrack line.

He stopped now, as caught in the spinning of the thread as she, as the spindle turned and wound their lives together.

He had travelled so far and for so long to meet this woman – hadn't expected to come across her like this, alone on the early-morning beach, some stars still holding fast to the darkness, but sunrise bleaching out the richness of pattern found in this clear, bright space.

Tongue-tied.

As their eyes met, both having been lost to their own

thoughts, before long they were lost in conversations. He confessed that he had come seeking her – she was astonished that, hundreds of miles away, in the city where he lived, there were stories of her craft. He explained that it wasn't the craft he had come for, though, but the music. He told her of the beauty of the land he had passed through, the rivers he had crossed, forests, mountains. She had never been far on land from the shore. She was like the seabirds, who come only to the cliffs to nest, never crossing land. She'd tried, but a curious land-sickness overwhelmed her. She was never sure if this was the pull of the shore, or whether she was tethered to her selkie skin in some way.

He was, he told her, a collector, a singer. It was the songs of the island he had come for, and songs, in particular, of the people of the sea.

As the day wore on, he told her of his journey. Their conversation was illuminated by some of the songs he had gathered, and sometimes by fiddle reels he had picked up, and wished to play to the wave's rhythm. And sometimes she would sit and spin and sometimes rise and dance on the sand.

In the doorway of the cottage by the sea, the old woman leaned in the sunshine, content to watch from a distance, delighting in the snatches of song and laughter, caught on the wind.

She watched as the younger woman set down her spindle, took up her needles, began a new garment. The old woman smiled.

As the day wore on the young man asked to be taught the songs of their people. There was laughter and learning between the two. He was invited to stay, for supper.

This was the first day of their lives together.

He stayed on the island, learning songs and reels. Music is made to be shared. He brought so many new sounds, a thread of music like a river from city to shore. Some days he would sit with the women, helping wind up the skeins of wool, of sea silk, marvelling as they knitted seaweed mats from the kelp. Sometimes he would help out with the fishing boats, lending a hand when a crew was short. Always a song close to the surface.

Cuckoos came and went, and wheatears, nesting in the old stone walls where the weasels hunted. Fulmars flew in with their own stories, greeting life partners, laying an egg, sharing the caring, then away out around the world again. Ravens gathered, sharing their lore. There seemed more than ever, and the great colony that formed wheeled and circled and called, and some said that they saw among them a white raven amidst the murderous murmuration. Thrift bloomed, and campion faded, and honeysuckle scented the bracken, and heather blushed the land where the owls nested.

Sometimes he would wander alone, gathering up driftwood to spark up a witch-fire of salt sparks in the women's hearth, for they had welcomed him into their hearts and their home.

It was during one of his wanderings that he discovered the box.

Beautiful it was, washed up at the back of a cave. Even beneath the crusting of barnacles and young mussels he could see the intricate patterns carved into the wooden surface. Mahogany? Oak? Hard to tell, so soaked by the sea. Shaped like a small boat, closed shut and swollen by water and wrapped in kelp ribbons, with a rusted catch and a carved pin. Heavy in his arms, he carried it carefully, having prised it out from the cleft in the rock where it was wedged and weighted, deep in a sea cave.

He was afraid of what he thought might be inside. And he thought he knew to whom the box belonged. All of the songs he'd ever learned of selkies informed him of what he should do next.

Careful he was to open the box without doing damage to its beauty. Sure enough, there inside, a sealskin. Rich, soft, thick skin, scented with brine and sandalwood, storm, wave, sea and, somehow, also of her.

He'd known from the first day that he loved her, wanted to spend the rest of his life with her. Now he held the means to do so, warm in his hands, a gift from the sea. He could not imagine a future without her.

That night he slept on the beach, beneath the Milky Way, pale in the fading full moon, the selkie's skin stretched out beside him, breathing in the scent of her.

The next day he knew what he should do.

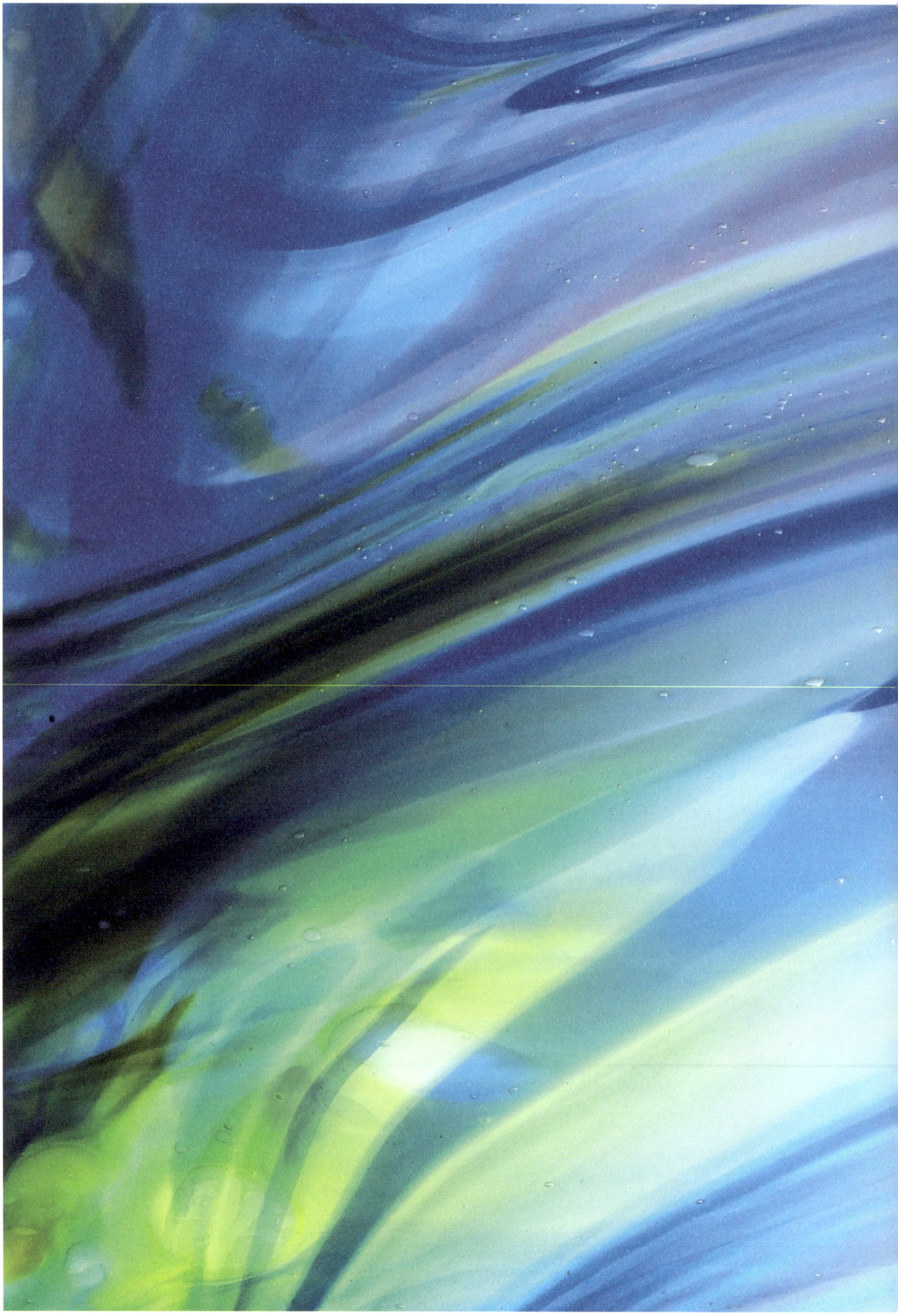

He found his love close to the tideline. She was watching the colours change on the skin of the sea as the sun warmed away the darkness, and the moon became so pale in the morning sky. She was knitting the most exquisite garment that seemed to echo all the colours of the sea, to shimmer with the wind's touch.

   Blue
   and silvered blue,
   and the memory of deeper blue
   blue-green
   glass-green caught in wind ripple
   smalt
   deep indigo towards the horizon
   silvered brown nearer shore and silver grey
   sap and ochre mixed with sunlight
   pale cerulean blue.

   All the colours of her soul, and he thought of the sight and the scent of the pelt in the box he had carried here.

She had watched him approach along the tideline, seen how he cradled something precious, heavy. A shiver passed through her, strange senses as if through whiskers and as if someone had walked over her grave. The sight of him, even so distant, quickened her heart. She loved his songs, and how they could sit together in silence.

   Small flocks of knot rose before him, wheeled over water, settled in his wake.

For a while they sat together, watching the colours grow rich on the water, seeing the tide beginning to turn. He summoned his courage.

   'I've something to ask you.'

He spoke between wave-lift and seabird's cry.

Sure he was of what she was, and he understood from the many songs what it meant to possess the skin of one of the people of the sea. He loved this woman with all his heart. He could not bear to lose her.

'Ask it, then,' she said, and lowered her hands, the better to listen, resting her stitches, looking into his eyes.

'First,' he said, 'I have something for you.'

He lifted the box, settled it on the rock between them, turned it to face her and opened the lid.

Fear coursed through her body as she saw the beautiful dappled pelt. She lifted the skin, inhaled the scent, ran her hand over the flippers, velvet smooth and dark as the rocks.

'Where did you get this?' Her eyes alive now with a dark storm of anger he had never seen in her before.

He stammered out his story, of the cave, finding it wedged in the cleft of stone.

She gathered the skin into her arms like a lost child returned, and fled from him, sobbing, away from the shore to the house she called home. And he watched as his love ran from him.

His heart sank like the heaviest of stones, down into the depths of despair. He'd taken the risk of giving her the skin, knowing that if he kept it, she would have been his for ever, but knowing that he could never keep something so precious from the one he loved with all his heart. And now he had lost her.

He walked away, sorrow flowing through his soul. Away from all that he loved, from the future he had hoped for, heart as heavy as the drowned.

In the cottage, the sea's child found her teacher asleep beside the fire. She knelt before her, lifted the skin, draped it heavily across the woman's knees, and took her friend's cold hands in her own. They were gnarled by age, twisted with arthritis, but beautiful with all the marks of a lifetime of work. Slowly the woman shifted out of sleep. She smiled to see her young friend, and as she moved to wakefulness from dreaming, sensed the weight of skin, the warmth of it, the scent of it.

'Ah, but I am dreaming still,' she thought.

'He didn't burn it,' the sea's daughter spoke with a whisper. 'He hid it, deep underground, in water, beneath earth, bound in wood. But he didn't burn it.'

The pain of loss of all those years shot through the old woman as she stroked her soul-skin, sealskin. She sobbed a weight of sorrow that shook her to the core, and relief and love for this extraordinary child she'd shared her last days on land with flooded her being. When the first of this storm of emotions had passed, the two walked together, the older woman leaning hard on a stick, the younger carrying the weight of the pelt, down to the land's edge. Together they wrapped the skin around her shoulders. The skin had missed its soul sister too and it clung where it touched, and moulded to the form of an old seal as she dropped to her knees; then, fully seal now, in a coat of darkest mottled grey, she entered the water. The first time in decades she felt the touch of the sea against fur. Homecoming. Salt, cold, sway and lift, and all around a chorus of seabirds and the song of the seals as they welcomed their grandmother.

As a seal she turned to face the sea's daughter, eyes filled with sorrow and beautiful longing. And she swam. Away from the land, out and away, towards the beautiful deep.

On the beach the sea's daughter turned. Her heart sought the man she loved. She saw the work she had abandoned in her haste to return the long-lost skin to her friend. She saw footsteps leading away, but then obscured as the tide had written new patterns over them.

She loved him even more now, as she knew he had thought the skin to be hers, but had offered it into her keeping despite that.

She gathered up her work, holding the bundle of it to her heart, and ran.

He wasn't in the harbour.

He wasn't by the ferry.

A storm was coming. The island folk had warned him, but he had wanted to flee, away from the land, away from his loss, away from the woman he loved and this island he loved.

Clouds as dark as a bruise were rising high with the wind, and the horizon was a maelstrom of chaos where sea met sky.

Then she saw him, crouched in the shadow of the wind on the harbour wall, great waves breaking over him, all the boats turning and pulling at their moorings.

She ran, between the sweeping rhythm of the crashing waves, drenched by the storm, into his arms, pulled him away, away from the water that threatened to take him, back to the fireside. To shelter.

She banked up the fire, and they took off their wet clothes and soaked up the heat. They needed no words, simply to hold each other close, then closer, as the wind raged outside and the waves crashed against the windows, and the old stone cottage shook and rattled in the teeth of the storm.

Next morning, when they awoke, he thought his life had become a dream as he held in his arms all that he held dear in the world. Sun slanted through salt-smurred windows,

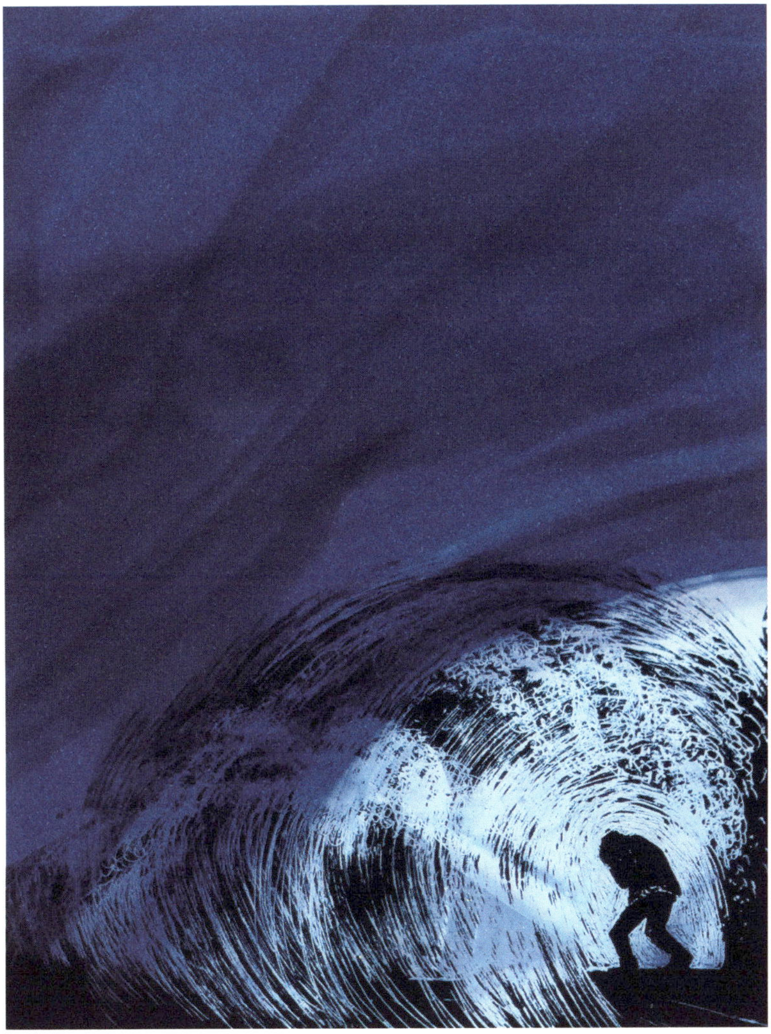

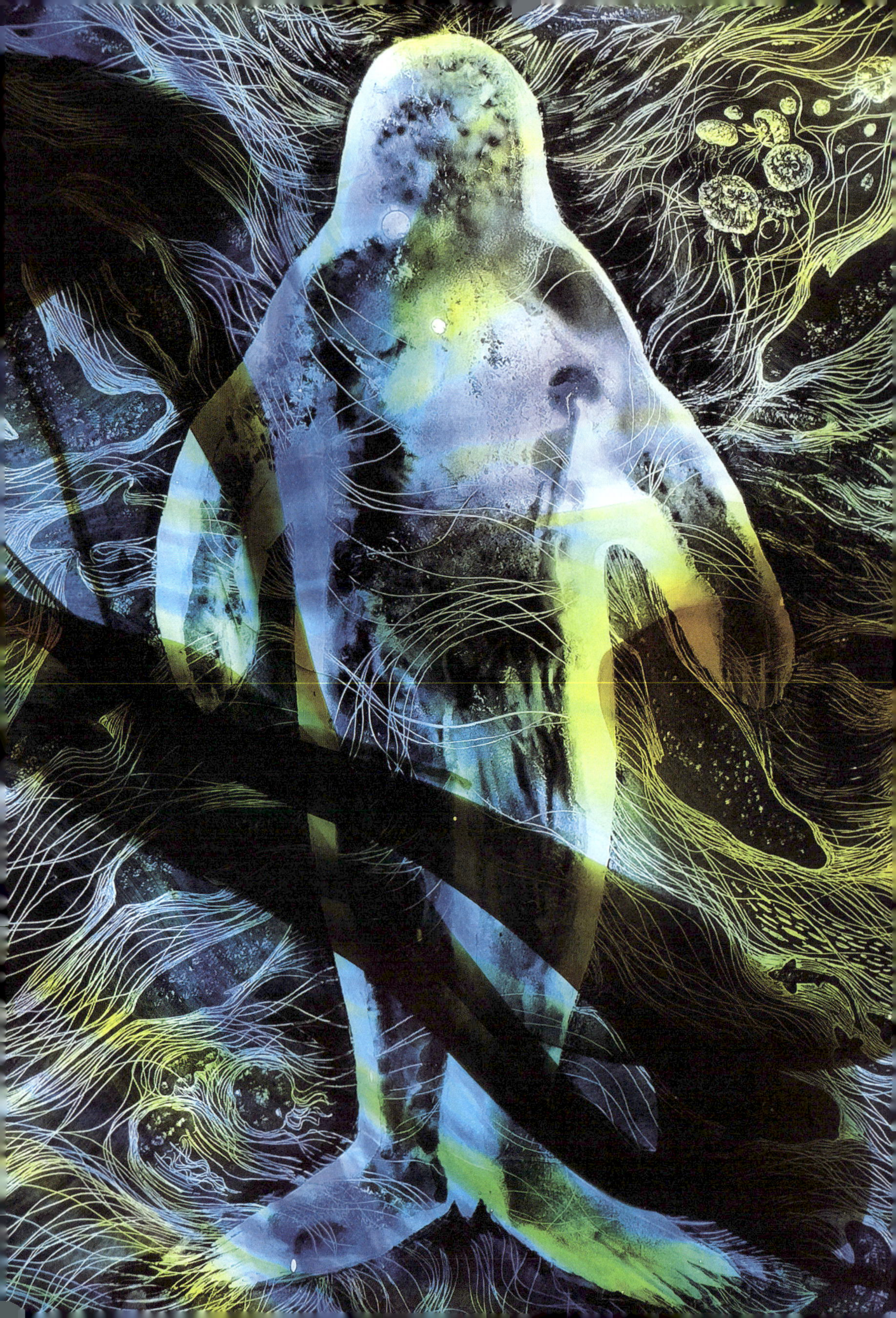

softening the glow of early light. Outside there was the special silence that comes after a great storm. He kept his hopes close to his heart, not wanting to wake from what he thought must be a dream. The warmth of her, the scent of the almost-dead peat fire, the silence. Then she stirred and stretched and opened her eyes and held him closer.

She brewed some tea. They sat outside, either side of the cottage door, watching the colours dance on the sea. In her hands the needles moved towards a finishing.

'I've made something for you,' she said. 'The like of it has never been made before. I made it for you, but you do not have to accept it.'

She held up the garment. It rippled in the light of the fresh morning, the new sun, all colours and every colour of the sea held in the fabric. He knelt beside her, reached out a hand to touch, thrilled by its beauty, but she stayed his hand.

'Before you touch, you need to know this – I am of the sea, born of the people of the sea. We people have our own lore, our own legends. One is that one day a miracle would happen.

'I have made a skin for you. A selkie skin with the magic to turn a land-born into a seal. I give this freely to you, that you may come beneath, learn our ways, see and understand what still remains of all that is life, of the deep ocean, the rivers, the roads of the sea, the forests, the hills, the mountains of beneath. To see, to learn, to return, with songs and vision. And so that we can be together, on land and in the water. Once you wear the skin, you make a promise that cannot be broken.'

Again he reached his hand forward, entranced.

'Wait. A friend once told me, there is a price to be paid for everything. So know, for this too will have a price that has to be paid. And that price is that you must speak for us, sing for us, take our songs and stories onto land, and help people learn what true wealth is, how they need the sea, and how to be more gentle in this world. Once you make this promise you cannot break it.'

Again he reached for the gift and, where his hand touched the garment, it melded with his flesh. There was pain in the joining of skin and of pattern, but also great joy. They walked to the sea and she lifted the selkie skin she had crafted, draped it like a shawl over his shoulders. Crafted with hope, with love, with magic. Where it touched his pale-skinned human self, flesh and cloth, sea and land, combined and a new myth was born.

She'd brought her skin too. Wrapping the pelt around herself, she felt the rush of joy, becoming one with the pelt, and, two seals now, they let the waves lift them, cool in the water, and swam.

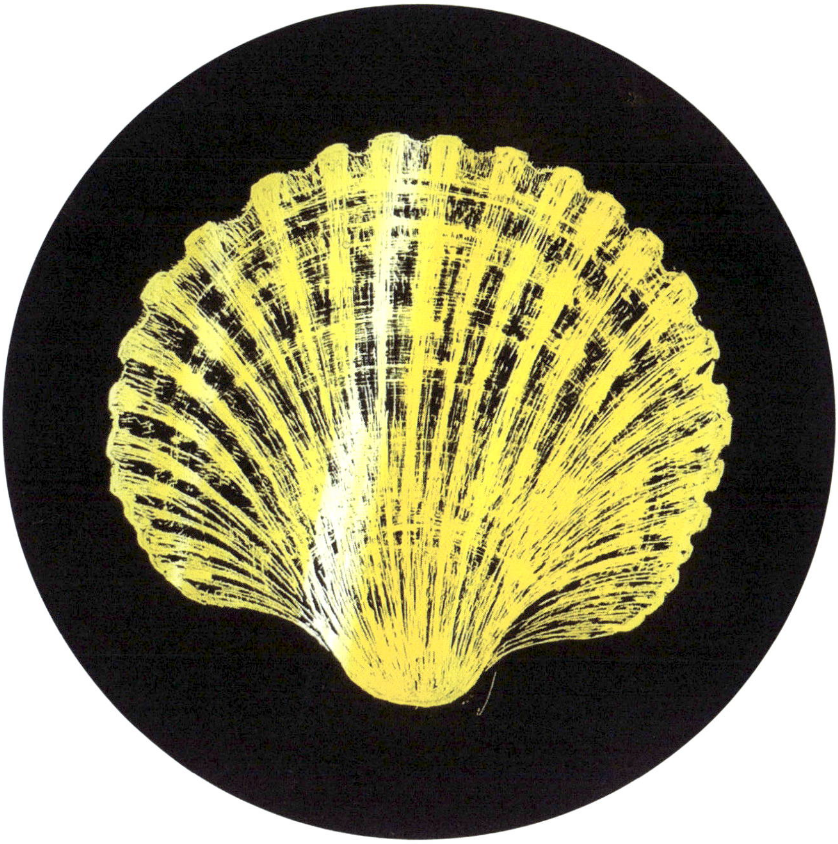

EPILOGUE

She continued to live in the small cottage in the cove, beneath the granite hill, so filled with memories and love.

To begin with her grandmother would return, coming ashore, always keeping her selkie skin wrapped around her shoulders like a rich fur cloak. Both understood that their time together was short now. The old selkie had chosen to die as her seal self, giving her whole soul back to the world's waters.

The soul of the singer thrived in this new element. All the rich music entranced the young man, not least how the world sounded through the ears of the seal, how sound beneath water travelled, how he seemed to hear through whiskers. He loved the water's touch, the endless movement and shifting moods and currents of water, the ease of movement, weightless.

Sometimes they swam together, sometimes he journeyed alone, while she remained on shore, making new garments for the children of the people of the land.

Their first child was conceived in a sensual underwater dance, deep beneath the ceiling of the sea, skin to skin, heart to heart, soul to soul, while the great whales sang.

She returned to her seal form to give birth, and the child was born, cream-white, soft. She grew fast with the rich magic of selkie milk.

On land the child slept, wrapped in her white selkie skin, in the wooden box that had once hidden her great-grandmother's soul-skin, refashioned to form a cradle, shaped like a rocking boat.

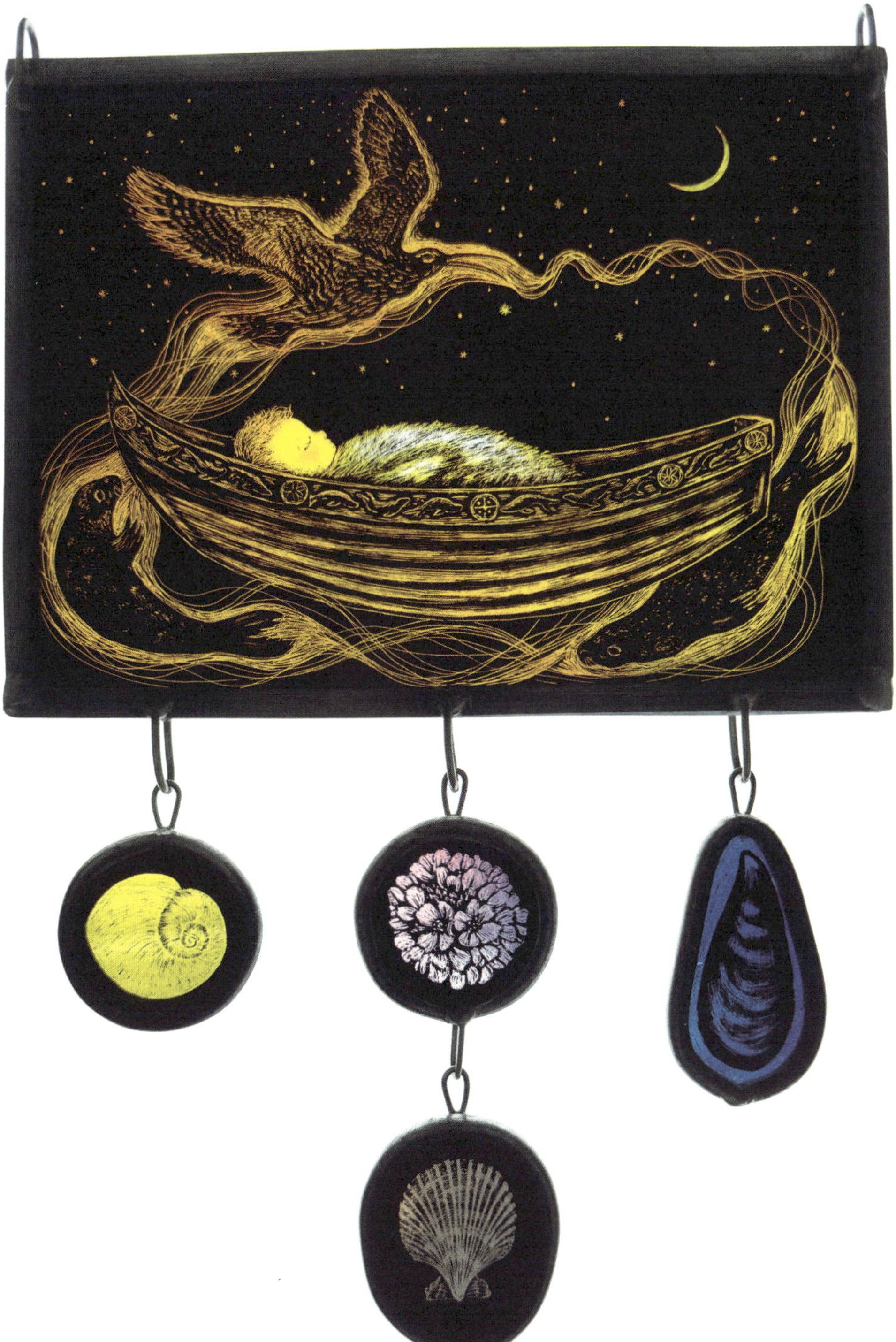

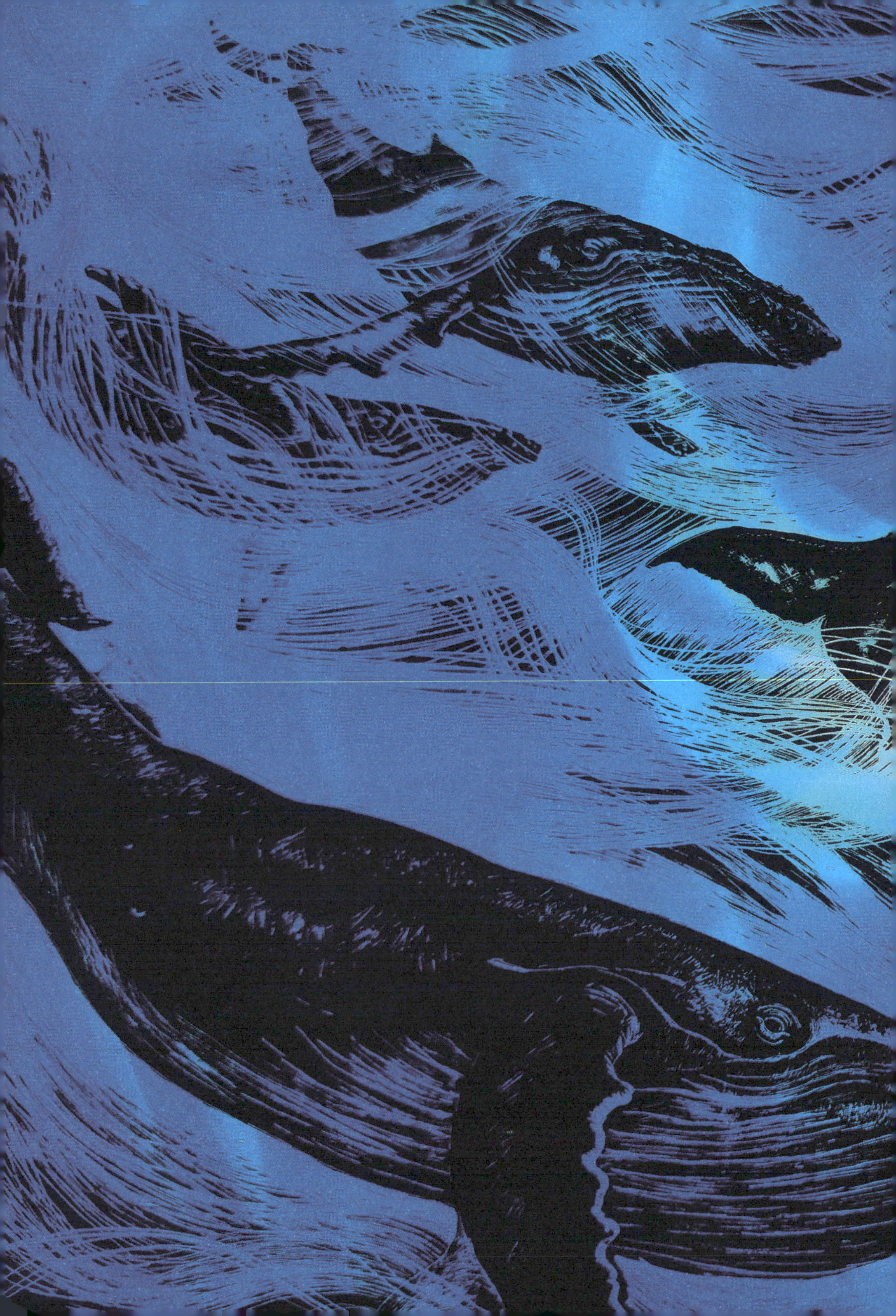

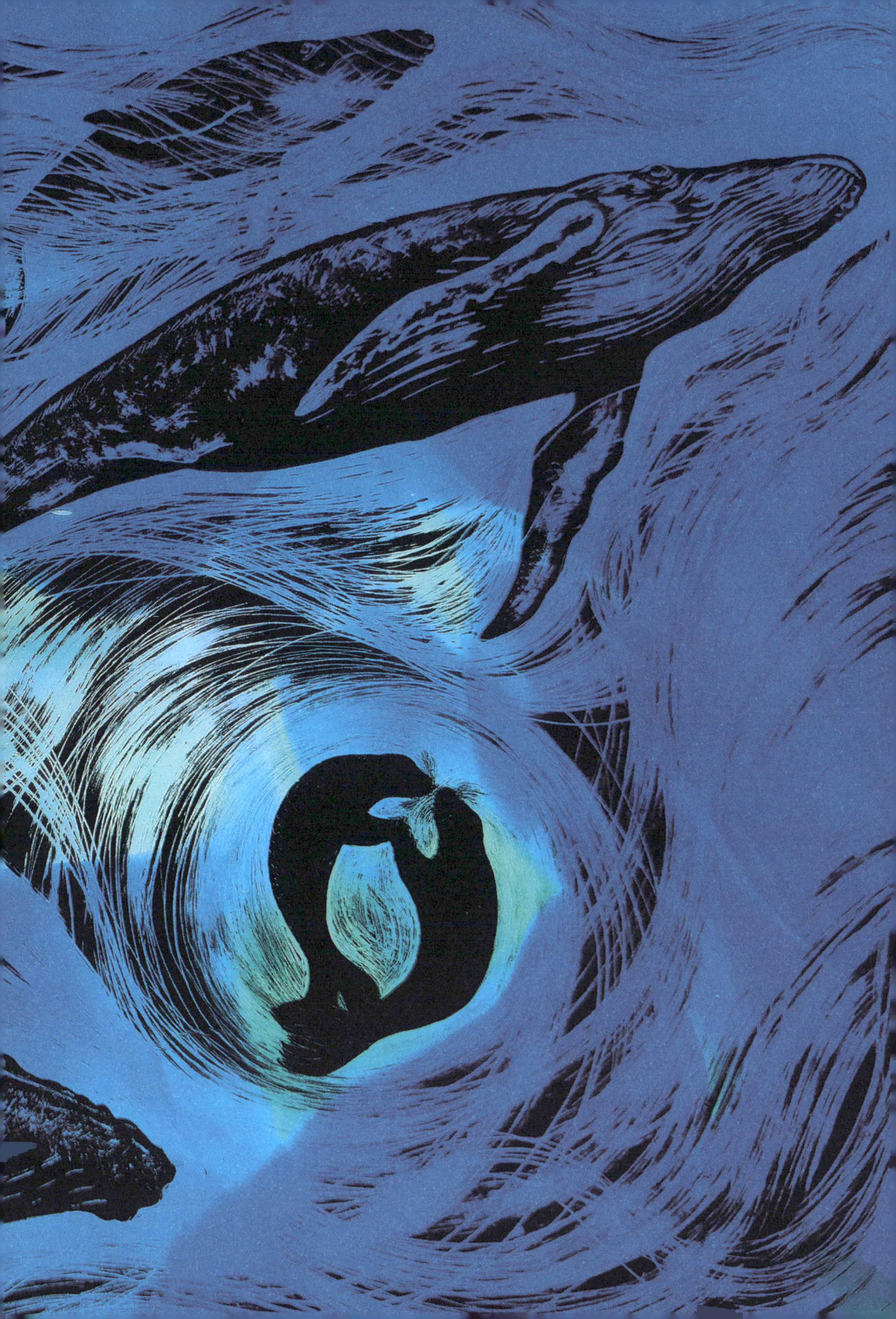

The last time they spoke together, the sea's daughter was watching her beloved rocking the cradle, singing so quietly a lullaby of land and sea, woven together with the notes of the fiddle. The old woman struggled on land now, happy though, to see the new life in her cottage beside the sea, loving the music and laughter. Side by side the two women sat, somehow understanding that this time was the last time.

'Years ago, when first we met, you said you knew me – knew what I was, who I was, what I wanted and what I desired most. I asked you once before, how did you know, when I was still so young and unsure? You said there was a price to be paid, to be careful. What did you mean?'

The old selkie pulled her sealskin shawl closer around her shoulders, rubbed her cheek against the knap of the fur.

'There is always a price to be paid when we follow our hearts. For me it was sorrow, pain, loss. Until you came.

'I feared you, too, were looking for that love the sea people only find from humans, that only sorrow would come of it. But no two people are the same.'

'All I ever wanted was to learn the magic and the skill of the making,' she answered. 'It was such a compulsion for me. I needed to create, to heal, to give.'

The sea's daughter looked across at her beloved, listened to his soft voice caught in the wind. Every movement of his beautiful soul brought her happiness, delight, as he rocked the cradle.

'I never knew before,' her friend said, 'that sometimes, rarely, the price to be paid is one of absolute joy.'

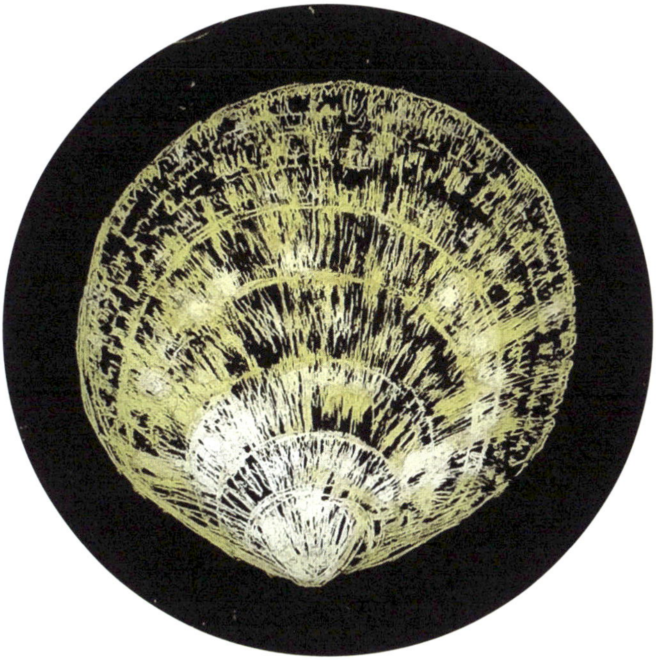

*Rainbows catch
in salt spray
seals rest
summer's day*

Loosestrife
meadowsweet
flow to sea
where seals sleep

As waves lift
gulls cry
seals sing
shapeshift

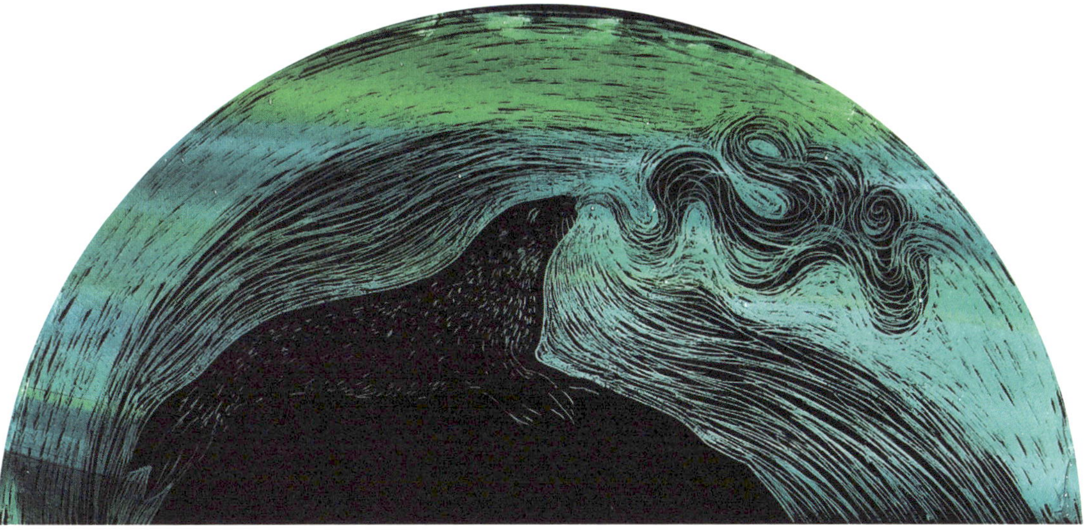

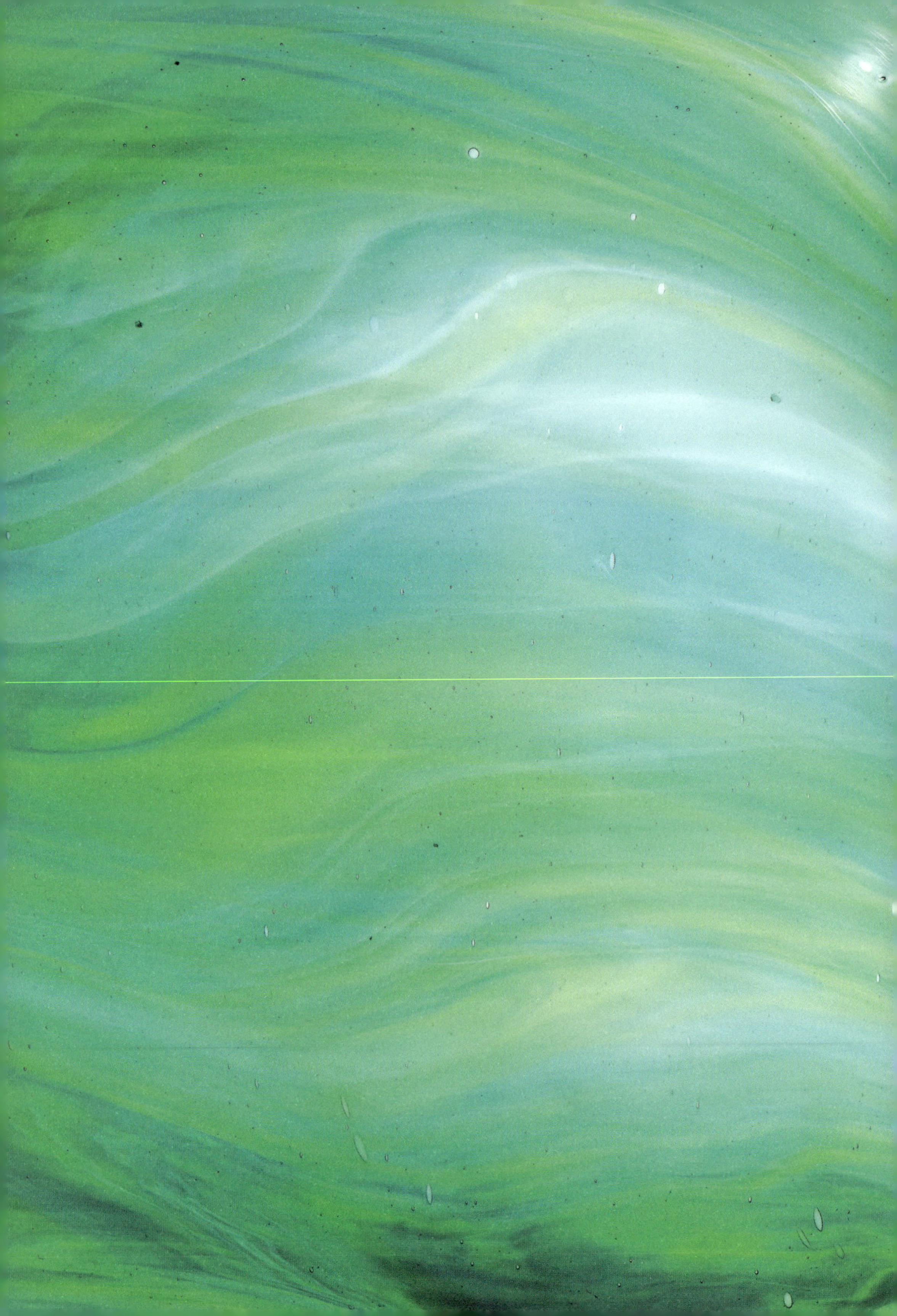

THE WHITE HARE'S TALE

FOR CHRISTOPHER JELLEY,
WHO WAS THERE WHEN IT HAPPENED

At home the air was pearl-bright, salt-clean, smelling of ozone. Even at night there was so much light, as stars reflected from the beach, and when you walked on the wet sand it seemed as if you were the centre of your own vast universe, and utterly insignificant at the same time.

But he wasn't at home. He was in a house in the woods and he hated it. The air reeked of damp, mushrooms and rot.

College was over. Real life about to begin. Until now it felt as if he had no autonomy. There was a path that went from school to university and then industry, work. He'd hoped for a summer of surfing before entering a new phase. Sea, sand, surf. Peace. Instead, his parents had asked him – no, they didn't ask, they told him they were having 'one last family holiday' before he became a grown-up. So much for autonomy.

Now he was here, landlocked, every bone in his body aching for the sea. Even the light here was different.

Four weeks.

The White Hare's Tale

The journey had taken five hours. It was dusk when they were almost there and he was convinced the satnav was bent on their destruction. They were following a map, printed-off instructions: go left by the bins and down a steep and narrow track. Understatement! Tree roots snatched at their tyres and plants swayed down from the high hedge banks to sweep the windscreen. More of a rutted rollercoaster than a road.

And then the road ended and there was the house. You could almost stand next to it and not see it, as if it had grown in the forest, out from the trees that enclosed it from the rest of the world.

The house sat snug on the slope of a steep-sided wooded valley. A rough clearing in the front passed as a garden. Late-evening light made a bright island of the space. They stood and watched as a great bird slow-flapped away across the valley. Huge, legs trailing behind it. It looked like a dinosaur, dragon bird.

Inside the house there was little to explore. Three bedrooms, his holding a narrow single bed. The place smelt of emptiness, damp? Maybe that was the scent of outside creeping in. He threw the window of his room open wide to let the air and the dusk in.

Nothing but trees, everywhere. He watched the light fade, then threw himself onto the bed, plugged in his earbuds and lost himself to music. This could turn out to be the longest four weeks of his life.

He could hear the sea as he woke on the first morning. It crept into his dreams. The sway and the lift and the dance of the waves and the water he could read so well. A rolling surf. Drowsy with sleep, he smiled. Then opened his eyes and remembered.

He was landlocked. The wind in the trees had tricked his ears as it rolled through the leaf canopy. He watched from the window. The treetops bent and rolled like deep green waves. He could hear each gust of wind coming.

It was early. Maybe midsummer. The rest of the household still slept. He went out into the garden, stood at the edge, where trees and garden met. The wood made him nervous, unsettled. He'd lived by the sea with its wide horizons all his life, apart from the brief spell at college. The light under the trees was emerald in the early-morning sun-slant. Things moved, all through the trees, always at the edge of his vision.

He went back into the house, closed the door on the wildness, made coffee, wondered how he would ever get through the next four weeks.

By the third day he was climbing the walls, ready to walk to the nearest train station, get the first train home. Every time someone opened the door something of the wood came into the house: leaves, twigs, bits of moss, insects. As if the wood wanted to grow inside the house.

Then he met the girl.

He'd been out for a walk with his mum and dad, down the track that led away from the house, into the heart of the wood, following the path and the hand-drawn map that was left in the house for visitors. He hadn't liked to admit that he needed to go with them, couldn't go alone into the wood, because he was afraid. Of what, he couldn't say. The trees themselves, perhaps? He felt they were watching him, waiting for him to do something. Maybe he was scared of getting lost? Perhaps it was just a residual memory of all those childhood tales of white pebbles in pockets and witches' houses and wolves? He knew it was irrational. Didn't make the feeling any less real. So he walked with his mum and dad, listened as they talked, and began to understand this wasn't really a holiday. His mum had come away to get some peace to work on a paper; his dad would come and go, back to work; and no, he couldn't join him, as his mum needed him to be there so she wouldn't be scared, being alone in such an isolated place.

They walked down the narrow track and the forest thickened around them until they reached a small mound, a thick wooded hump of a hill. The path ran around the hill, down beside a silvered stream, then back up the hill towards the house. He felt peaceful here, for the first time in weeks, years maybe.

Waking early next morning his bones itched with the restlessness to be back in the water. A fire burned in his brain. He decided to walk the route again, left a note, closed the door quietly behind him.

It was only just light, a blue-green dusky light with sun slanting through trees. A mist hung below the branches, as if the trees were trying to capture the clouds. He put in his earbuds, switched on the music and danced down the path to show the trees he wasn't scared. Spiderwebs stretched unbroken across pathways. Only a few steps away he looked back and the house was already swallowed by the wood. He followed the path down, away from the early rising sun. Movement caught his eye. Something large. A deer. An ear twitched in the bracken. Another deer. Three, four, more, a whole herd. Then branches lifted up from the forest floor into a shaft of light and there was the great head of an antlered stag. Both stood statue-still, watching each other. Amazing. Wild deer. Moments later something spooked them and they turned and flowed like a stream of wildness down the slope towards the heart of the forest.

He took a step and let out the breath he hadn't realised he was holding and walked on. And there she was, at the foot of the wooded mound, the girl, with eyes the colour of autumn leaves. He took the earbuds out and heard the forest speak.

'You took your time,' she said.

They walked together widdershins around the hill and down towards the narrow stream. They talked as they walked, with an easy intimacy, though at first he felt a little shy of this girl. When people asked him later what she looked like he couldn't say, apart from the autumn eyes. Meeting her there, this first time, it was like sitting offshore on the surfboard, waiting as wave after wave went past and then feeling the rush of knowing, the energy building and lifting to catch that perfect wave. She was like that.

He learned more in that one day – about the forest, about himself – than he had learned in his lifetime at school, at college.

Somehow the usual questions did not come to mind, nor seem important. She knew who he was better than he did, where he was staying, and when he asked her how she knew, she simply answered, 'The trees told me.'

So they walked. At first on the path he had walked with his parents, but then deeper into the wood. As she stepped from the path, she held out her hand to help him over a fallen log. He hesitated.

'Aren't you scared of getting lost?' he asked.

She laughed loud and a flurry of small birds flew up from the trees. 'No more than you are scared of drowning,' she answered. 'No one can truly get lost in the forests of Albion in these times.

This is a small island. But there was a time…' Her voice trailed away, lost in memories.

'Are you coming or not? I have such things to show you.'

He took a deep breath, threw caution to the wind, put his hand into the warm hand of this stranger, stepped over the log and off the pathway.

As he followed the girl deep into the heartland of the forest their voices became hushed, as if sounds were drowned by the density of leaves. Now and again a light breeze would blow through the canopy high overhead, where the tops of the trees touched the open sky.

He asked, 'Do you live here?'

She answered, 'Yes.'

'In the forest?'

'At Mounsey Castle.'

'You live in a castle?' He imagined something from old tales of knights and dragons.

She laughed.

'You are from the sea. I can smell the salt air on you.'

'Have you ever been there?' he asked.

'I live in the forest,' was her reply.

Trees thickened. So tall. He had never really looked at trees before. Where he lived the salt winds stunted and twisted and wove the trees. You could tell by how they grew the prevailing wind direction. Even old trees were short on growth, as salt winds and summer storms damaged the leaves.

'Don't you long for open space?' he asked.

'There are clearings,' she said, 'but no. Not really.' She stopped on the path, held up her hand to the leaf-canopy sky. 'Listen.'

Around them the forest light glowed. He could feel the sun,

higher now, though the sky was invisible, light softened by the huge weight of leaves.

He wondered how long he had been walking. Time seemed strange with this girl. The air was so still he could hear a leaf fall, touch the earth.

'So many trees. They all look the same to me.'

'That's because you don't look,' she said. 'The trees would say the same of people. And I would say, so many trees, each one different, unique, and much more besides.'

She smiled, crouched down, lifted a single fallen leaf from the ground.

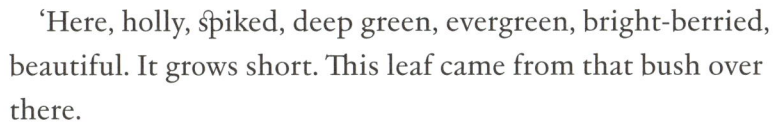

'Here, holly, spiked, deep green, evergreen, bright-berried, beautiful. It grows short. This leaf came from that bush over there.

'Here, oak, see the difference of the pattern. And this one too is different, and each and every leaf on a tree is individual. No two the same. So many of these trees are oak. Look up. See how the leaves pattern the sky.

'Here, beech, smooth, slightly glossed, smells different from the oak, though both have a tannin scent. Breathe it. Know it. Name it.

'Here, hawthorn. Smaller, much smaller than oak, red-berried, but different to holly berries, a swathe of blossom in spring and a feast for birds in winter. This one was planted by a song thrush many years ago.'

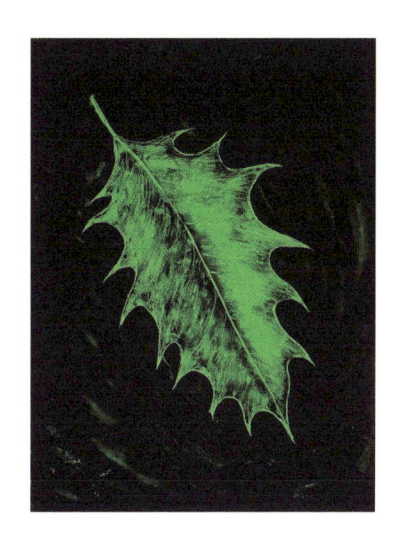

She passed each leaf to him. He traced its pattern with his fingers into his memory, learning the shape and the name, the colour and the scent of it. Their progress through the wood was slow now, as she would stop to show him each fresh thing, and he began to see the wood through new eyes.

'Here, anemone. Its seeds are carried by the wind's hands. Here, wood sorrel. Taste it. Lemon.'

The freshness of the leaf on his tongue seemed to awaken his senses wider to the life of the woods.

She found a small brown shell, a hole in one end, hollow.

'Acorn. This would have grown into an oak had it not become food for a squirrel or jay. This, star moss. So dense a cushion you can push your fingers deep into that green pillow and not feel the rock it grows on. Cool, moist. See the small beads of water still held in the green. And lichen. So many kinds of lichen and fungus, slow-growing.

'You know a single oak gives home to so many beings? They are their own small universe. Moth, butterfly, bird, plant. All find a home here. All are welcome.'

He began to see the different patterns of the trees, the small plants that had been hidden from his eyes by his own ignorance, the ferns and brambles and all the life in the wood.

Small bright-green spears of leaves pushed up through the earth. 'Bluebells,' she answered, before he could ask it. 'In spring the ground blushes blue with their flowers and evening air hangs heavy with perfume and bee-song. The wood is always changing.'

'Like the sea?'

'Yes, I suppose so.'

'Once,' he said, 'after a few weeks of storms, I went to the beach. The tides had ripped away the sand, leaving tree stumps and roots of an ancient forest standing proud. It looked like those war paintings by Nash. Just blasted stumps where the sea had claimed the land. The whole bay had once been a forest. This was all that was left, sleeping beneath a blanket of sand. I couldn't imagine how it would have looked all those years ago when it was trees, not beach. Until now. Now I can. All that life. It's covered again now. The sea smothered it again with a weight of sand.'

She shivered, as if a cold wave had washed over her.

For a while they rested on a fallen log, beside a clear, shallow river, in a small clearing where a white horse grazed.

'The best way to see is to be still,' she said.

She drew his attention to the small lives around them, as they came into the clearing while the two sat, side by side, almost in silence. He had never felt so at ease with another person. No pretence. No showing off to impress. Just being himself.

Curious and well out of his depth. Learning. He watched the wood. He watched the girl.

'Dipper,' she said, nodding towards a small brown-and-white bird balancing on a mossy rock midstream. 'Don't point at them. Wild things don't like it when you point. They consider it rude.'

A flash of electric blue. 'Kingfisher.' A branch across the river caught the bird mid-flight, holding them still. He had never seen a creature so beautiful, so otherworldly, in his life.

They heard a call, high, high in the sky, looked up, seeing the blue through the clearing. Midday, midsummer, almost. 'Buzzard.' She smiled and they both watched as the buzzard's mate lifted from a low branch, slow-flapped through the pathways between the trees, then up, up to ride the thermals, out into the elegant sky.

He thought of the great bird they had seen on the first evening, slow-flapping across the sunset.

'Heron,' she answered, before he could ask. 'It was a heron.'
Then, 'Otter. Like a river wolf. Hunting fish.'
The otter lifted a head above water, aware of them but unafraid, continuing the hunt along the gold-green waterway.

Minutes passed. Maybe it was hours.
He learned more names, saw animals, trees, dog roses planted in the clefts of branches by birds. He watched squirrels run across treetops, leaping through the branches. Jay, blackbird, thrush, nuthatch, treecreeper, raven, sparrowhawk, dragonfly, rook, robin, wren.
'How do you know so much?'
'I told you. I live here. Have done for years.'
They sat in silence for a while longer. The air around them cooled.

'We're waiting for something, aren't we?'

She answered him with a smile.

A wren flew up, perched in her hair. He began to understand. The sun dappled shadows through the trees. He felt a sense of peace fill his whole being.

A herd of deer came down to the river to drink, wild and beautiful, passing so close he could have reached out to touch. The stag looked straight at him. He felt its challenge, assured the creature he meant no harm, looked away.

'The trees. They talk to you, don't they?'

'Yes.'

'How?'

'Trees don't have a mouth through which to speak. Their language is not one of words. Trees speak with their whole being. Beneath the ground they talk with a myriad of fungi who share the earth with them. Their language is more nuanced than yours. Their language is chemical. To hear it you have to choose to listen with your whole body, not just your ears, and you have to give it time. It can be visual, in the patterns of leaf growth. What we would call a sentence might take a season to form. Their sense of time is different to yours. Their language is so far from the self-serving language of humans. Human words are not rich enough to even describe it. Here, let me show you.'

She reached out again to hold his hand. He offered it willingly. Eager to learn.

'Listen. With all of yourself.'

Together they laid their palms on the roughened bark of an oak tree, perhaps a thousand years alive.

Peace. An open mind. An open heart. And then he felt the surge of power that came with knowledge. No, not a language.

Images – he couldn't describe it, the wonder of it, so he took his feet from the ground and just lived it; root and branch and leaf and blood and bone. All through his body he felt a deeper connection with the land than ever before. The language of trees.

Their wait was over. As he took his hand from the oak and turned, bright at the edge of a clearing a silver birch glowed. A lightning strike of a tree, silver in the green. As he watched the bark shifted and shimmered and a wild god stepped forward, out from the bark, into the light. Part man, part stag, a crown of antlers on a powerful head, wreathed with leaves that danced with small birds and moths. A green spirit of the forest. He knew now he was alone in the presence of the ancient ones.

He looked to the girl.

'Go with them,' she said. 'Take the next step.'

The creature reached out his hand and the human put all of his trust into it. Together they flowed back into the birch and became the forest.

How long did he travel with the wild god? Time an irrelevance. Every second seemed an hour. Every moment a learning. Awareness bright, light-changing truth. Never could he have imagined such a world, and yet this was the world in which he was born, had lived, but seen through different eyes. This was a world where all life became visible to him, from the rising sap to the wing-flicker flight; a world where humans were so small a detail in the tapestry, so insignificant. The wonder and web of the interconnections of life was made gloriously visible to him, and he began to understand the planet on which he lived in a new way. A single living organism, connected to so many parts – river, mountain, forest, shore, desert, ocean, moor… he began to comprehend the pathways that linked tree to forest, forest to whale, whale to bird, bird to fish, fish to ocean,

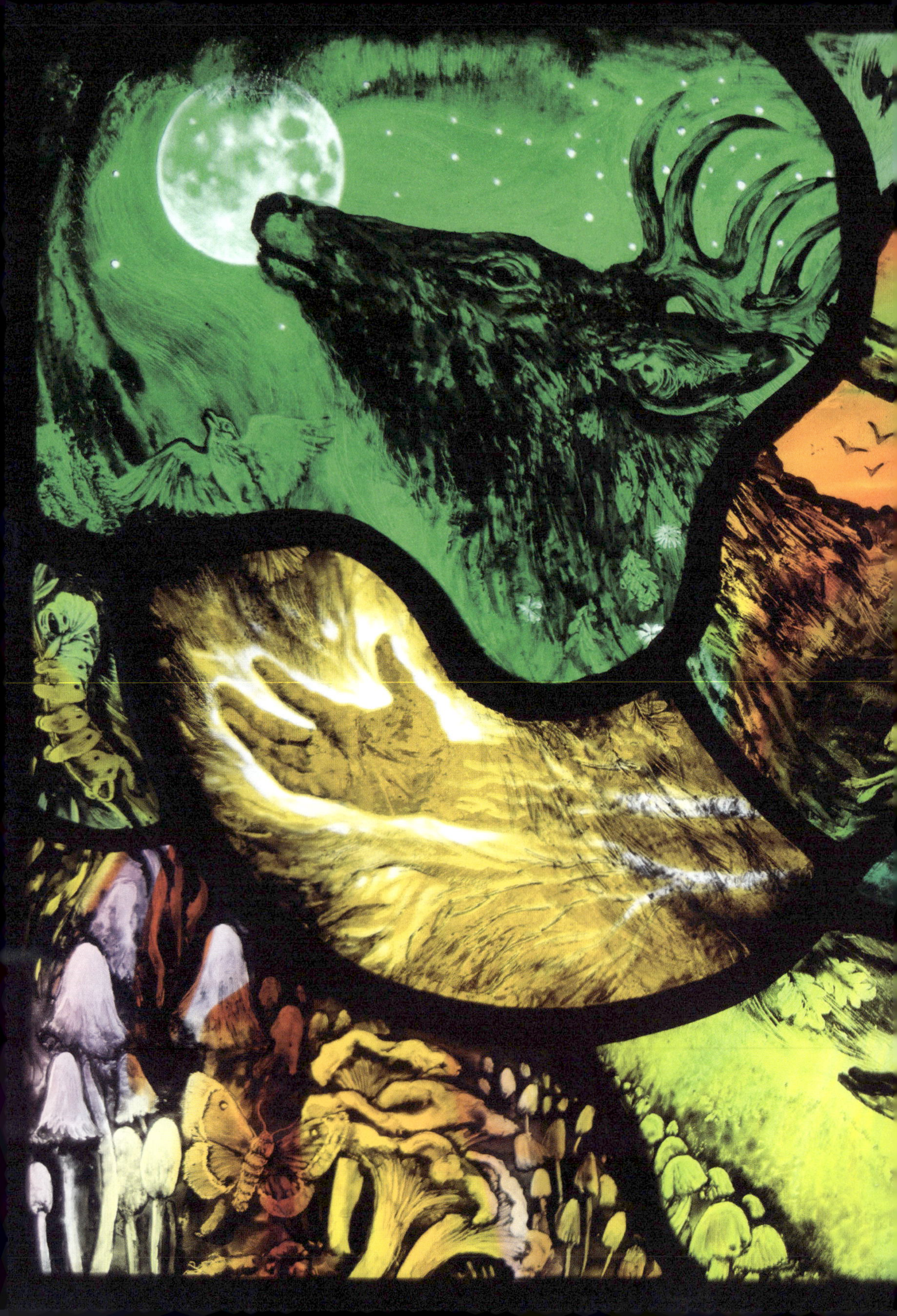

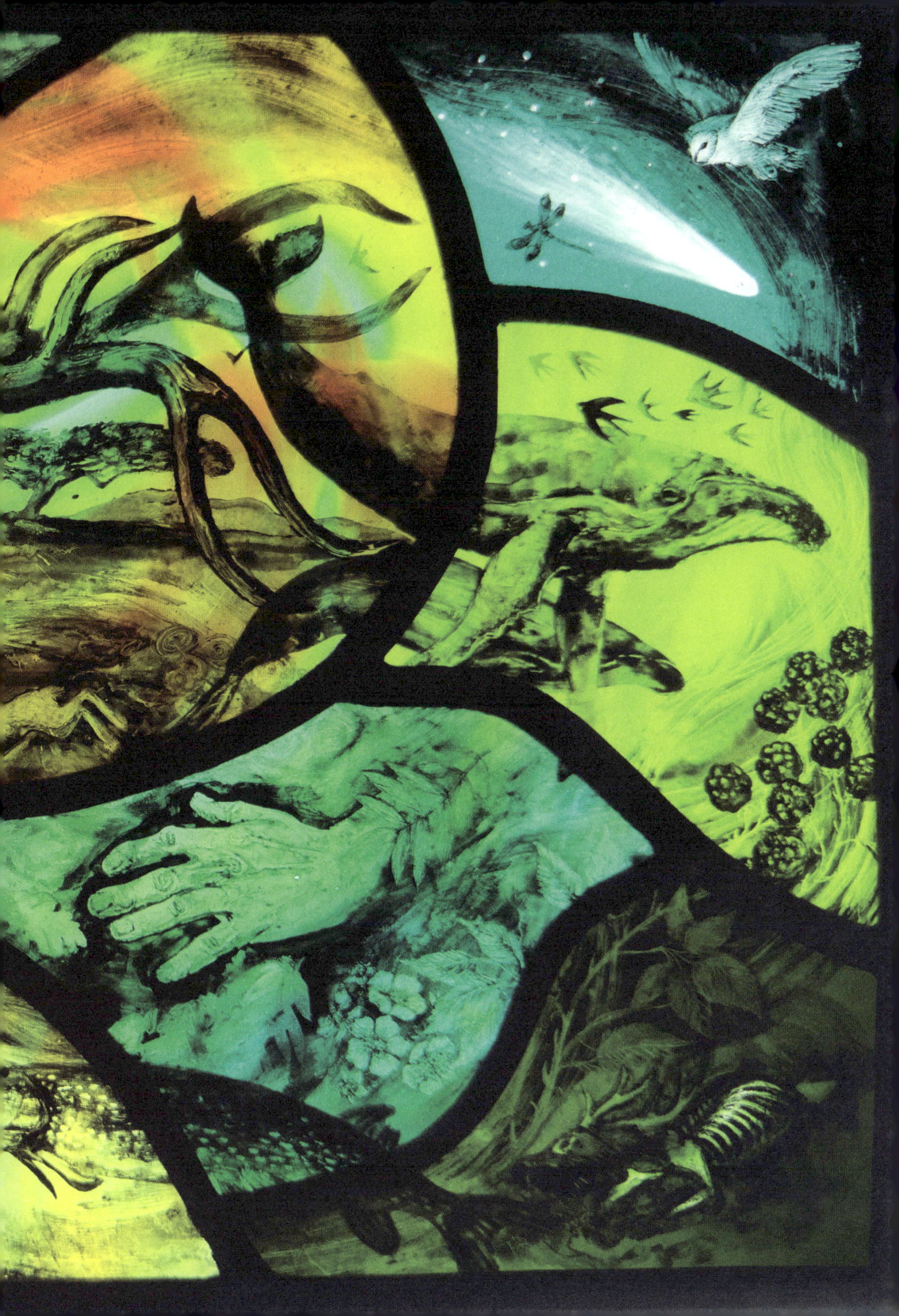

ocean to shore, shore to river, river to otter, otter to eel, eel to stream, stream to meadow, meadow to bee, bee to flower, and on in a curious and beautiful cosmic dance.

They spoke with the creatures, they spoke with the ancestors, those who had more knowledge, and he learned the language of birds, weather, trees, bees and so much more. He grew strong with the knowing and understanding. A wild wisdom. And all the time he felt in his bones the seasons come and go, the light move around the world on a chorus of birdsong.

Then one day the wild god led him back, out through the silvered barkskin into the clearing and the waiting girl.

No longer alone in the forest, he sensed now all the life around him, tasted the weather, disorientated by feeling the sun warm on his skin for the first time in – how long?

They began to walk back to the house. He was exhausted, hungry.

'Who are you?' he asked.

'I am the forest,' she said. 'We've been waiting so long for you. There was a time when these woods ran with wolves who hunted deer, with bears, and beavers who braced the river with dams.'

Around them, on either side of the path, he could feel the ghosts of the wolves, layered by time, hunting the deer.

'Time will always change things,' she said. 'You know that. You have seen the wood beneath the waves. But things are changing fast now, too fast. Too many people fail to hear the forest speak, the voices of trees. Humans are losing their way, trapped in a web of screens, cars, worries. They control the environments of their homes even as their true home, the planet, spins into a climate of chaos. They forget to look outside of themselves. Street lights block out stars, dams change the course of rivers, ancient forests are swept aside to build roads and railways for the convenience of humans, with no regard to the millions of lives blighted. Marshes are drained to build cities in deserts. It's a sickness that threatens us all.'

He remembered how there had been times when he was in that other place when he had felt through the earth a great fear, a profound sadness, and realised that another great being of a tree had been felled, a forest burned to clear land for crops, a river poisoned by sewage, mining. The feeling was an intense, visceral sorrow that wracked his bones.

'You know what we need. Someone to speak for us. To help people to see us. To know us and name us. To restore a balance.'

The weight of the responsibility felt heavy on him. But he thought of what he had experienced, this day that had lasted centuries. The gift of wisdom he had been granted.

'You know the way back from here. Just up the track to the house.'

The lights of the windows caught the sun.

He was weary, so weary.

'This is where you live?'

'Yes. Mounsey Castle.'

They were at the small mound of a hillock, tree-dense and holly-coloured, alive with the bright song of small birds.

'What now?'

'For now,' she said, 'rest. You've more time here. We can walk again tomorrow. And at night. You must hear the wood at night. It comes alive in a different way.'

'And after? When I go home? I'll not see you again?'

'I live here,' she answered. 'Now go, rest. Tomorrow.'

She turned from him and he began to walk up the hill, aware now of all the life around him. An owl called. It was twilight. He stopped and turned to wave. She was gone, but through the trees at the brow of the hill he caught a glimpse of a white hare, sitting, watching.

'Tomorrow,' he thought, 'yes. Tomorrow.'

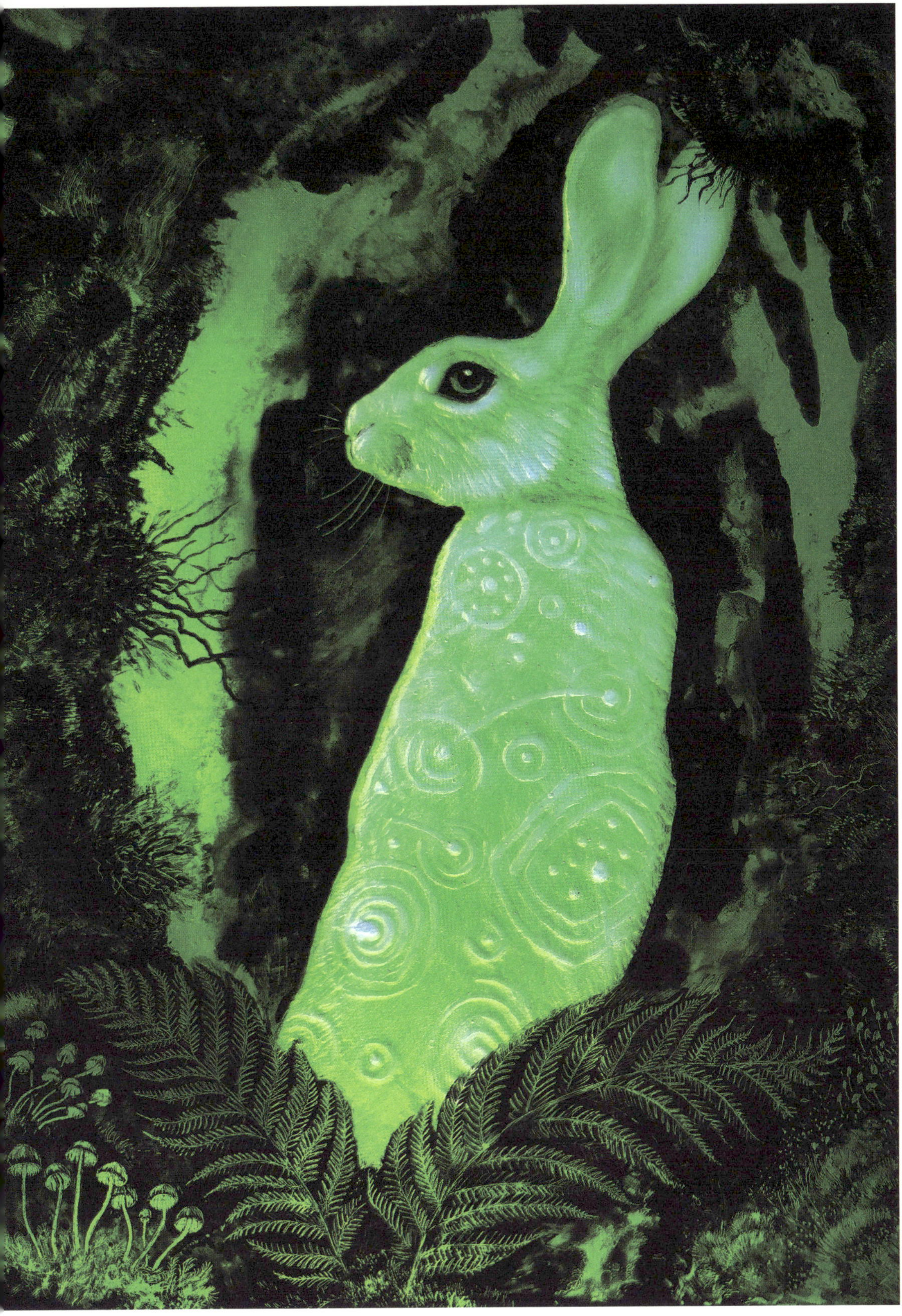

Field fare
white hare
dragonfly
wild eye

*Busy wren
quick flight
holly dense
green light*

Holly leaf
hawthorn berry
oak seed
wild cherry

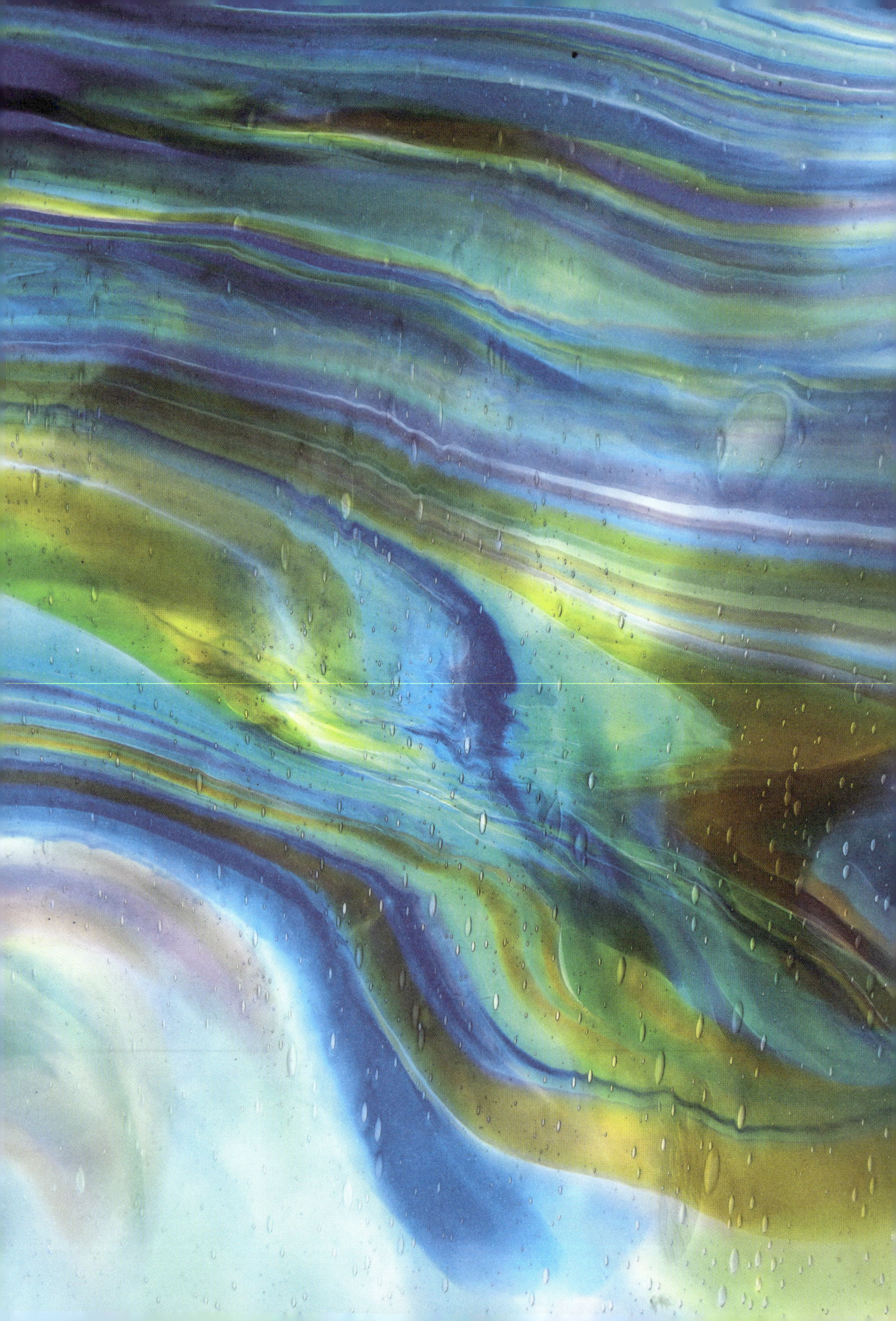

THE SILVER TROUT'S TALE

FOR ROBERT MACFARLANE,
WHO FOLLOWED THE RIVER

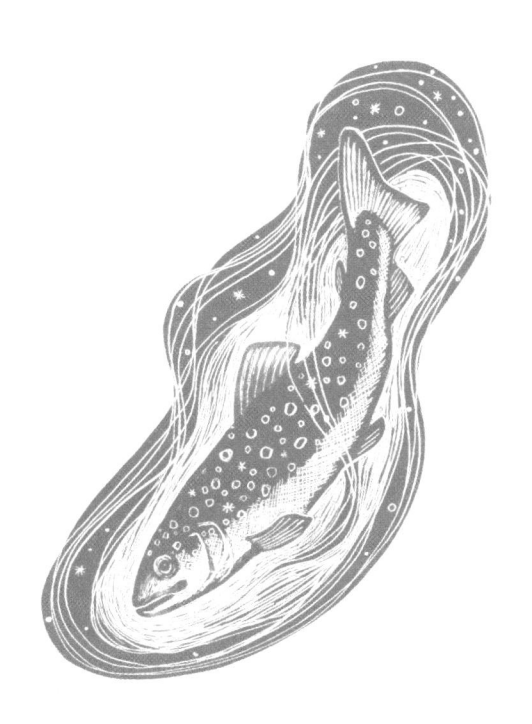

She sits, still, beside the river.

He wanders, hollow lands and hilly lands,
barrows and burial mounds,
circles and stones,
searching.

Did he question how
she knew his name,
a stranger, who,
as fire burned inside his mind,
had come to this place?

Apple blossom at the time of red berries –
river's edge
day's edge
mothlight
and starlight
and the time of full moon
in daylight sky,
the time of wild magic.

A hazel wand,
a berry bright,
stars aligned,
owl flight.

She sits, still, beside the river.
She remembers the lure
of the berry, bright
its taste in her mouth,

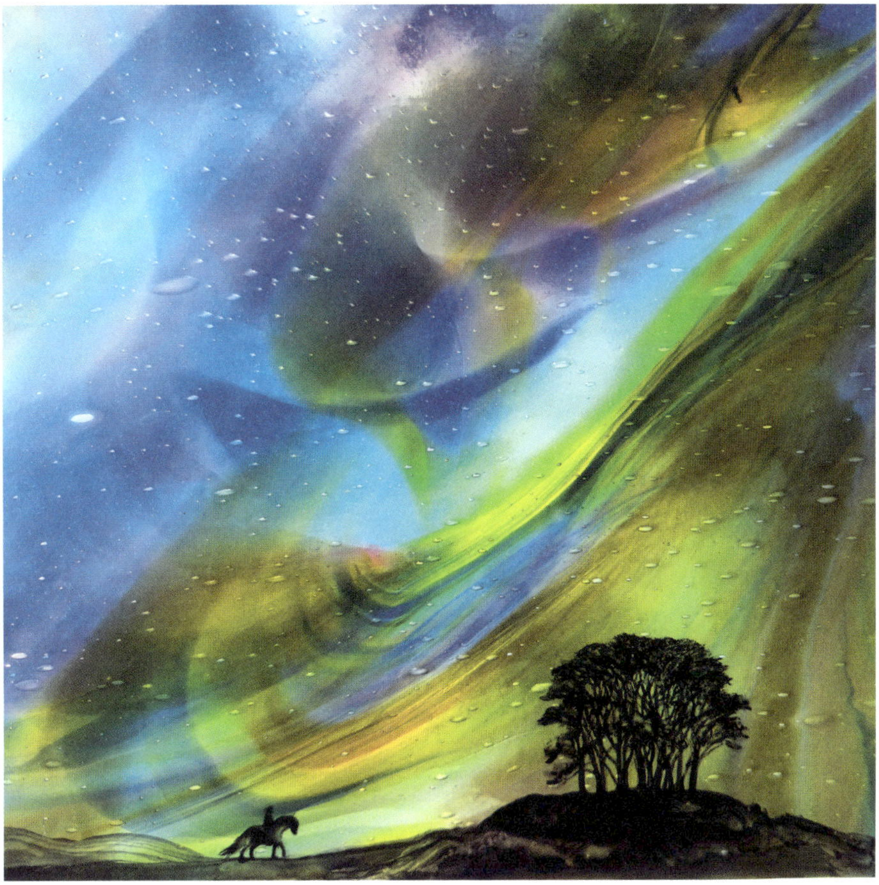

the lift and the shock
as water became air
and, silver, she rested
on riverbank.

Full moon.
Bright moon.
Light on the water,
and falling star,
as she turned,
silver scales shimmering,
lungs tasting air.

How did she know his name?

She watched him
kindle flame from gathered twig,
blow the flame to dance
with light.
Fireglow glimmered on her dress,
silver like the scales she wore
in riverlife –
apple-blossom crown resting
on wet hair.

She swayed in the current of air.
He looked up,
across flame-light.
Rising moon made a halo
for her head.

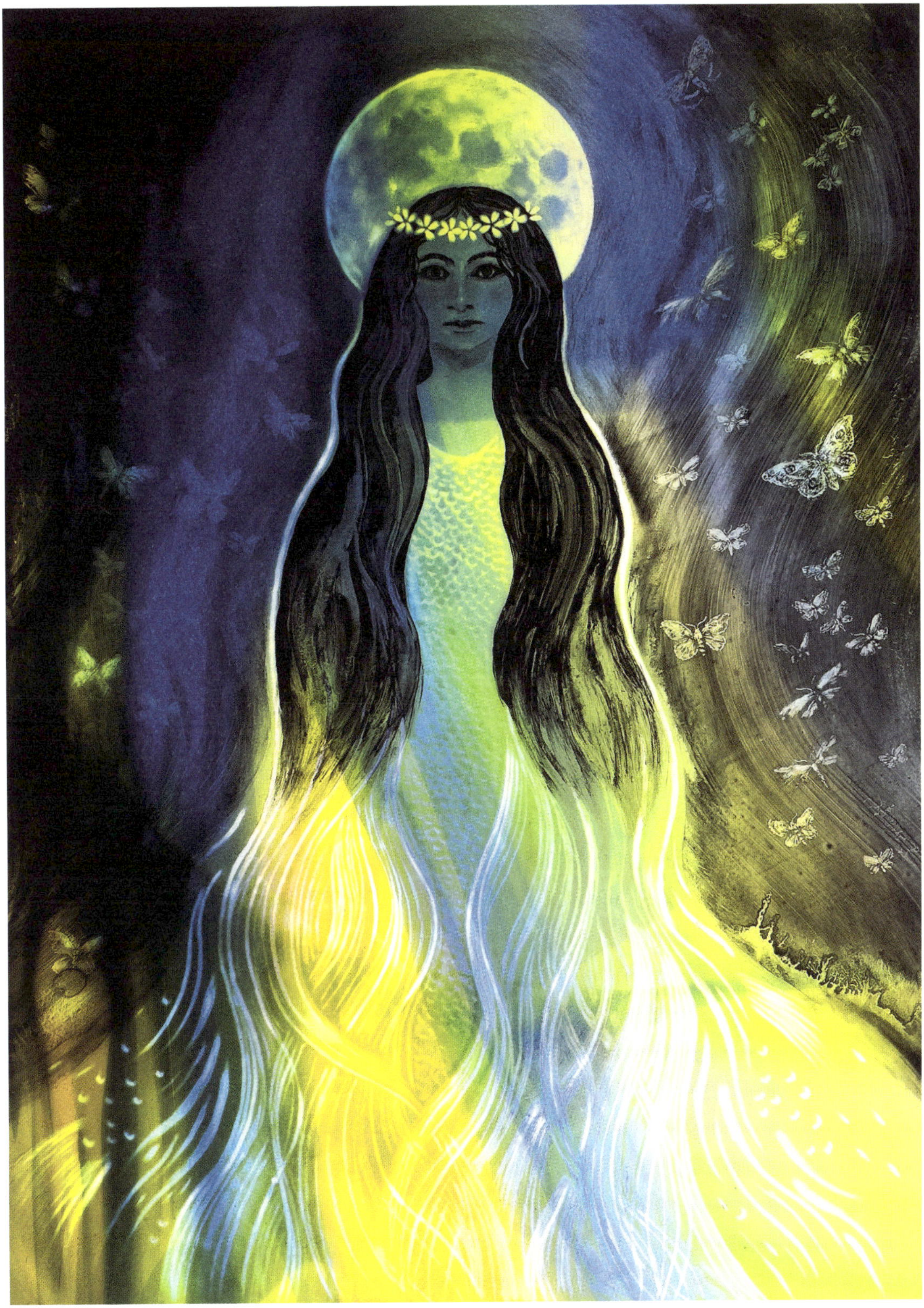

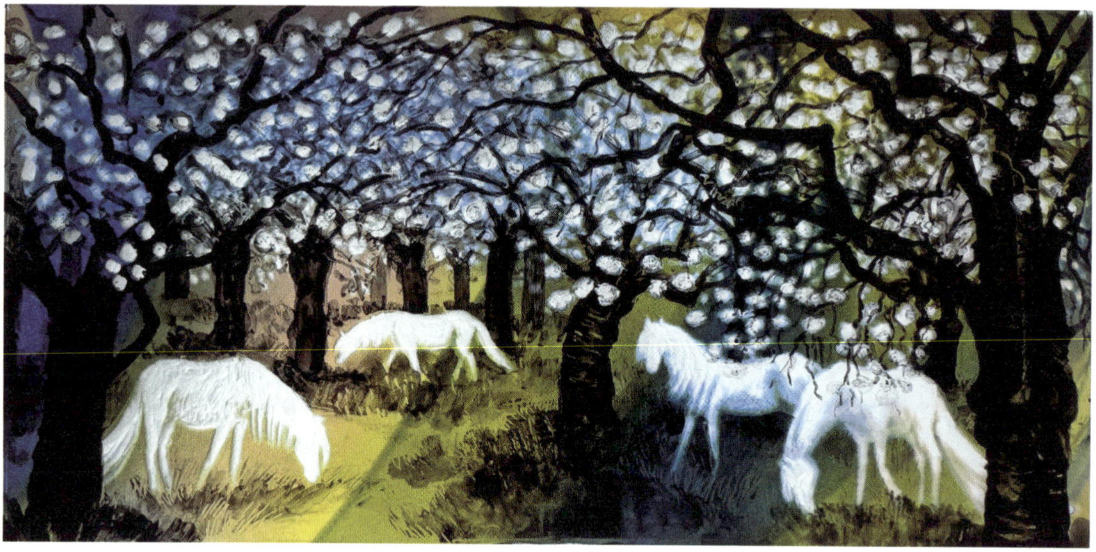

The Silver Trout's Tale

Dark beauty,
silhouette,
apple blossom.
Desire.

Mothlight
bats fly
otter's breath
heron's cry.

Into this moment she spoke his name,
then turned upstream
and ran,
fading as the morning star
into the mist,
taking his heart,
his longing,
his breath, away.

He wandered,
hollow lands and hilly,
asking, searching,
seeking, yearning,
for the apple-blossom beauty of her
that never faded in his memory,
wishing only to
hold her hands,
to kiss her lips.
He searched, following
the paths of moths.
He followed dreams and streams,

from Swallowhead Spring to Winterbourne,
across narrow becks and
rivers wide,
and down beside the sea he spoke
with fishing folk.
In spring, seduced by scent,
he found himself in orchards
blossom-heavy
and whispered to the bees
who danced a pattern
that sang of his longing.

She sat still,
on riverbank, beside the trees,
as water moved,
restless.
Through long summer days,
sun-warmed, short nights
through autumns,
harvest moon heavy, full,
leaf fall
berry bright,
listening as river song
changed with the seasons
with falling rain
with winter freeze
with summer drought
with autumn leaves.
When ice wrapped river's bank
in glowing light,
when summer seeds caught in river's flow,

The Silver Trout's Tale

Still she sat,
statue-still,
waiting.

Birds came and went, and some
brought news of him.
And all the while the water rushed,
restless, full with life,
towards the sea.

And still he searched,
beneath the fairy hills,
in caves, water-carved from stone,
through winter freeze
through summer rain.
At Callanish he asked
the Shining One,
who simply pointed back,
along the path
his footprints left
through spiderwebs
rich with diamond dew.

In northern lands he
spoke with Coventina,
drank at the well where
the white hart drinks,
listened, watched,
hope in heart,
to rook call,
raven flight,

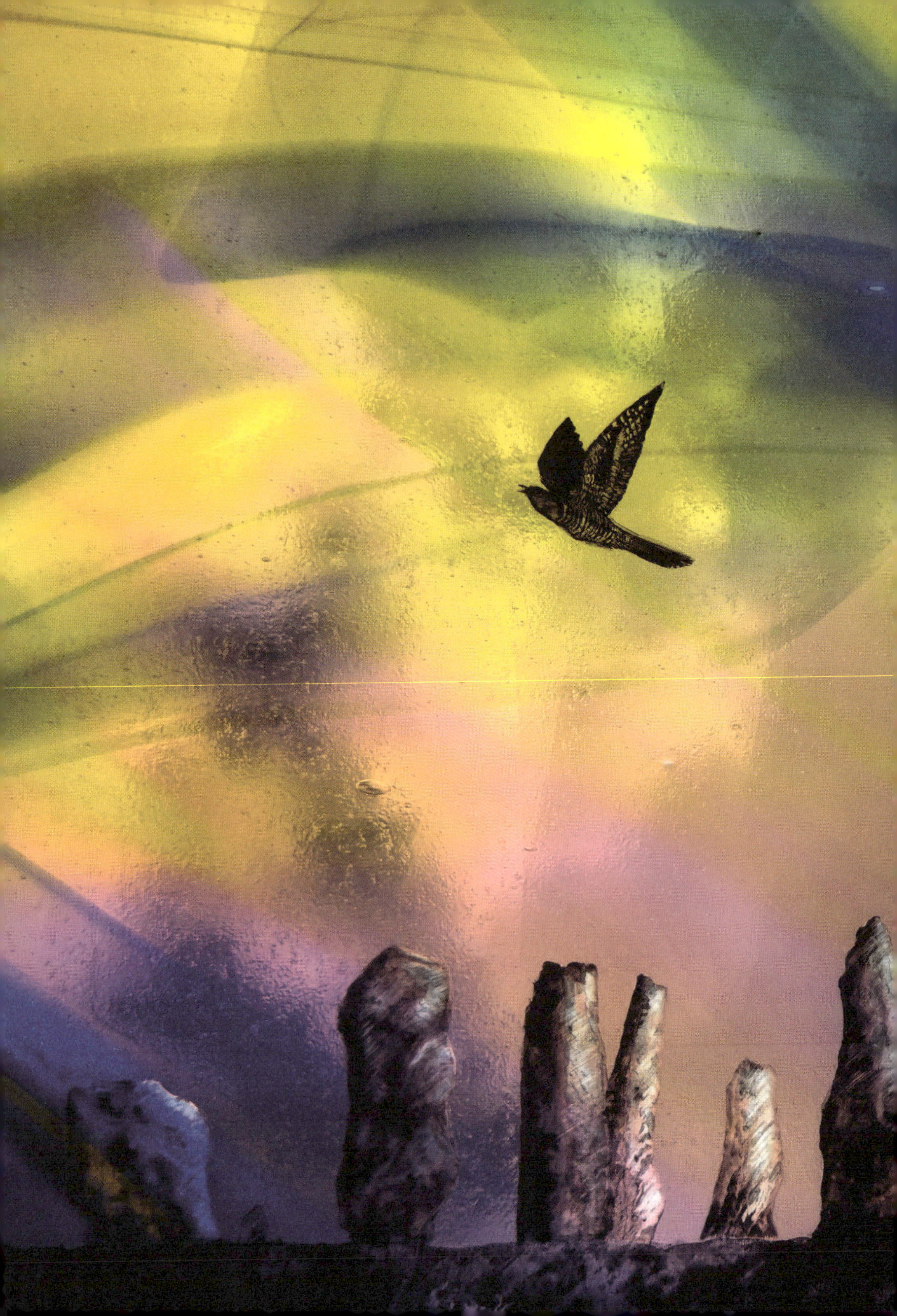

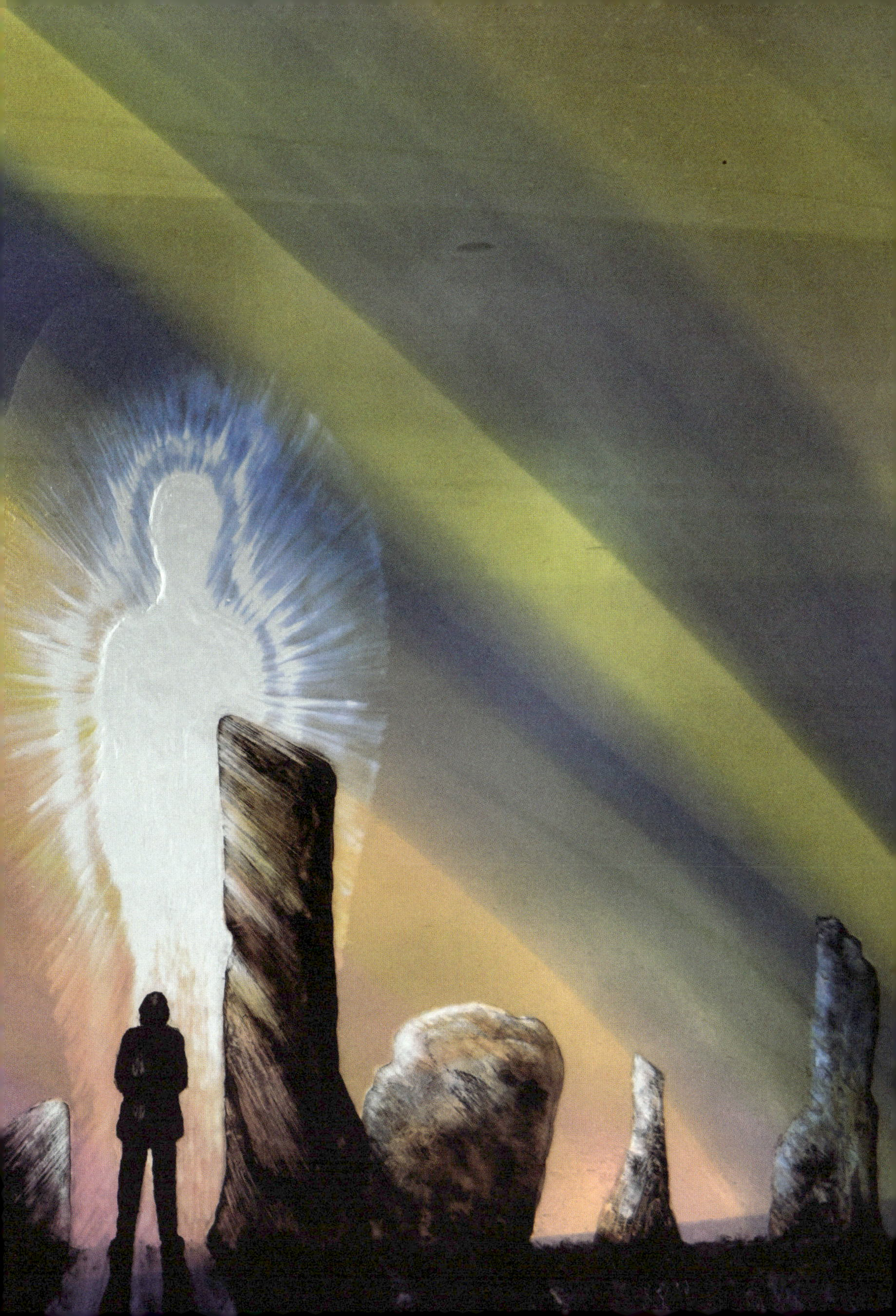

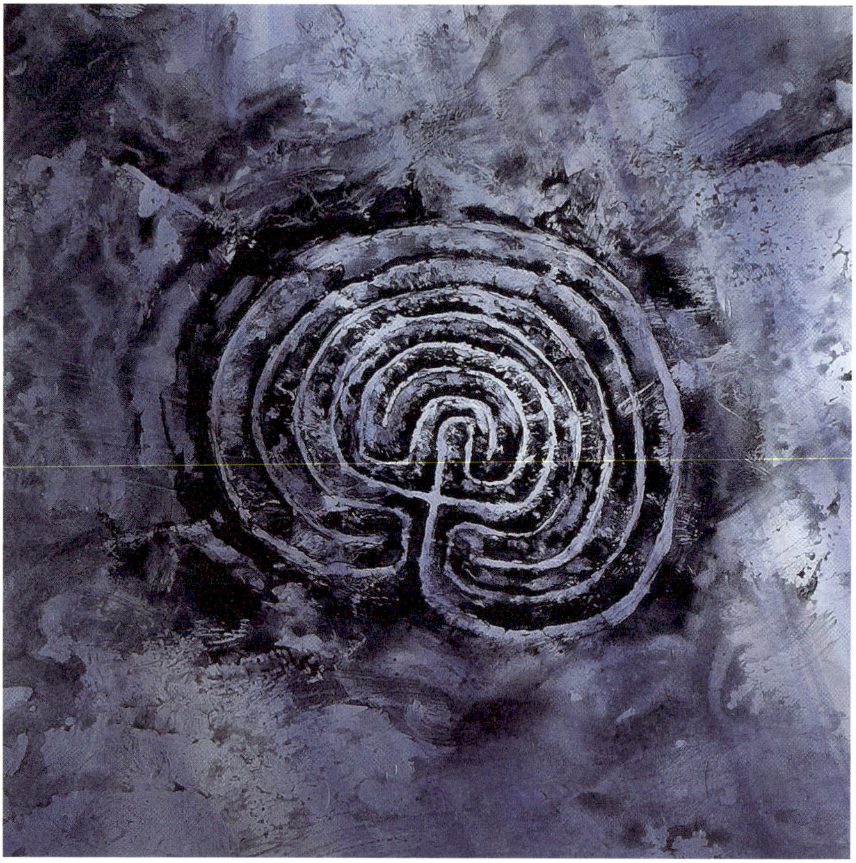

The Silver Trout's Tale

jay feathers
eyes bright
with longing.

And when the acorns came
he ſpoke with the ſpirit
of the Whiteleaved Oak,
whose leaves sang,
'Go back.'

Through borderlands to Cymru,
to Alba, and the islands,
and Albion, where,
his horse lame,
he paid a silver coin
and Wayland made bright shoes.
But when he asked the smith
about the silver lady of his dreams
he ſtilled the hammer.
A wren sang into the silence.
Looking skyward, he simply said,
'Go back.'

With these words hammering in head,
to Kernow, where, on a ſtone
he found a labyrinth.
Weary now, with wandering,
in hollow lands and hilly,
he lingered,
traced the pattern's pathway in,
the pathway out,

and in his mind –
'Go back.'

Old now, weary with wandering,
fire still burning in mind,
body aflame with the pains of age,
fire in joints,
hair thinned and grey
and back bent,
eyes dimmed,
he sought again the place,
of hazel wood and rowan berry,
and bright stream.
Moonlight on water,
moths on the wing,
trout rise,
owl call and
the slow flight of heron,
as water moves and
she sits, still,
apple-blossom crown,
otter curled in arms,
still as fresh as that first day
when stars were fading in
the brightening air.
Through clouded vision he saw,
or thought he saw,
the moth-like stars,
the glimmering in gloaming,
the girl.
She called him, by his name again,

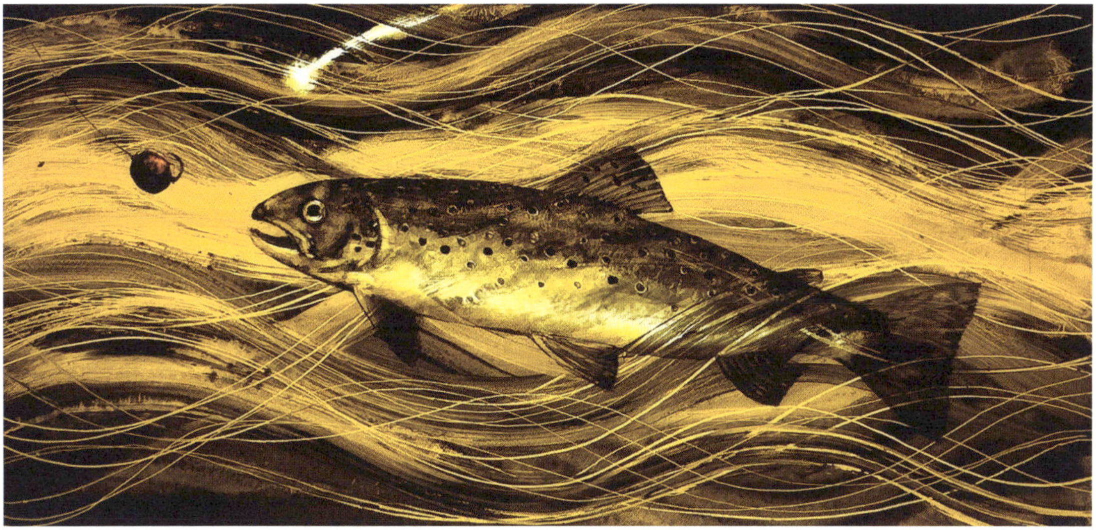

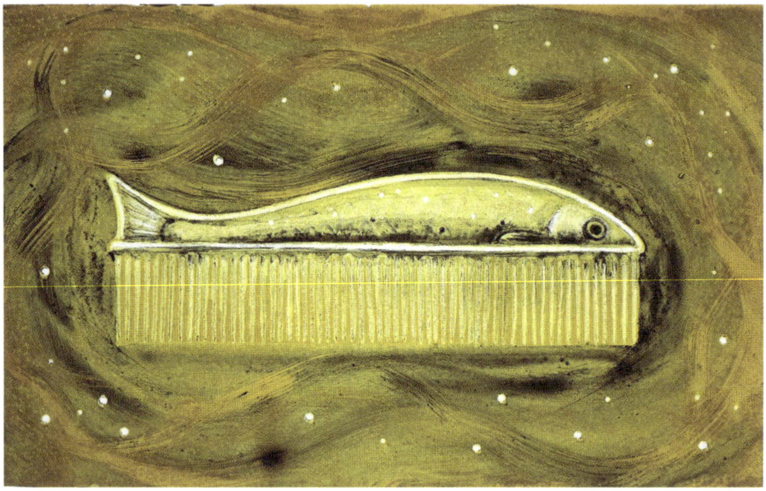

but words were lost in river flow.
A third time, and
held out her hand
as he stepped towards the vision
and placed his old, unsteady hand
in hers.
As otter slipped to stream,
she cradled his body,
sat him down
in moonlight-dappled grass,
and he wished only now to
die in the curve of her warm arms.
Here, where water flowed,
between the light of night and day,
she took out a comb,
began to comb the ragged grey,
and with every stroke the hair
grew longer, thicker, stronger,
darkened in the wakening light.
And each movement of the comb
eased the fire inside the mind,
dulled the burning joints until,
as stars flickered out,
blinded by day's light,
he became again the young man
who, so long ago,
had hooked the berry to a thread.
She turned his face towards the light,
and kissed his lips,
and held his hand.

*Heron's brook
kingfisher's stream
wild-rose thorn
brown trout's gleam*

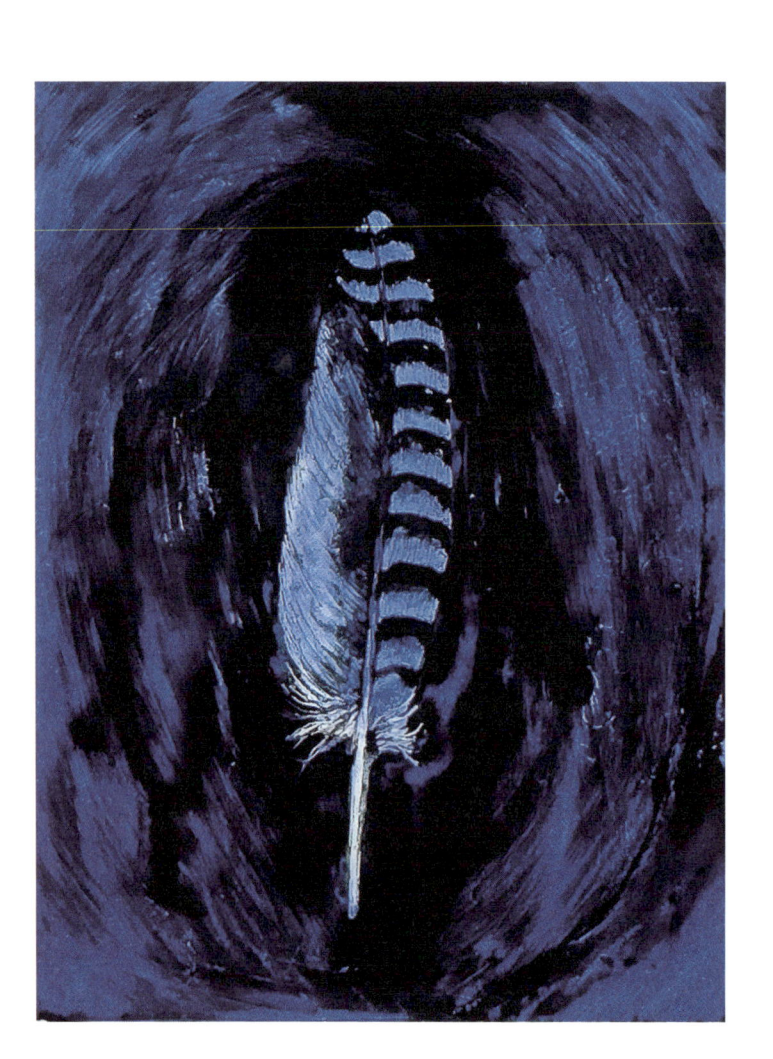

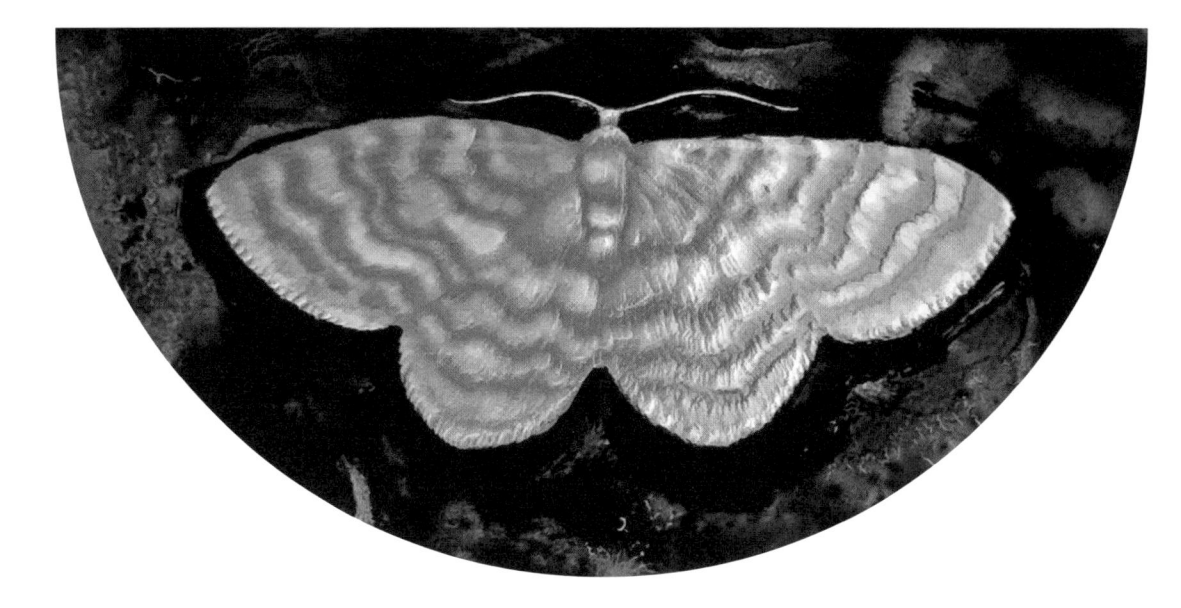

*New moon
star bright
ink dark
moth flight*

*Slow flight
heron's wing
deep in wood
owl sings*

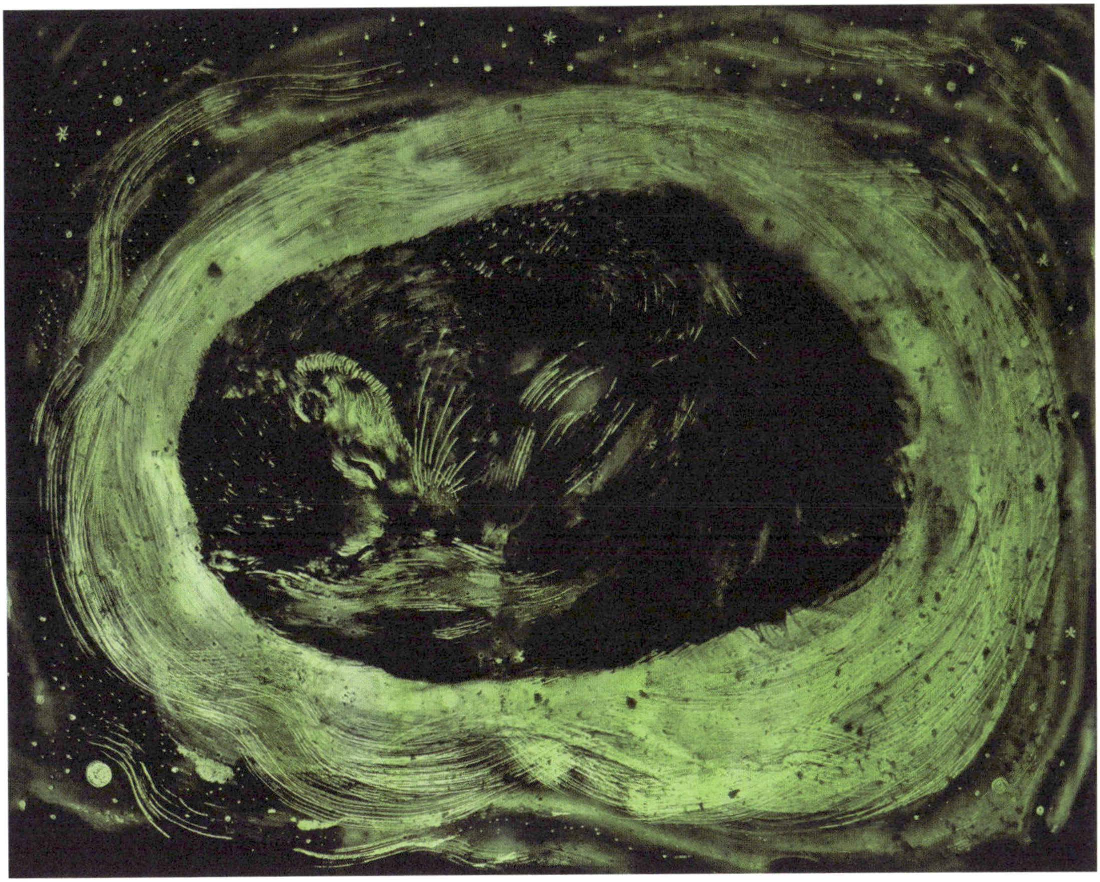

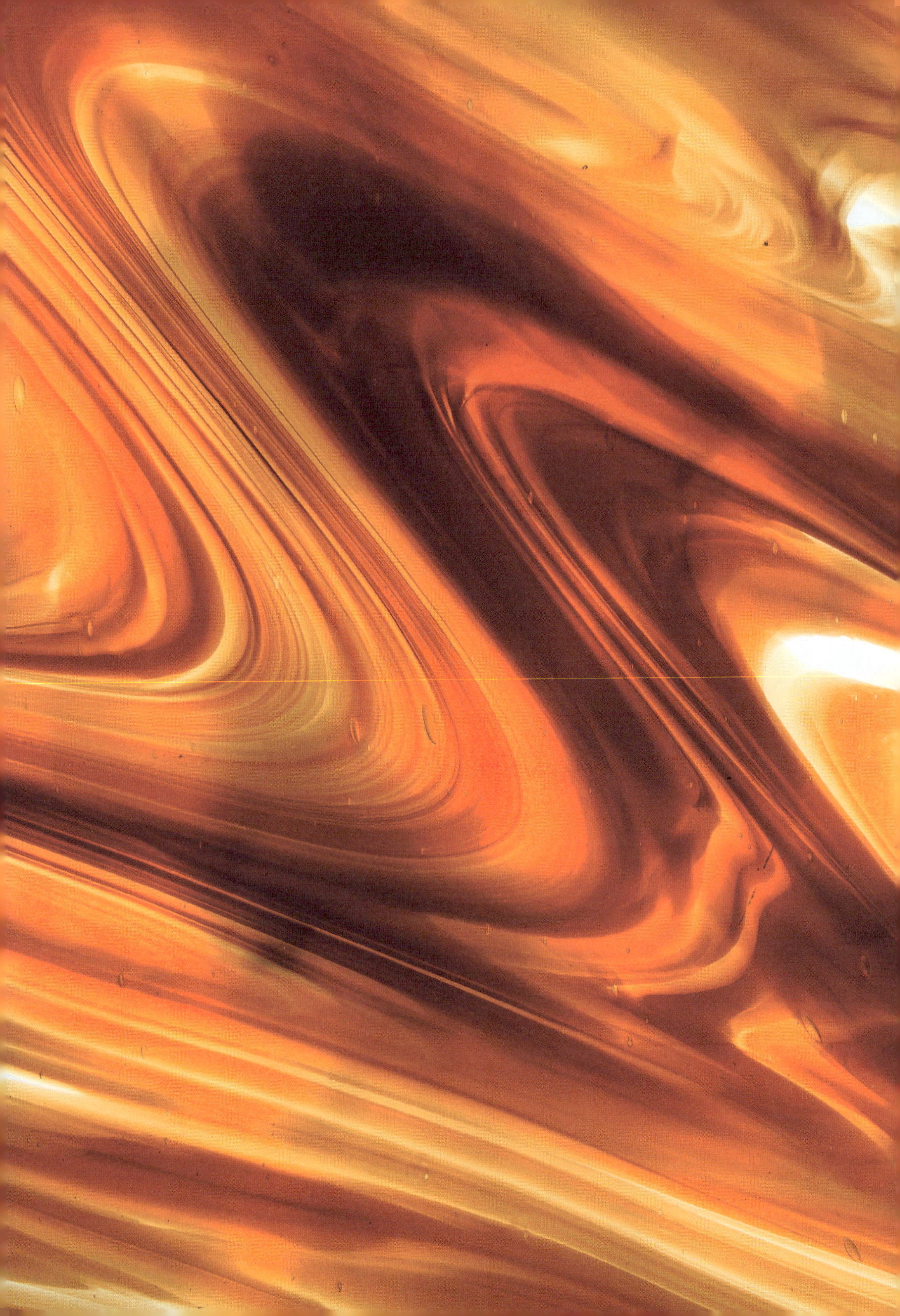

THE RAVENS' TALE

FOR ROBIN STENHAM,
WHO WAS THERE WHEN I SAW HER

First step from boat to shore, and beneath her feet she felt it. No word in her mother tongue, but in Cymraig, *hiraeth*.

The island knew that moment too, through stone and lichen, heather and gorse. All the birds, small mammals who lived on this place, turned their heads towards the harbour, for a moment.

Like stepping through time,
from sea to shore,
where the veils are thin.
Land's edge,
sea's edge.

The air held the taste of gorse, golden, and a promise of heather. The land belonged to the birds. Wheatears bobbed, smalt-blue, white-rumped, along stone walls, bone-white with lichens. At the seaward side of the island a tangle of chough tumbled in turbulent air over the wild sea.

She'd loved birds for as long as she could remember, from the moment a fledgling wren, new from its nest, perched on her shoulder as she stood statue-still in her garden, wanting to keep company with this creature, delighting in the delicacy of the nut-brown feathers, pattern of wings, bright eye. Unafraid, her child self had loved the weight of the bird, the claws that caught. Such a small bird to carry such a mighty song.

There were wrens here too.

Everywhere she walked she could see, taste, hear the sea. The air felt different. Such a clean smell after growing up in a city.

When she was a child she had a book, with pictures. A story of selkies. The shape of the land here seemed so similar, and there were seals here too, a breeding colony of greys.

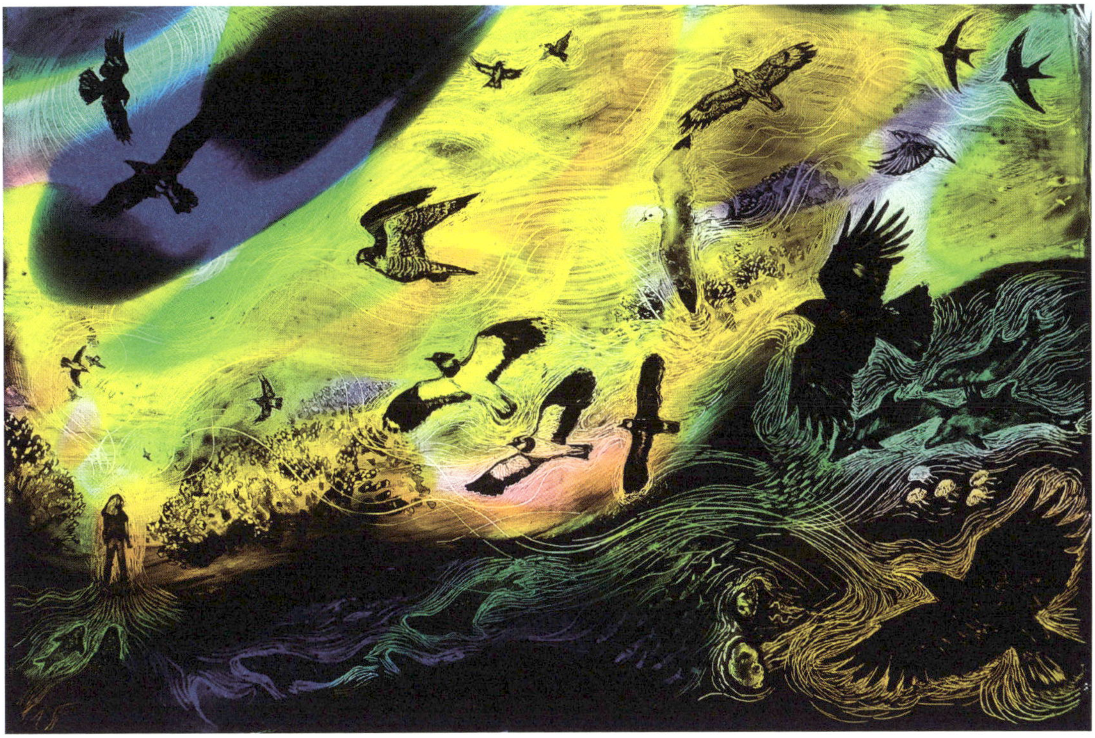

She closed her eyes, the better to hear:
buzzard
chough
wren
lapwing
lark song
kittiwakes
sea, racing through rocks
waves on shore
wind over land
and
in a moment of stillness
air, through the feathers
of raven wings
and that deep call,
the language of ravens.

She didn't want to think of the city, didn't want to remember. Wanted only this moment, this now, this here, to drink it in, taste it, hold it, stop time.

Warm sun on face, and the lull of wind and wing.

Worry snapped her back into time's river. This was just a holiday. Lovely as it was, her parents said, no one could 'live here'. No work, they said. And yet people did live here, and she'd seen so many adverts in shops and cafés offering work.

She thought about her future. Her parents wanted her to go to university, then a job, marriage, mortgage. This path of their desires led through a maze to a cage, trapped in work to pay for a house.

She loved it here. Perhaps a different path was possible? Out to sea, specks of bright white became the shape of gannets, hunting. Beneath them porpoise rose. Possibilities, hope. Through the touch of her body where she lay on the earth, sun-warmed in wind's shadow, the sense of belonging took root – a feeling she had never known anywhere, any time, before. So out of place in her family, in the city, living between the lives of others, trying to get by, to understand.

Earth under hand, sky above, and a wish for wings, her mind began to drift into dreams as she watched ravens dance in the rising thermal at the cliff's edge.

She slept.

And while she slept the island filled her dreams with a story…

It began with an egg, green porcelain, fragile, mottled, deep in a tangle of twigs lined with moss and wool, on a high cliff on the seaward side of Hrafen's Ey.

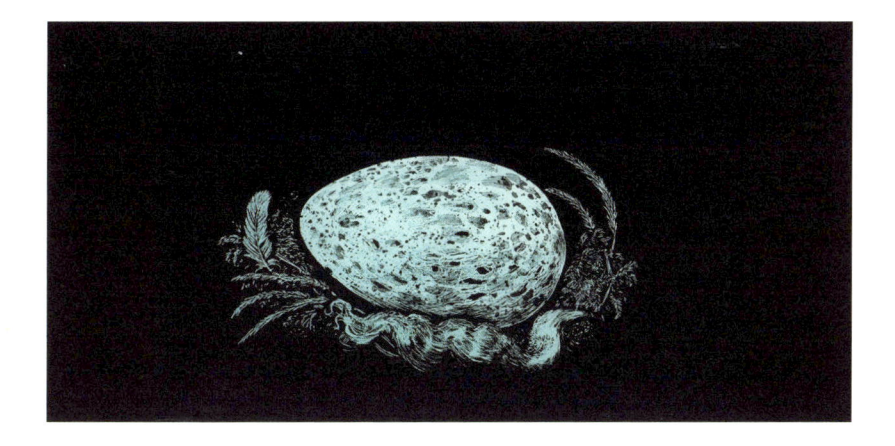

Raven grew up with the sound of the wind and the call of the birds and the song of the seals. Sea below and sky above, he was wild.

And he grew up with the island's legend deep in his mind, raven lore, the legend of a king sleeping under the hill, waiting for the return of the white raven, the magical one.

> *Far away, long ago,*
> *white feathers,*
> *dark eyes,*
> *gold bars,*
> *lock and key,*
> *impossible creature,*
> *myth in feathered form,*
> *dreaming always of freedom.*

Strong and fierce, Raven flew, highest of all the birds. Black feathers gleamed with gold dust in the sunshine. He gloried in flight, tumbled and turned and played with the wind.

He looked to the east and saw the sun rise. He looked to the west and watched the sun sink into a fiery sea. And when he slept, he dreamed of the white one.

Then one day men came to the island. Across the Sound in a boat they came, to catch peregrine for the king in England. The falcons on Hrafen's Ey were the fastest, the fiercest.

They baited their traps and waited.

And Raven saw the rabbit, flew down to feast and was caught.

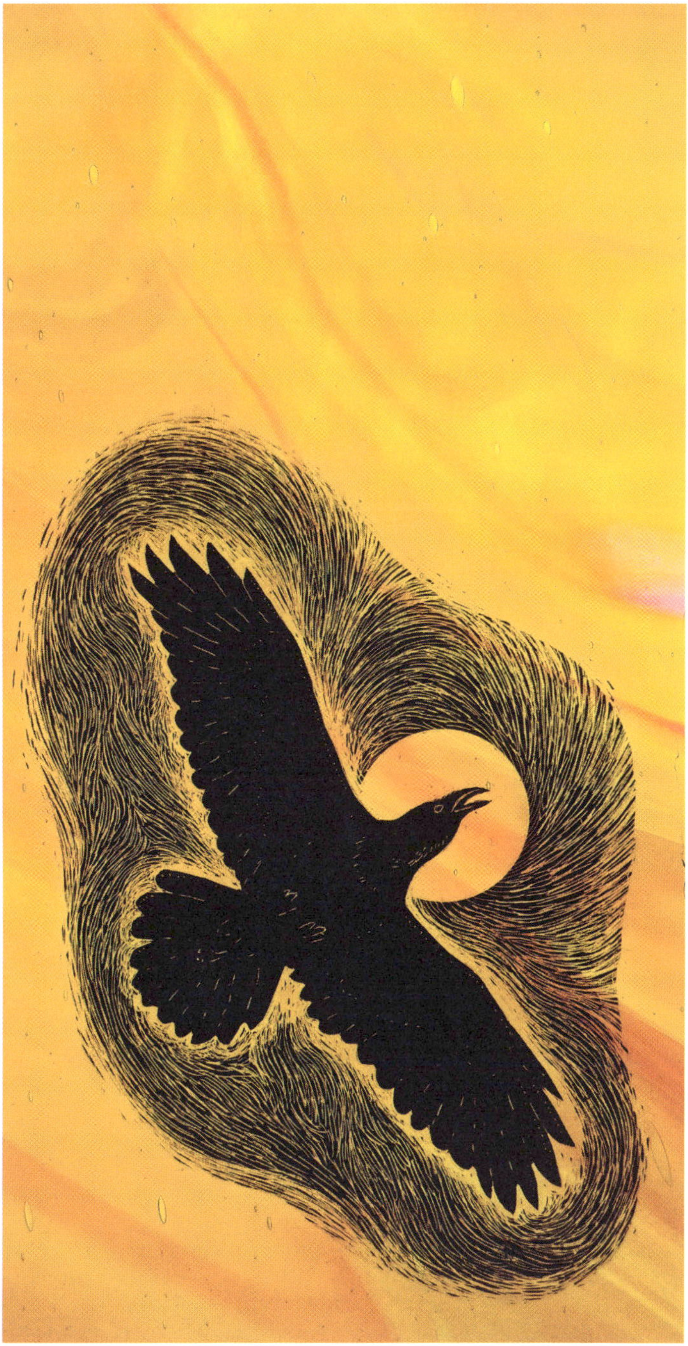

Bundled into a basket, his world became dark. He could smell the fear of other captive birds. Hunting had been good for the men. They had four fine peregrine, a merlin and a remarkable raven to take back to the king. A new raven was needed for the Tower.

He heard their laughter as they placed the baskets of birds in the boat and left the wild island for the long journey to London.

Long days in the dark weakened the raven. Meat and water were put into his cage, and after many days of travelling on boats and carts, through villages and towns, they entered the city. Journey over, the basket was opened and the light bit into his brain. He ruffled his soot-black feathers and strutted. Noise was everywhere: people talking, shouting, dogs barking. He saw the Tower like a cliff, human heads on spikes decorating its walls, rotting in the sunshine, and a strutting king in rich robes.

He saw ravens, well-fed, fat, pale imitations of his wild brothers and sisters.

The Ravens' Tale

And then he saw her, the white one, dazzlingly bright, beautiful and strange. Like a ghost raven.

In the cage
  White Raven knew
    no past,
      no future,
        only the now,
          trapped in a spell
            in the cage
              by weird magic,
                not knowing
                  what her wings were for,
                  each moment her first
                until she saw
                  through the space between
                gold bars
                  the jet-black
                    mirror form.
                    Where she was light
                  he was shadow.
                    Light stealing dark.
                  She saw freedom
                    where he perceived myth
                      in feather, beak and bone.

He watched. Saw the bars. Understood the trap. He waited, growing stronger each day. Saw the human take her food, turn the key, open the bars, close, twist and lock.
    He sang quiet raven songs to her, close to the cage, a courtship, tales of flight, of freedom, of home.

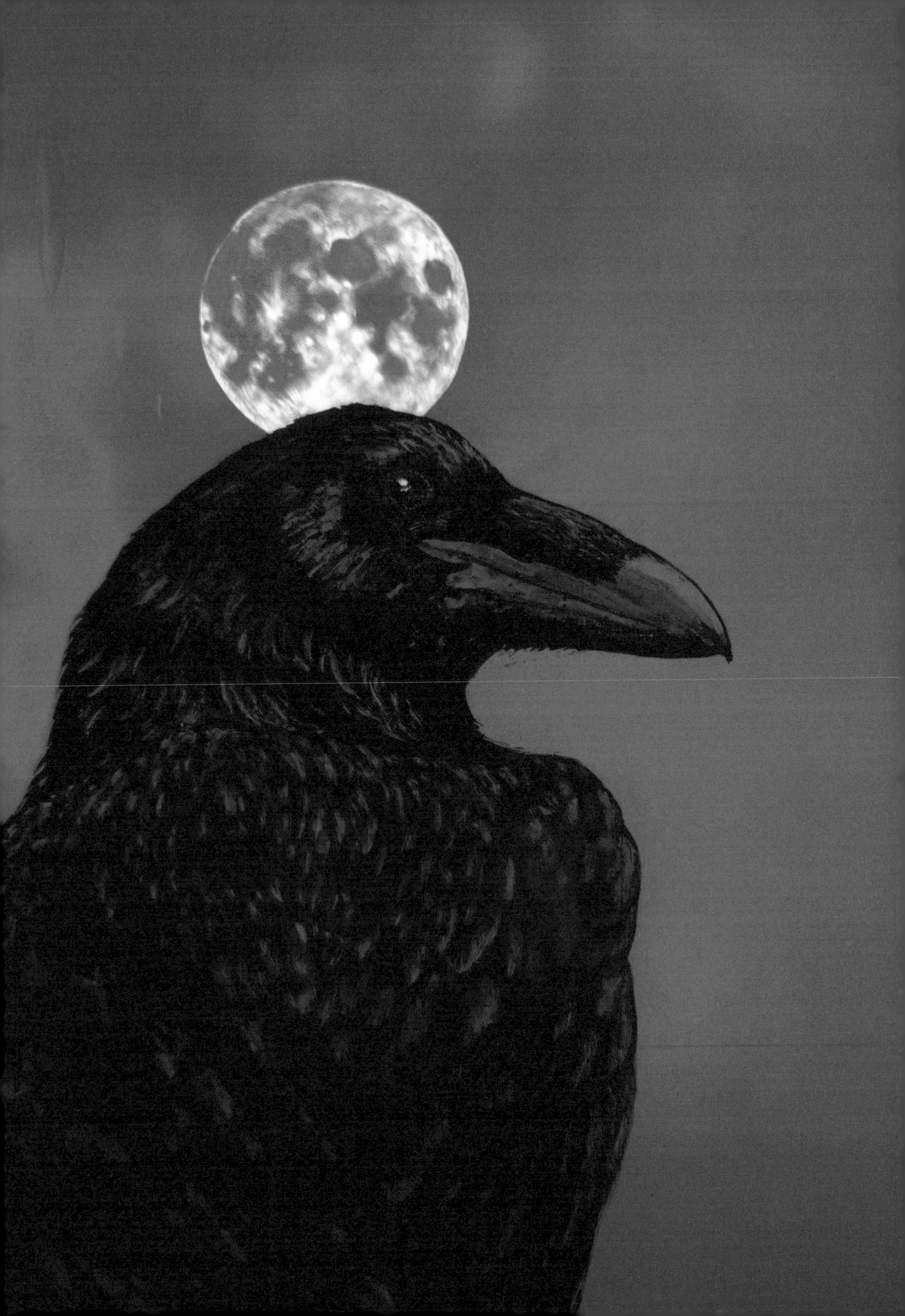

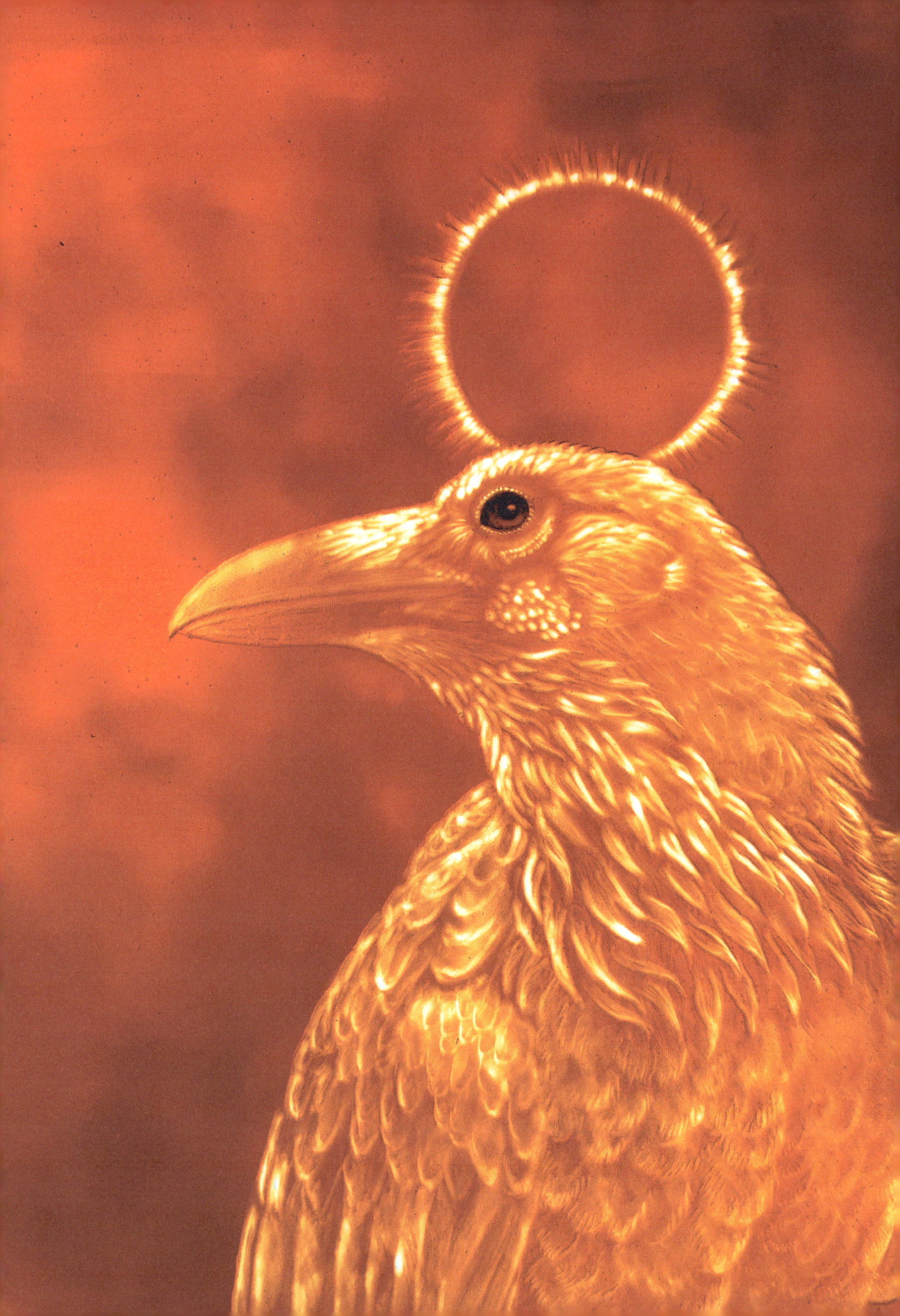

Closer and closer,
through the bars,
as beaks touched,
spell broke
as a raven's beak
breaks the shell of an egg,
cracks a bone.

Sunrise, midsummer, he turned the key.
She took the key from his beak,
spread wings wide,
lifted from stone sill
into waiting air
that welcomed her form,
holding her gentle
in the wind's hands.

Up
and
up
and all the ravens in the Tower
followed,
a spiral dance of flight to freedom.

Swooping low to river
she opened beak,
let golden key fall into tide's mud,
and where it fell
time began to ripple and shift.

The Ravens' Tale

He marked the rising of the sun,
wheeled them west.
Land folds and time folds
isobars of years
centuries.
They flew through time to the building of barrows,
saw great stones lifted,
earth's bones shifted,
white horses drawn in chalk on hillsides,
saw forests rise from planted acorns seeds
to become great trees,
cut down and cleared,
regrown.
They rested by an ancient mound,
where a blacksmith forged
a sword with the heart of a wren,
a weapon to end the wars of men,
and later saw it thrown into water,
where an arm rose to snatch from the air,
clothed in white,
and watched peace drown.
And time folded,
twisted, turned and tumbled,
fluid as a raven's flight.

Black Raven,
White Raven,
now flew alone.
Each day stronger, wilder,
fiercer, wiser.
Time steadied in their wake,

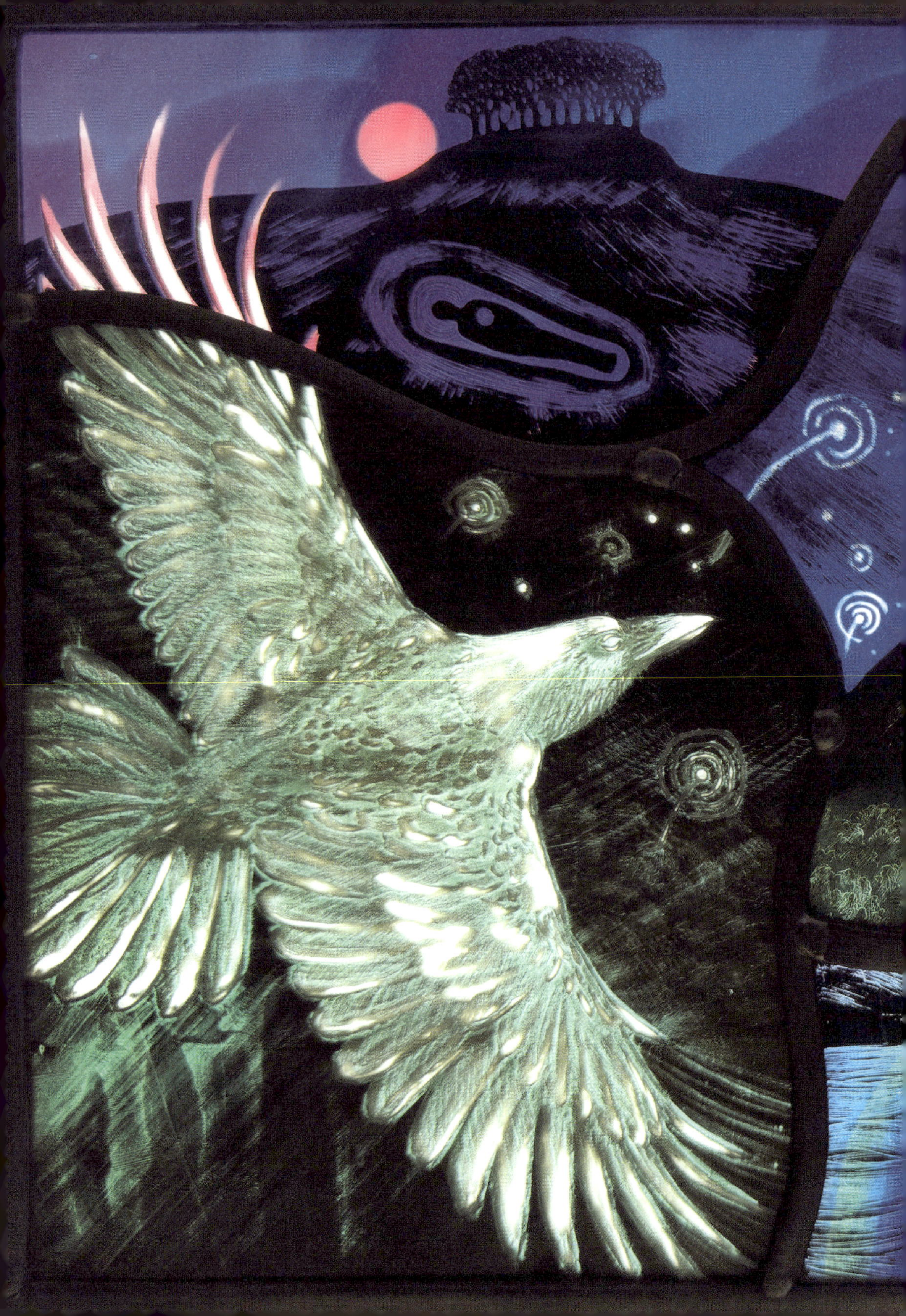

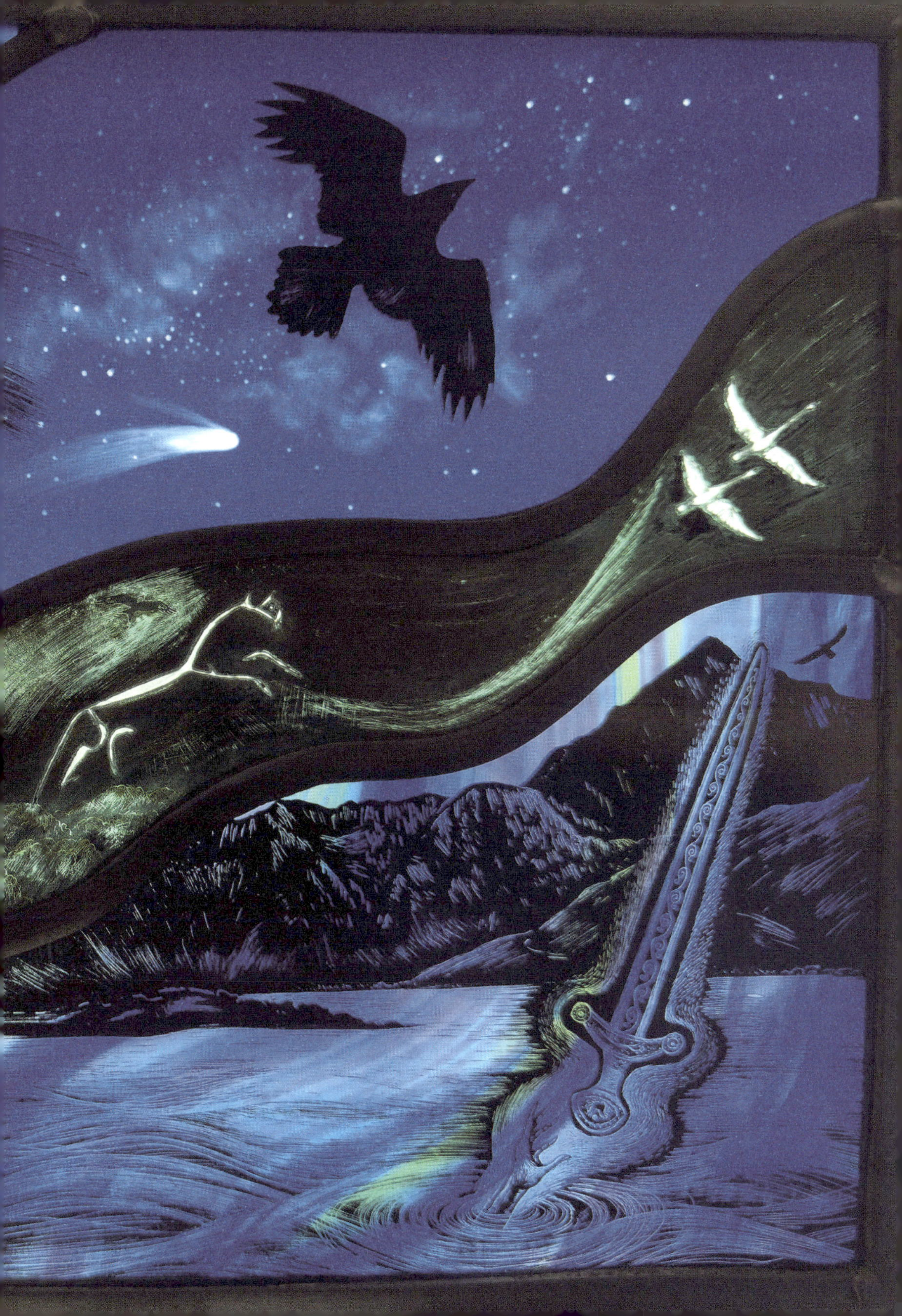

and she now woken from the binding spell,
gathered threads of time
in mind and memory.

At land's edge they dropped to earth
to rest on an open barrow.
Power gathered around the pair,
in this place,
over sea, over stone,
skin of the land,
bones of the earth.
Across a ribbon of sea, the shape of home beckoned,
over water that echoed the rippled patterns
of time and tide.
Above sea, over stone, wings beat.
Island ravens flocked out to welcome them.

Waking into evening light, the girl saw the white one, high above, pale in the fading day, eyes as blue as the sky, a dream made flesh. She saw the wild black raven wheeling at her side. She stood and they flew to her shoulders, one to the left, one to the right, and all three felt the sleeping king waking, the old wild gods waking. And she knew that this was only the beginning.

The old gods rising.
The old gods rising.
The old gods rising.
The old gods rising.
The old gods rising.
The old gods rising.
The old gods rising.
The old gods rising.
The old gods rising.
The old gods rising.
The old gods rising.
The old gods rising.

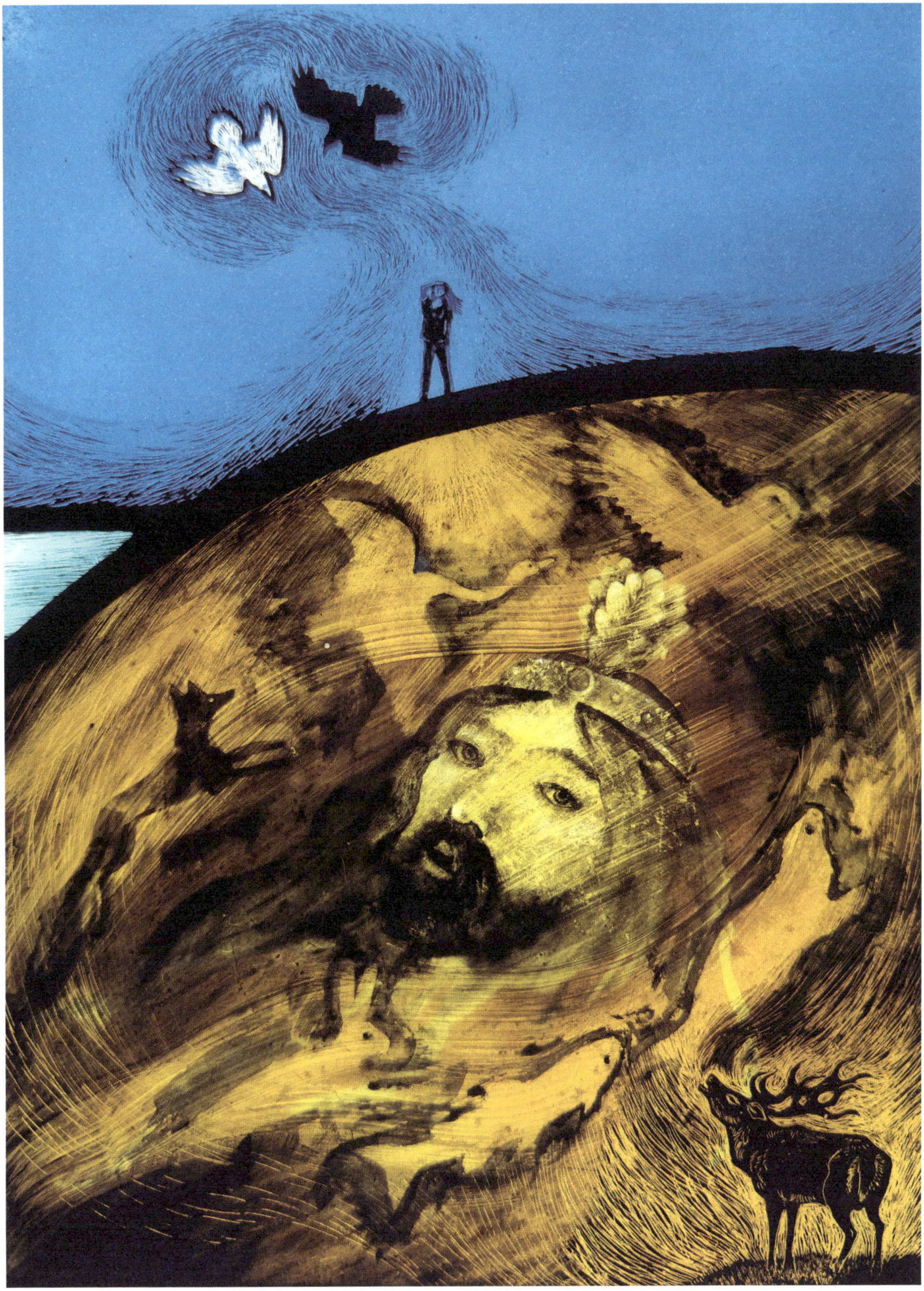

The old gods rising.
The old gods rising.
The old gods rising.
The old gods rising.
The old gods rising.
The old gods rising.
The old gods rising.
The old gods rising.
The old gods rising.
The old gods rising.
The old gods rising.
The old gods rising.
The old gods rising.
The old gods rising.
The old gods rising.
The old gods rising.

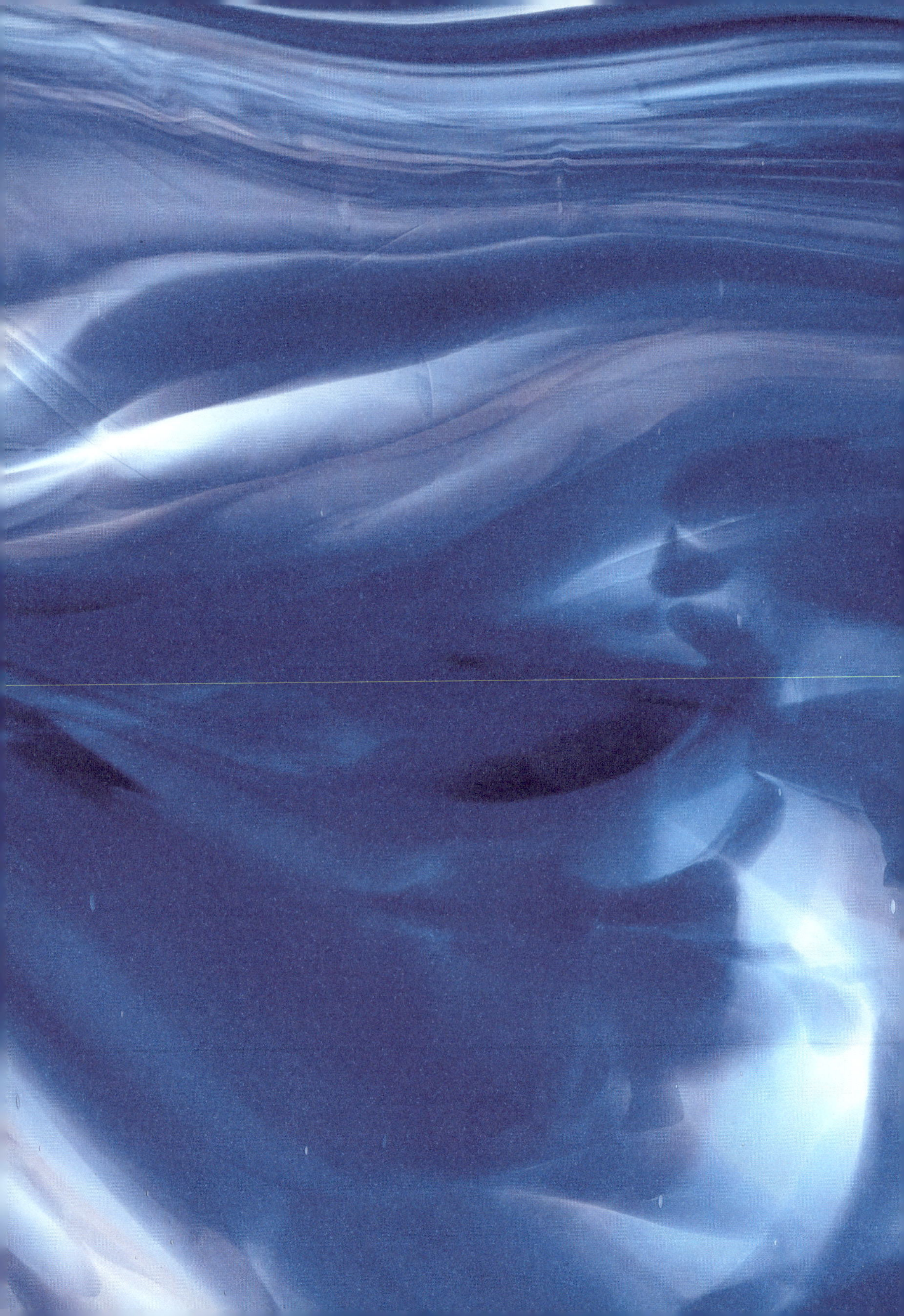

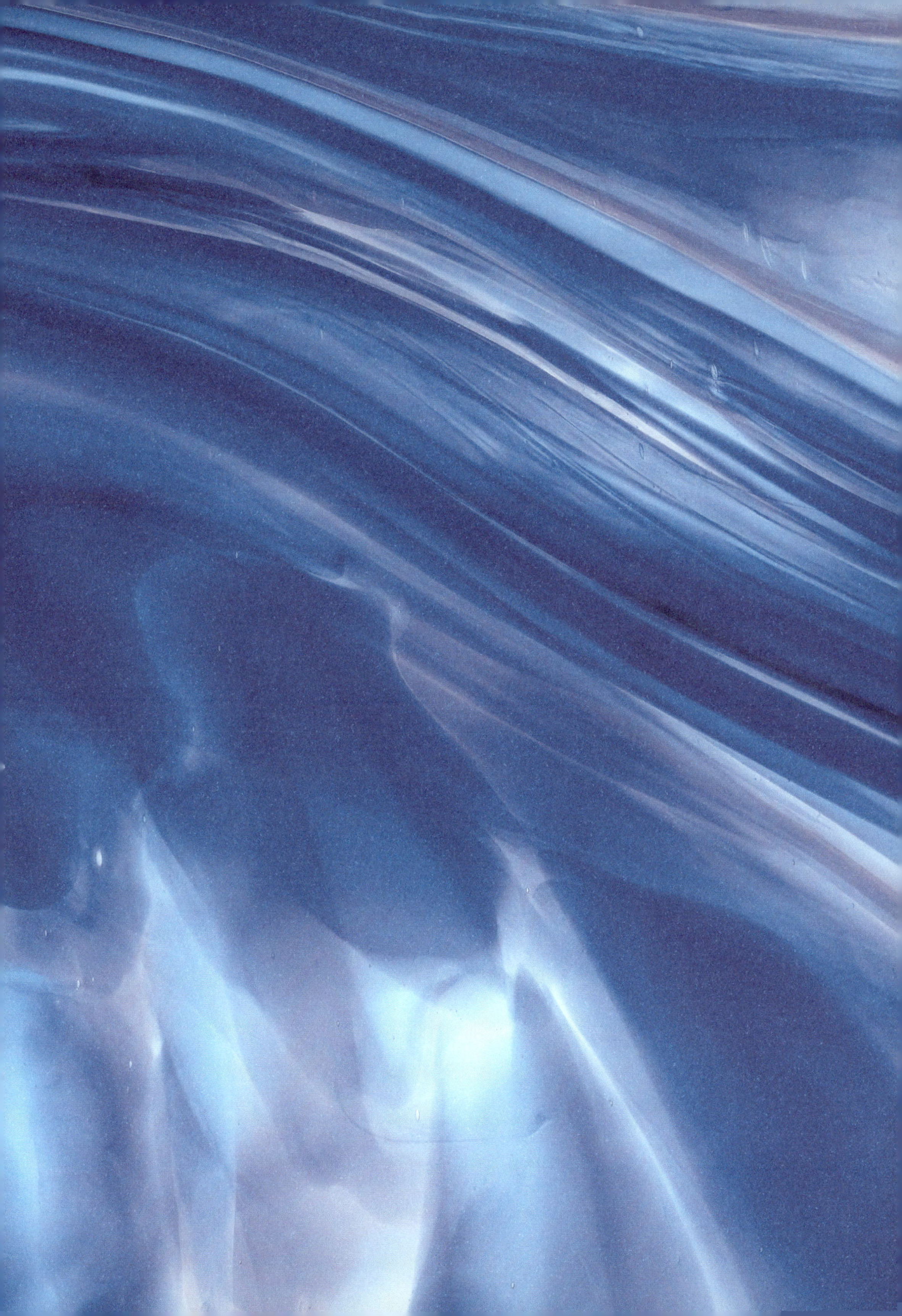

FINDING THE WORDS

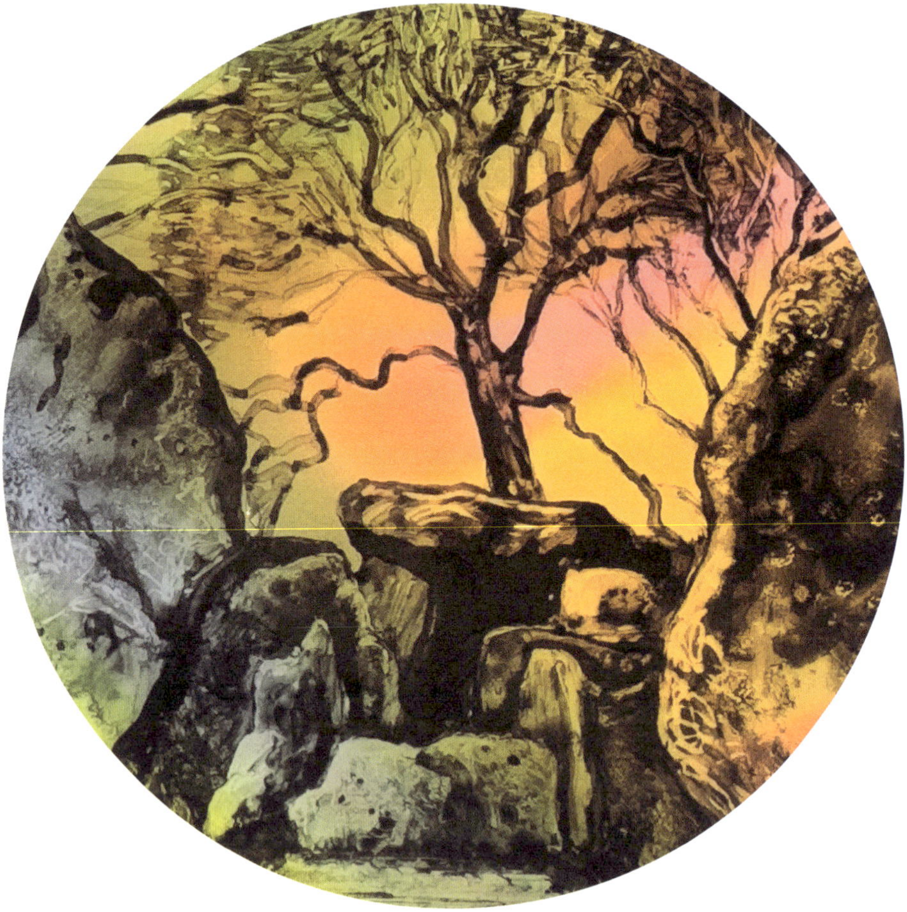

The Smith's Tale
An adaptation of a traditional story about Wayland, the smith who inhabited the stone barrow now called Wayland's Smithy.

The Black Fox's Tale
Born in a kitchen in Herefordshire, the roots of this tale are two-fold. The label on a cider bottle, and a walk in Pembrokeshire in early twilight, searching for badgers and finding instead a great, dark fox in the low blackthorn, hunting.

The Owl's Tale
The story of the woman made from flowers has its roots in the *Mabinogion*, an old series of tales from Cymru, when magic grew rich on the sides of the valleys.

The Selkie's Tale
Wherever humans and seals meet, there are stories of mythical creatures called selkies; both seal and human at all times, but sometimes appearing as one, sometimes as the other, they are ocean-born shapeshifters. The singer in this story is based upon a real singer.

The White Hare's Tale
Mounsey Castle is a place of green magic on the edge of Exmoor, a place where deer run and the shades of wolves haunt the trees. Through the wood, close by, runs a clear stream, the haunt of the kingfisher and otter. This tale was found in the dappled shade between autumn leaves, while the red deer called, and a mist rose up into the valley from the water, and owls threaded their song through the dawn-light and dusk.

The Silver Trout's Tale
Written as a response to questions arising from the work of a poet, the source of 'The Silver Trout's Tale' is 'The Song of Wandering Aengus' by W. B. Yeats. The words took their own route through my imagination, beginning with the question: how did she know his name? And why was there blossom at the same time as berries? Words, like water, sometimes find their own way.

The Ravens' Tale
The island of Hrafen's Ey is more commonly known as Ramsey Island, a small island about a mile off the coast of Sir Benfro, Cymru, across a treacherous tide-race. It is the haunt of many a beautiful bird, surrounded by seal song. Ravens build their ragged nests here, of twigs that cling to the cliffs, raising their children over the wild waters.

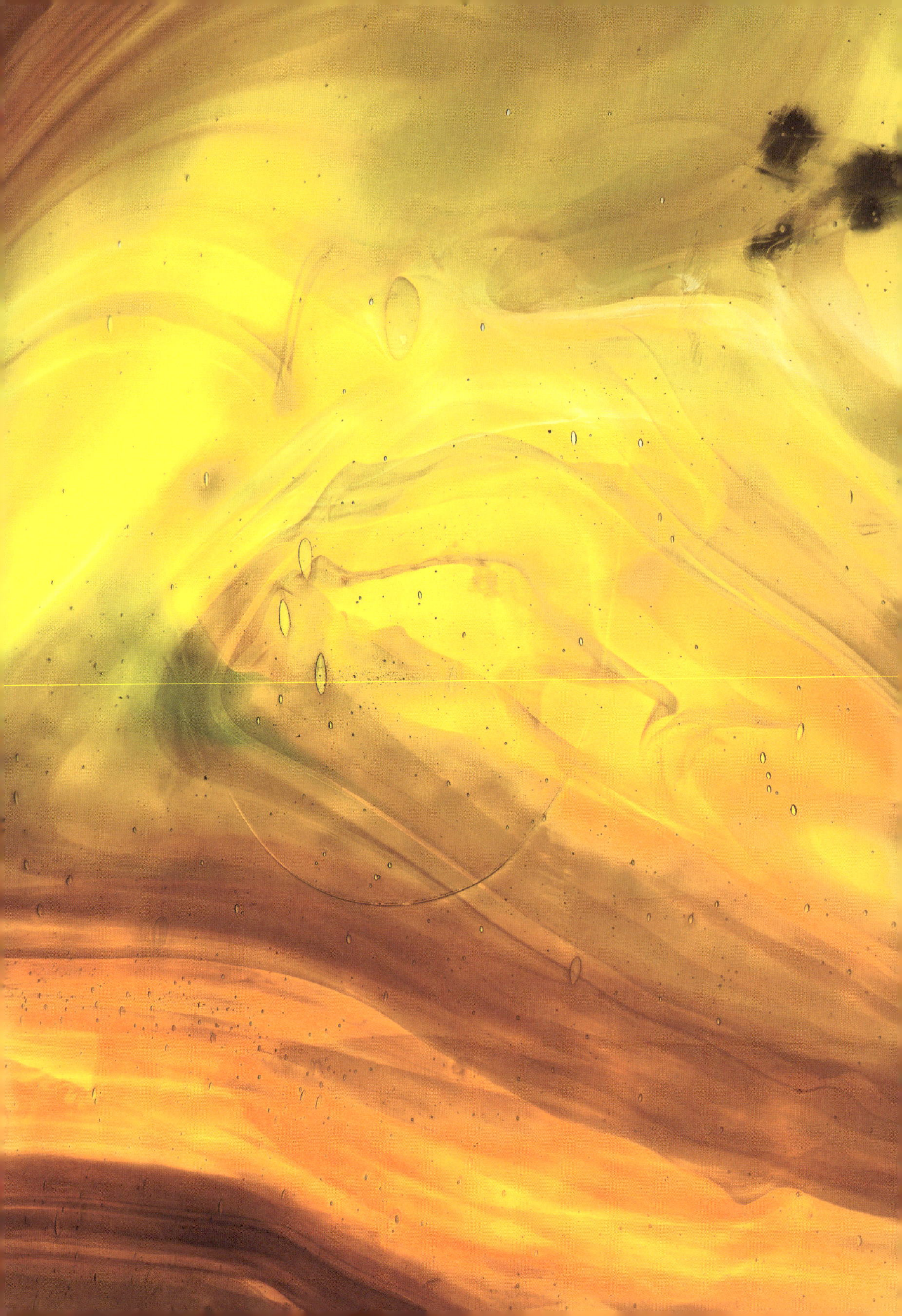

THE GLASS

All the illustrations for *Wild Folk* are created on glass. Glass seems an appropriate choice for a selection of tales concerning shapeshifting and transformation in that it is itself an alchemical material endowed with mystical properties. It comes in a myriad of jewel-like colours which, when combined with light, glow with a crystal clarity even though it is made from the base materials of silica (sand) and minerals. It appears to be solid, but it is in fact an incredibly slow-moving liquid. Many of the techniques, materials and tools used in working with stained glass, have changed little since medieval times.

The glass used in the book is all mouth-blown. A little of it is made by Saint-Just, near Saint-Étienne, France, much of it is made by Lamberts in Waldsassen, Germany, but most of it is the rarified product of an incredibly skilled mouth-blower called Walter Pinches (now retired) for English Antique Glass, a company that is not producing flat glass at the moment. The flat glass used in the book was produced in the works near Alvechurch, West Midlands, but development of the site into housing forced the works' closure, and all remaining stock and glass-blowing is now with the parent company in Oxfordshire. The work in this book is a hymn to the glass-blowers and the glass they produce.

The illustrations on the glass are created by several methods, two of which involve painting and one of which involves engraving. Often the methods are combined for effect and both sides of the glass may be utilised to create a sense of depth in the work.

The black line or paint is a traditional glass glaze that can be applied in a free, painterly manner or by blacking the entire piece of glass and scratching the image through the paint, sgraffito style. In both instances the paint is fired into the surface of the glass to create a permanent image.

The white lines and textures are created by engraving away the surface colour of a special kind of glass called flashed glass. Flashed glass is mainly one colour (usually clear) with a fine layer of colour on one surface. Using drills made of diamond and stone, the colour can be removed in varying degrees to create tones or white areas.

Most of the glass was photographed against the sky using natural light, some of it was photographed on a lightbox.

In 2023 'historic stained-glass window-making' was added to the red list of endangered crafts in the United Kingdom by the UK-based Heritage Crafts Association (HCA). The HCA defines endangered crafts as those 'which currently have sufficient craftspeople to transmit the craft skills to the next generation, but for which there are serious concerns about their ongoing viability'.

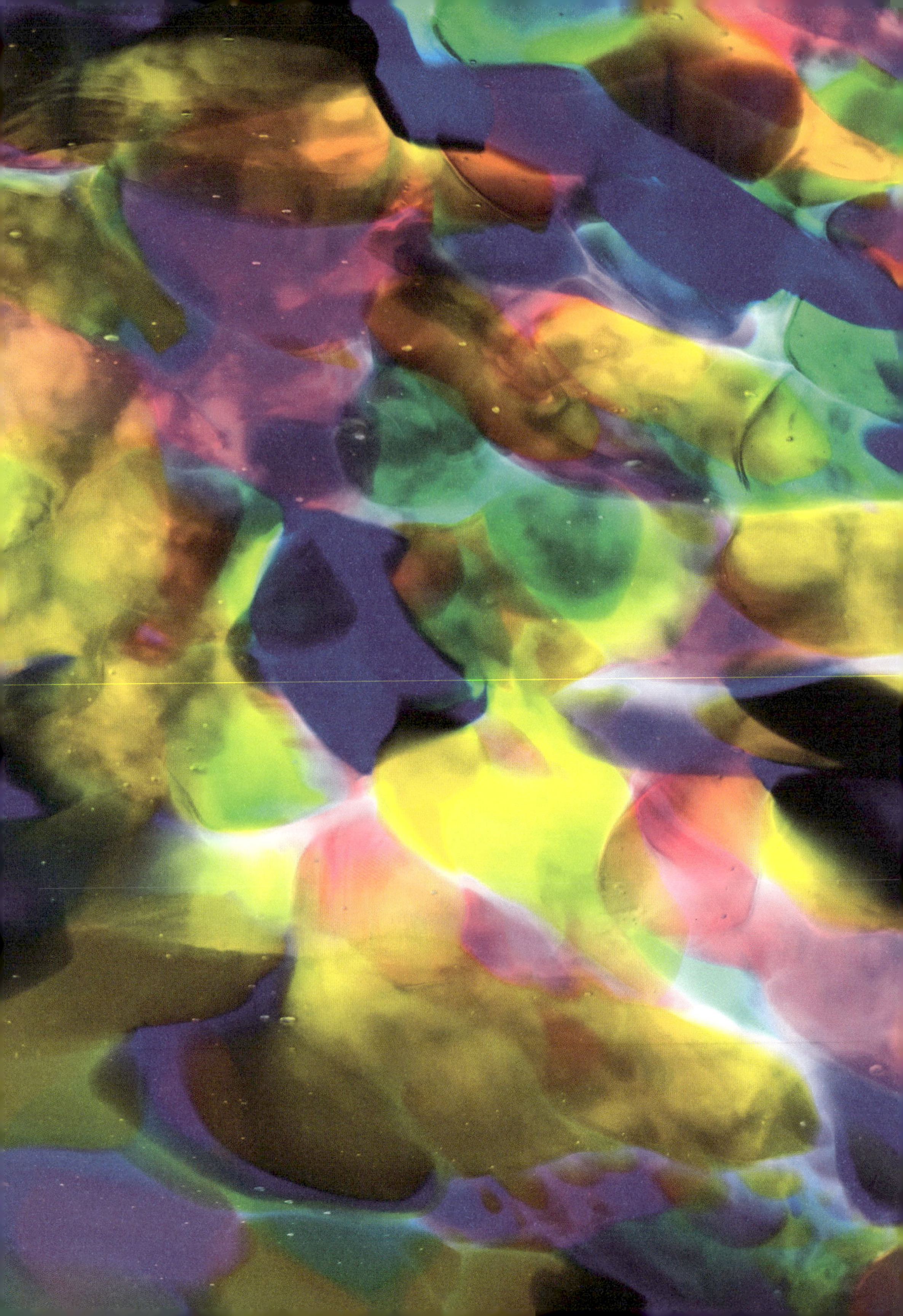

SUPPORTERS

Unbound is the world's first crowdfunding publisher, established in 2011.

We believe that wonderful things can happen when you clear a path for people who share a passion. That's why we've built a platform that brings together readers and authors to crowdfund books they believe in – and give fresh ideas that don't fit the traditional mould the chance they deserve.

This book is in your hands because readers made it possible. Everyone who pledged their support is listed below. Join them by visiting unbound.com and supporting a book today.

SUPPORTERS

The Accidental Bookshop, Alnwick
Booka Bookshop, Oswestry
Books & Ink Bookshop, Winchcombe
The Book Nook, Stirling
the bound, Whitley Bay
The Edge of The World Bookshop, Penzance
Falcon Boats, Pembrokeshire
FOLDE Dorset, Shaftesbury
FORUM Books, Corbridge
Gloucester Road Books, Bristol
The Golden Sheaf Gallery, Narberth
Jaffé and Neale Bookshop and Café, Chipping Norton
Kenilworth Books, Kenilworth
The Literature Laboratory, Hay-on-Wye
Mr B's Emporium Bookshop, Bath
The Nairn Bookshop, Nairn
Newham Bookshop, London
Norfolk Children's Book Centre, Alby
Old Chapel Gallery, Pembridge
The Old Electric Shop, Hay-on-Wye
Rossiter Books, Cheltenham
Rossiter Books, Hereford
Rossiter Books, Leominster
Rossiter Books, Malvern
Rossiter Books, Monmouth
Rossiter Books, Ross-on-Wye
Sam Read Bookseller, Grasmere
Seven Fables, Dulverton
Sherlock & Pages, Frome
Solva Woollen Mill, Solva
Tinsmiths, Ledbury
White Horse Bookshop, Marlborough
The Yellow-Lighted Bookshop, Nailsworth
The Yellow-Lighted Bookshop, Tetbury
Country Bookshelf, Bozeman, USA
Point Reyes Books, Point Reyes Station, USA

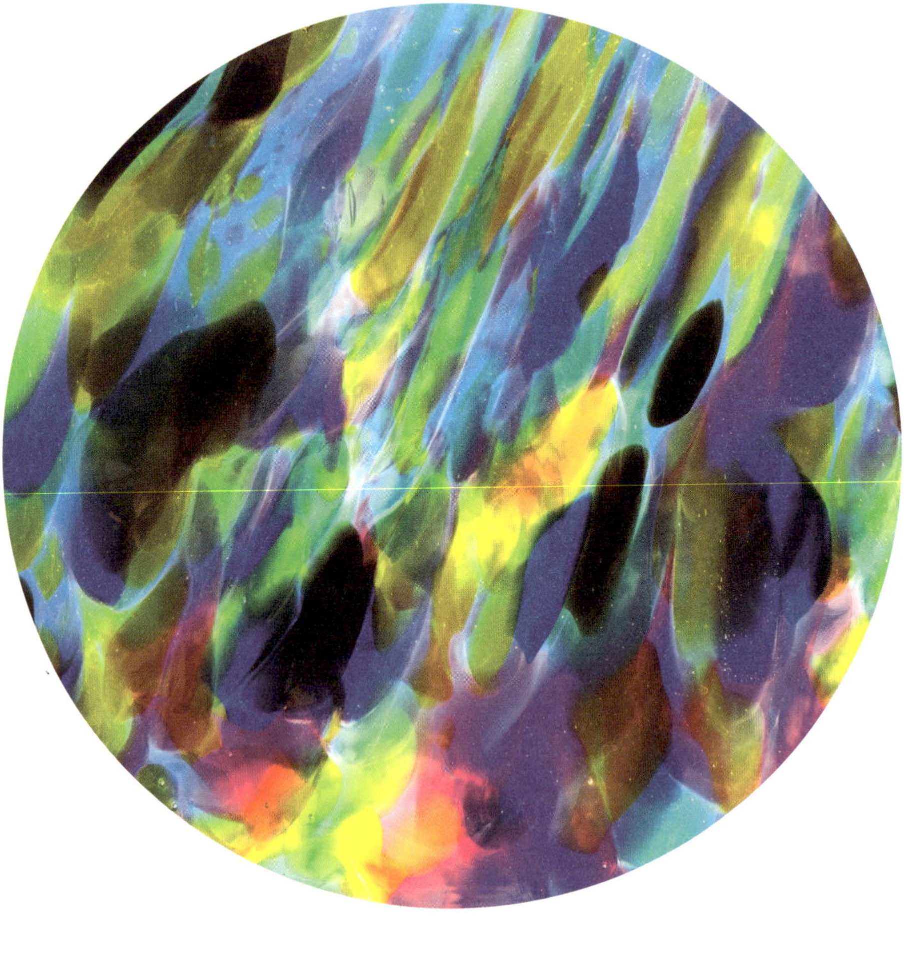

SUPPORTERS

Dougal Abbott
Nettie Abbott
Liz Abdey
Clara Abrahams
Jess Abrahams
Ace
Jose Acevedo
Meredith Ackroyd
Alexis Adams
Adriane
Steven J Agius
Karen Aicher
Sue Ainley
Saad Akhtar
Miki Akimoto
Sue Alder-Bateman
Belinda Aldrich
Holly Aldridge
Sarah Alexander
Shona Alexander
Alix
Joey Allaire
Ash Allen
Cerys Allen
Jane Allen
Siobhan Allen
Lorraine Allister
Kathy Allso
Clare Allum
Jeremy & Mary Allum (Tamsin's parents)
Ruth Allum-Johnson
Alexandra Allum-Pearce
Hugh Allum-Pearce
Meraylah Allwood
Robert Amling
Abigail Anderson
Andrew
Angelika
Janie Angell
Anna & Evelyn
Annie
Anouk, Iwan & Ottilie
Savannah Anthony
Sarah Arkle
Diane Armitage
Frances Armstrong
Sue Armstrong
Deborah Ashton-Cleary
Siobhan Ashton-Cleary
Gordon Askew
Kate Aspinall
Lucy H Atherton
Caitlin Atkinson
Davey Atkinson
Katie Attenborough
Beth Aucott
Emily Audsley
Anne Louise Avery
Ashley Avis
Veronique Avon

Catherine B.
Carolin Backhus
Karen Badenoch
Allison Bailey
Jackie Bailey
Rachel Bailey
Steve Baines
Anji Baker
Ellie Baker
Suzan Baker
Tamsyn Ball
Sarah Ballance
Deborah J Ballantyne
Jason Ballinger
Sara Bankes
Avril Banks
Anne-Marie Bannister
Leah Barabasz
Ruth Barak
Diane Barker
Helen Barker
Tracy Barker
Sandra Barlow
Maria Barnard
Mattie Skaff Barnes
Ann Barr
Shirley Barr
Janet Barraclough
Sara Barratt
Ruth Barrett
Alison Barry
Amy Barstow
Sue Bartell
Amanda Bartlett
Mikaela Bartlett
Julia Bassett
Sofia Batalha
Jenny Batchelor
David Bates
Jennifer Bateson
Jennifer Baumgard
Mandi Baykaa-Murray
Steve Bayley
Emma Bayliss
S Beale
Anna Bear
Rosemary Beardow
Charlotte Beauchamp
Naomi Beaumont
Bob Beaupre
Samuel Becker
Simon Beckford
Yvette Beckley
Anna Beddow
Dawn Beedle
Amy-Jane Beer
Sarah Beeson
Shahin Bekhradnia
Victoria Belcher
Derrienne Bell
Julie Bell
Bella in the Wych Elm
Ronnie Bendall
Carole Benham
Felix and Gideon Bennett
Connally Bush Bennison
Stephanie Benvenuto
Rosie Bergson
Ari Berk
Patricia Best
Bev, love from Av x
Gemma Bevan
Karen Beynon
Clare Bhaoilligh-Sander
Harriet Biddington
Connor Biggin
Jenny Bigwood
Bill, Dave, Hannah, Clarence, Dorothy and Dala, Hugo, Bec, Ava, Finn and Jakey

SUPPORTERS

Su Billington
Ann Clare Bills
Heather Binsch
David Birch
Eloise Birnam-Wood
Simon Bisson
Carrie-Ann Black
Ryan Blackburn
Sharon Blackie
Emma Blades
Kim Blain
Amanda Blair
Milli Blake
Melody & Raven Blanchard
Alice Blears
Sarah Blenkinsop
Lee Blincow
Amélie Blossom
Lynne Bly
Carl & Elizabeth Boardman
Katharina Boehm
Denise Boggs
Yvonne Bolton
Rachel Bond
Laura Elizabeth Bos
Helen Bosher
Lucy Bourne
Ruth & Stewart Bourne
Julia Bovee
Karl Bovenizer
Stephen Bowden
Jo Bowen
Deborah Bowes
Brenda Boyd
Eric Thurso Boyd
Kit Boyd
Angela Boyden
Vivien Boyes
Kat Bradbury
Eleanor Bradley-Cox
Sarah Bramble
Sarah Branton
Nicole Christine Bratt
Caroline Bray
David Brazier
Jane Brewer
Adrian Briggs
Karen Bright
Lynda Britnell
Easkey Britton
Harriet Brooke
Amy Brooks
Sharmaine Brooks
Antonia Brotchie
Deborah Brower
Carla Brown
Karen Brown
Myra Brown
Nicky Brown
Shawn Brown
Sue D Brown
Vix Brown
Anna Browne
Daphne Browne
Lucy Browne
Suki Bruce
Kathleen Bruno
Isobel Brunsdon
Jonathan Brusby
Marlene Brussaard
Hazel Alice Buchan
Bonnie Buckingham
Erica Bullivant
Angela Bulman
Rachel Burch
Andrea Burden
Will Burdett
Sarah Burgess
Kathleen Burke
Karen Burkhardt
Rob Burney
Abi Burns
Adele Burrell
Theresa Burt de Perera
Jennifer Burton
Sarah Bush
Mark Butler
Tracey Jane Butler
Jenna Butler, Karen Loucks
Janina Byrne
Kit Byron
Pam Bzoch

Paul Cabuts
Sarah Cadwallader
Anna and Oscar Caig
Amanda Caines
Kate Calico
Kate Calico and Helen J Gaunt
Alanda Calmus
Aidan Cameron
Cary Campbell
Fiona M H Campbell
Hilary Campbell
Lucinda Campbell
Lucy Campbell
Trish Campbell
Claire Card, Hannah Nibloe, Elizabeth Ruffell
Ruth Carden
Catherine Cargill
Claire Cargill
Claire Carlile
Caitriona Carlin
Gemma Carlin, Neil Carlin
Chris Carlton
Liz Carroll
Lorrie Carse-wilen
Catherine Carter
Jill Carter
Margie Carter
Nicholas Carter
Rachel Carter
Ruth, Mabel and Tabitha Carter
Sally Carter
Ande Case
Sabrina Casserley
Belle Cattell
Karin Celestine
Susan Chadwick
Saoirse Chalcraft
Barbara Challender
David Lars Chamberlain
Barbara Chamberlin
Caroline Champin
Gaynor Chapman
Scarlett Chapman
Kenny Chapman – for Amber
Karen Chard

SUPPORTERS

Sheeryn Charize
Siobhan Tan
Thalia Charles
Elizabeth Charlesworth
Gillian Charters
Greg Chernoff
Donna Cheshire
Ann Chidgey
Alison Chidwick
Beth Childs
Joanne Chittenden
Roger Chorley
Chris & Judith
Angela Christian
Rebecca Christie
Leela Churchill
Jane Churchill and Helen Smith
Ali Cillov
Jay Clancy
Katie Clare
Clarey Marey Quite Contrary
Amanda Clark
Ellie Clark
Martin Clark
Natasha Clark
Amanda Clarke
Catherine Clarke
Jenny Clarke
Louisa Clarkson
Michael Clayton
Sam Clayton
Justine Clement
Gill Clifford
Greg Clifford
Phoebe Clive
Freyalyn Close-Hainsworth
Allison Clough
Angela Coates
Lucy Coats
Julie Elizabeth Cobbin
Larri Cochran
RS Coen
Daniel Cohen
Kate Coleman
Alexander Coles
Brigitte Collazo
Dorothy Collins
Mark Collins
Jennifer Elwell Comeau
Lisa Compton
Tom Computer
Pierre Condou
Dom Conlon
Gillian Connelly
Linda Connelly
Jill & Graham Cook
Joni Cook
Kirsten Cooke
Sue Cooke
Jaqueline Cooley
Debbie Coolman
Jo Thompson Coon
Cathy Cooper
Denise Cooper
Paula Cooper
Sheryl Cooper
Su Corcoran
Bev, Rod, Tom & James Cornaby
Tyler Cornelius
Kate Cornish
Amanda Corp
Sarah Corrigan
Caroline McDermott Corry
Teresa Cotterell
Laura Coulson
Sarah Counter
Amaryllis Courtney
Jane Cowan
Catherine & Andrew Cowling
Steven W. Cowling
Serena Cox
Wendy Craig
Suzy and Billy Craik
Pamela Holm Crawford
Mike Crawley
Ruth Crawley
Annie Creary
Dawn Cripps
Cora Crisman
Melissa Crocker
Susannah Croft
Sandy Crole
Anne & Julian Crook
Alasdair Cross
Louise Crossley
N. Crotty
David Croughton
Maverick Crow
Karen Crowley
Judith Cuddihey
Jane Culpan
David Cummings
Gill Cummings
Cindy Curren
Elaine Currie
Deborah Curtis

Robina D'Arcy-Fox
Alissa Dalton
Alexandra Dance
Lucy Danes
C Darsley
Katelyn Daugherty
Andrea Davies
Cathy Davies
Deborah Davies
Gareth Davies
Ian Davies
Karen Davies
Katrina Davies
Nia Davies
Penny Davies
Nicola Davies and Dan Jones
Emma Davies, Helen Bates
Patia Davis
Sarah Davis
Simon Davis
Stephanie Davis
Alexandra Dawe
Victoria Dawes
Gill and Grendon Dawson
Aimi de Lacy
Emma Gibbs de Oliveira
Celia Deakin
Evenstar Deane
Sheila Dearden

SUPPORTERS

Sarah Dearling
Katherine Dearness
Debbie
Anne Delekta
Anne Deneen
Maureen Denning
Elena Dent
Julie Dent
Alexandra Derby
Graham Devine
Patric Ffrench Devitt
Sharon Devo
Annette Dewgarde
Jules Dickinson
Samantha Dickinson
Tom Dillon
Mary Dinneen
Cathy Dixon
Leigh Dodds
Philippa Dodds
Becky Doherty
Suzanne Donnelly
Aleta Doran
Amanda-Jane Doran
Ben Doran
Laura Doty
Linda Doughty
Eleanor Dourish
Rosalind Draper
Andy Drumm
Rebekah Drury
Allan Dryer
Tracy Duddridge
Kim Duffell
Seven Fables Dulverton
Deena Duncan
Helen Jane Duncan
Tess Duncan
Anne Dunn
Barclay A. Dunn
Guy Dunning
Hayley Dunning
Louise Dunsire
Val Duskin
Mike Dyer
Sarah Dyer
Katy Dynes

Jane E.Ward
Helen Eaden
Heather Eagland
Ginger Earl
Dan Early
Michael Earp
Amanda Earps
Tim Easton
Jutta Eberhards
Kim Eddy
Liz Eddy
Emma & William Ede-Smith
Raven Edgewalker
Rhona Edney
Debby Edwards
Finn Edwards
Gwen Edwards
Rachel Edwards
Eva Eensaar
Amanda Eglite
Charlotte Eimer
Ekaterina
Nicola Eldridge
Richard Elen
Kate Elizabeth
Mark Elliott
Mary Elliott
Suzanne Elliott
Cherie Ellis
Jo Elphick
Gillian Ely
Rachel Emanuel
Elisabeth England
Ali English
Catherine Masterson Ennis
Meriel Ensom
Theresa Entriken
Christine Entwisle
Jennifer Escoubas
Deborah Esdale
Ethan
Jayne Etherington
Andrew Evans
Gillian Evans
Jennifer Margaret Evans
Kathryn Evans
Karen Ewing
John and Sue Exton

Rachel Fairbank
Frost Familia
Susan Farley
Ryan Farley-Harper
Charlie Farquharson-Roberts
Anna Farthing
Lisa Faught
Fiona Feather
Joanna Fenna-Brown
Lorna Fergusson
Charles Ferris
Mollie Ferris
Sharon Fienman
Gillian Finch
Caroline Burke Findlay
Renate Fink
Arlene Finnigan
Paul Finnis
Emma Firmin
Cathy Fisher
Colin Fisher
Matt Fisher
Brid Fitzpatrick
Nick Fitzsimons
Christine Flavel
Jenny Fletcher
Jo Fletcher
Regina Fletcher
Sara E Fletcher
Caroline Flexman
Andy, Jo and Django Flint
India Flint
Vicky Flood
Ricardo Flores @ EngelAnael
Cora Flory
Ann Flowers
Nicholas Flynn
Phyl Foley
Catriona Foote
Jean Forbes
Stuart Forbes
Fiona Ford

SUPPORTERS

Kitty Ford
Juliet Forrest
Helen Forshaw
Angela Forster
Jaci Foster
Virginia Foster
Claudia Fountaine
Amy Fox
Roz Fox-Bentley
Holly Foy
Rachel Franchi
John Francis
Philippa Francis
Lene Frandsen
Stephanie A. Frank
Jill Franklin
Fern Frase
Chris Fraser
Katie Fraser
Jacqueline Freeman
Christopher French
Rachel Frigot

Julie Gabrielli
Jim Galbraith
Georgia Galus
Majda Gama
Emilia Gan
Barbara Ganley
Thomas Ganter
Rachel Gardiner-Hill
Craig Gardner
Jennifer Garland
Dan & Barbara Garner
Graham Garner
Karen Garner
Sophie Katrina Garner
Sarah Garnham
Amelia Garretson-
    Persans
Christine Garretson-
    Persans
Kate Genevieve
Dean Geoghegan,
    April Chaplin
Amelia Gersema
Laura Gibbs
Suzie Gibbs
Lyn Gibson
Oliver Gibson
Ruth Gilburt
Julie Giles
Shonagh Giles
Jane Gill
Rina Gill
John Girardeau
Rupert Gladstone
Juliana Glanfield
Andy Glazier
Lara Gledhill
Vivien Gledhill
Alex Glendinning
Bramble Glendon
Richard Glet
Matt Goddard
Menna Godfrey
Anat Goldflam
Lynne Goodacre
Julie Goodall
Helen Goodchild
Louise Goose
Stella Goose
Katherine Gorman
Stacy Gormley
Rachel Goswell
Vicki Gottlieb
Dorothy Gracey
Gill Graham
Kevin & Karen
    Grahame
Lauren Granillo
Jane Grant
Elizabeth Gray
Simon Gray
Stephanie Grayling
Deborah Green
Samantha Green
Stephanie Green
Louise Greenaway
Marion Greene
Alison
    Greenmystwitch
Helen Grierson
Jane Griffin
Mike Griffiths
Julie Groom
Jen Grosz
Matty Groves
Diana Guibord
Nancy Guinn,
    Shannon Guinn-
    Collins
Nadja Gunneberg
Philippa Gurney
David Gwilt

Steven H
Haagbeukie
Stephen Hackett
Jules Haddon
Kathrine Haddrell
Tassos Hadjicocolis
Linda Haecker
Sam, Helena & Eira
    Wren Hale
Joanna Hall
Martine Hall
Dorothy Hallam
Christine Halliday
Hilary Haman
Louise Hamblin
Shannon Hammond
Nicky Hampton
Liz Hankins
Barbara Hann
Hannah & Hunter
Hannah and Rowan
Ewan Hannay
Jamie Hansell
Jenifer Hanson
Mathias Hansson
Gerri Hanus
Kate Harbottle-Joyce
Paul Hardaker
Chris Harley
Candy Harman
Helen Harper
Harper & Maisie
Rachel Harrington
Claire Harris
Elizabeth Carolyn
    Harris
Jessica Harris
Kirsty Harris
Ruth Harris
Sarah Harris

SUPPORTERS

Emily Ruth Harris-O'Malley
Mathew Harrison
Rebecca Harrison
Rhian Wyn Harrison
Toni Harrison
Nancy Hart
Sarah Hart
James Harvey
Rebecca Harvey
Tim Harwood
Tracy Haskell
Deborah Hawkins
Jennifer Hawkyard
Jessica Hayden
Alys Hayes
Cate Haynes
Caroline Hayward
Sue Hayward
Alice Heal
Cathy and Steve Heard
Andrew Hearse
Maria-Teresa Heather
Anna Heaton
Sharon Heels
Richard Hein
Elizabeth Henderson
Christine Hendra
Daisy Henry
Julie Hesse
Audrey Hetherington
Andrea Hewes
Cecilia & Graham Hewett
Jan Hilborn
Bethanne Bethard Hill
Dale Hill
Jem Hill
Justine Hill
Lyn Hill
Stuart Hill
Charlotte Hills
Nicola Hills
Hannah Hinsley
Leenie Hirst
Kate Hobbs
Natasha Hobday
Sean Hockett
Em Hodder
Melanie Hodge
Anne Hodgkins
Michaela Hoeher
Louise Hoffman
Richard Hoffman
Gaynor Hogarth
Olwen Holland
Samantha Holland @ Nairn Books
Catherine Holland-Bax
Rebecca Hollely
Anne Holliss
Claire Holliss
Erin Coughlin Hollowell
Helen Holman
Joanne Holman
Anna Holme
Caroline Holmes
Fay Holmes
Hilary Holmes
Sophie Holroyd
Eryl Holt
Tracy and Martin Homer
Steph Hooton
Jenny Hope
Mark Hopwood
Xenia Horne
Lottie Hosie
Stuart Hough
Jocelyn Houghton
Sue House
Valerie Housley
Georgia Howard
Suzanne Howard
Julia Howell-Cortelli
Lucie Howes
Rebecca Hoyle
Louise Hozhabrafkan
Jo Hudek
Kath Hudson
Lucie Hudson
Nancy Hudson
Sue Humphries
Isobel Hunt
Maggie Hunter
Laura Hunter-Thomas
Bee Huntley
Elizabeth Hurst
Tim Hurst
Paula Hutchinson
Catherine Hyde
Liz Hyder
Damien Hyland

Claire Louise Inglis
Julia Inglis
Katie Ingram
Ann Ishiguro
Farah Ismail
Iverson

Jackie
Melanie Jackson
Netty Jackson
Su Jackson
Laura Jacobs
Rachel James
Kristina, Jan
Guinevere Lindley Janes
Shimrit Janes
Tracey Jardine
Rainey Jayne
Lucy Jeal
Jane Jeans
Lisa Jefferson
Vicky Jenkins
Holly Jennifer
Lynds Jennings
Christine Jensen
Loretta Jensen
Catherine Jessup
Jill
Jo W, Karen S, Lucy C
Joey, Danny and Jake
Eva John
Elaine Johnson
Heather Johnson
Joy Johnson
Laurie Johnson
Pauline Johnson
Sue Johnson
Zoë Johnson
Graham Johnston

SUPPORTERS

Ruth Joiner
Casey Jon
Brian B Jones
Cindy Jones
Daniel Jones
Eddy Jones
Kathy Jones
Laura Jones
Leigh Jones
Michael Jones
Nicola Jones
Nye Jones
Paula Josa Jones
Sarah Jones
Terry Jones
Ryan Jones-Casey
Marie Jordan
Michael Jordan
Tina Jordan
Mary Jordan-Smith
Anne Louise
   Jørgensen
Haley Jorgenson
Mary Jowitt
Gabriele Joy
Judith
Julie
Genevieve Jung

Holly Kahya
Eileen Kaner
Louise Karuna
Kat
Jennifer Kates
Lizzie Kathiravel
Nemie Kavanagh
Lesley Kay
Stephen Kay
Phil Kaye
Charlotte Keane
Sonja Elizabeth Keck
Katherine Keenum
Steve Keller
Nayara Kelly
Seamus Kelly
Angela Kemp
Grace Kemp
Hilary Kemp
Julia Davison Kemp
Helen Kennedy
Jane Kenneway
Chris Kent
Martha Kenyon
Karolyne Kerr
Mary Kersey
Ruth Keys
Jane Kimberley
Karen-Serena Kincaid
David King
Sally-Ann King
Sharon King
Trevor King
June Kingsbury
Emma Kirk
Pete and Jackie
   Kirkham
Nerissa Kisdon
Alex Knight
Mitzi Koch
Rosalie Kohler
Anuradha Kolhatkar
Liane Kordan
Jennifer Krieger

Kristine Loeb Krozek
Laura Krstovska
Claire Kruse
Matthew Kruvczuk
Jane Kuesel

Pamela L
Sheryl Labouchardiere
Katherine LaBrie
Katherine Lack
Sumitra Lahiri
Gill Laker
Ann Lally
Demelza Craven Lamb
Jane Lambert
Elizabeth Lambrakis
Marina Lambrakis
Julie Laming
Riversteadt
   LaMoreaux
Emily Lancaster
Angela Lane
Susanne Stingl Lane
Emma Louise Lane,
   Forest Sprite
   Crafts
Jennie Langdon
TJ Langrill
Skooby Laposky
Sybil Lark James Todd
Matt Larsen-Daw
Zena Binny Lavinia
   Lascelles
Lauren
Rhiannon Law

Bridget Lawlor
Alison Layland
Gwendoline Leach
Louise Leach
Mya, Rose, Will &
   Frank Leach
Gavin Lees
Carol Lenox
Robin Leveridge
Jeremy Leverton
Sandy Levesque
Anna Lewis
Diane Lewis
Marilyn Lewis
Phil Lewis
Rupert Lewis
Sally Lewis
Tanya Liddle
Jonathan Light
Bronwen Lilley
Susan Lim
Clare Lindley
Simon Lindsley
Alison Lingley
Anna Linskens
Clare Lipetz
Jane Littlefield
Dorothy Livingston
Rowan Jay Llewellyn-
   Logan
George Lloyd
Joanna Lloyd
Emma Lobb
Emma Loder-Symonds
Valerie M. Loew
Rose Logan
Cath Lomas
Clare Lomas

SUPPORTERS

Gillian Lonergan
Daphne Long
Jacquie Long
Lucie Loopstra
Frank Lopez
Stephanie V Lopez
Louise Lord
Amanda Lorimer
Lorna Faye Dunsire
Anita Loughrey
Melanie Louise
Racheblue Love
Jane Loveday
Tamsin Littlebird Loveday
Cate Lovett
Janet Lowe
Jacquelyn Loyd
Mezzie Elen Lucerne-Lambourne
Brigitte Colleen Luckett
Victoria Ludlow
Kelly Ludwig
Jen Lunn
Val Lupton
Donna Lynch
Murray Lynes
Sarah Lynett
Lynette
Lysanca

Yao Ma
Olivia Mabey
Tina Mabey

Rebecca MacDonagh
Mary MacDonald
Robert Macfarlane
Rosamund Macfarlane
Fiona MacGregor
Mary MacGregor
Richenda Macgregor
Araminta Mackay
Donald Mackay
Alex Mackenzie
Harriet Mackenzie
Becky Mackeonis
Rhona MacLennan
Laurie MacLeod
Aileen A MacNicol
Kirstie Macqueen
Daniel Madden
Maddy
Hannah Maggs
Sonia Mainstone-Cotton
Philippa Manasseh
Kev Mann
Steve Manners
Laurie Manton
Penny Maplestone
Oileàn Mara
Magdalena Marczewska
Lisa Hinkle Maria
Marie-Eve Mark
Sarah Markham
Tish Ferry Marrable
Anne-Marie Marriott
Shelley Marsden
Alex Marson
Cathryn Marson

Grace Martin
Frances Mason
Lu Mason
Sophie Mason
Francesca Matteoni
Susanna Mariam Matthan
Vianne Max
Emily Maycock
Marta Dittert McCabe
George McCallum
Susan McCarthy
Trevor McCarthy
Janet McCarthy (Kurz)
Jan McCartney
Callum McCaul
Marcus McCauley
Jill McCombie
Kirsti Ryall McCool
Marlene McCormick
Eamonn McCrory
Amy McCune
Meg McDonald
Corrina Cop Rain McFarlane
Fiona McGavin
Jo Chopra McGowan
Patricia Hunter McGrath
John D McHugh
Mary McKane
Deborah L. McKay
Kerry McKenna
Lucy McKeown
Ella Mckernan
Catherine W McKinney
Helen McLachlan

Alison McLaren
Jennifer McLaren
Paul McLeman
Fiona McLeod
Lynda McMahon
Morag McMahon
Amanda McMillan
James McNally
Hettie McNeil
Jac McNeil
Paula J McNulty
Hazel McSporran
Anne Meade
Meadow & Autumn
Tom Medlicott
Sarah Meehan
Christine Meerman-Cooper
Mary Megarry
Dylan Meggison
Lucy Meikle
Ian Mella & Margery Thomas
Lucy Meller
Pearl Melvill
Peter P. C. Mertens
Kristina Meschi
E. C. Messer
Michaela Meyer
Rasma and Ari Meyers
Johan Meylaerts
Derwyn Mhurain
Susan Middleton
Kizzia Mildmay
Celia Mill
Rory Millar
Rebecca Miller

SUPPORTERS

Claire Millington
Jane Elizabeth Miloradovich
Fleur Milsom
Polly Mineau
Sarah Mitchell
James Moakes
Farn Moldaschl
Francesca Monn
Alan Montgomery
Michelle Moore
Rhiannon Moore
Jessie Moorhouse
Paula Moorhouse
Jenny Moran
Malcolm More
Maya Morgan
Tracey Morgan
Morphosita
Alison Morris
Siân Morris
Sue Morris
Erin Morrison
Janet Morson
Alison Moss
Julie Moss
Lorraine Moulding
Deborah Anne Moussous
Adele Mower
Emma Conway Mowlam
Bernard Moxham
Rebecca Moyle
Kim Mullen-Kuehl
Catherine Mullis
George & Tommy Murphy
Joseph Murphy
Una Murphy
Gus and Julie Murray
Teryn Murray
Jennifer Muscato
Maureen Musson

Nathan
Carlo Navato
Sarah Naylor-Hagger
Jacqui Newberry
Stephen Newell
Ducky Nguyen
Haulwen Nicholas
Julie Nicholson
Mark Nicholson
Bodenham Nicki
Gilly Nickols
Gary Nicol
Kes Nielsen
Gwendolyn Noble
Emily Nolan
Lesley Northfield
Christa Norton, Clara Basset
Meredith Norwich
Somewhere Nowhere
Alice Nunn

Annabel O'Docherty
Dawn O'Donnell
Margaret M O'Donnell
Noah Micheal O'Donnell
Carol O'Driscoll
Ruth O'Leary
Rachel O'Meara
Rachel O'Reilly
Rebecca O'Rourke
Kato O'Driscoll
Toosie O'Morchoe
Katie O'Sullivan
Karen Oakley
Patricia Oakley
Sarah Oates
Adrian Oliver
Amber Caraveo Oliver
Lynne Oliver
Marjolein Oorsprong
Bee Operanto
Annabelle Oppenheimer

Kelly Packer
Allison Carolina Elliot Page
Paula Page
Richard Page
Kate Paice
David Palmer
Eileen Neil Palmer
Rosaleen Palmer
Sarah Palmer
Paula Palyga
Catherine Park
Julia Parker
Sophie Parker
Steph Parker
Suzy Parker
Mrs Emily Parkyn
Julie Parr
David Parrish
Jeni Parsons
Kate Parsons
Margaret Parsons
Suzanne Parsons
Morag Paterson
Adam Ross Patterson
Peg Payne
Michelle Payne-Gill
Carol Peachee
Jenny Peall
Oliver Pearcey
Emily Pegues
Judith Pendrous
Penwing
Katja Pepper
Ashleigh Pepper-Bowen
Amanda Percy
Constance Perenyi
Anne-Marie Perks
Nadia Permogorov
Caroline Perrington
Helen Perry
Shelley W. Peterson
Carol Phillips
Katie Phillips
Rachel Phillips
Robert Phillips
Nadine Phoenix
Claire Pickton
Anne Piecuch
Karen F. Pierce
Maria Pietocha

SUPPORTERS

Pip
Susan Pitt
Karen Pittaway
Elizabeth-Anne Platt
Shannon Marie
    Plummer
Karine Polwart
Angela Poole
Amanda Porter
Becky Potter
Dion Potter
Fiona Potter
Henri Potvin
Linda Powell
Tracy Powell
Jayne Power
Sean Power
Mari Prackauskas
Andrya Prescott
Debbie Prestwich
David Prew
Popi Pribojac
Thea Prothero
Chenie Prudhomme
Rosy Prue
Kathryn Pryce
Claire Pulford
Gillian Pulford
Christina Pullman
Andy Pym

Erin Quan
Kitti Quarfoot
Lisa Quattromini
Joe Quinn

Quinne
Sophie Quinnell
Nicky Quint

Rachel & Doron
Rebecca Rajendra
Riana
    Rakotoarimanana
Tim Ramsdale
Wynona Randall
Luke Randell
Petronella Randell
Pierce Randell
Anastasia Ratcliffe
Kate Rattray
Stephen Raw
Sue Rawley
Matthew Read
Ailke Shira
    Rechenberg
Debz Michaela Reed
Neil Reeder
Tracey Rees-Cooke
Emily Reid
Tania Reinert
Teresa Reiter
Cornelia Rémi
Damaris Revell
L A Rhodes
Julie Ricard
Rebecca Richard
Beth Richards
Kate Richards
Lynette Richards
Sue Richards-Gray

Geri Rinna
Hanne Kristiansen
    Risvik
Christine Rivett
Stefanie Rixecker
Marie Roberts
Rachel Roberts
Amanda Robertson
Doug Robertson
Marie Robertson
Nick Robins
Penny Robinson
Elisabeth Robson
Laura Roddenberry
Sue Roe
Charlotte Rogers
Paula Rogerson
Judith Rognstad
Carla Rohde
Flick Rohde
Barbara Roidl
Jessica Rolfe
Sally Rollinson
Kathy Rondel
Angie Rooke
Lucy Rooke
Joanne Roper
Julie Rose
Vikki Rose
Chris Ross
Gary Ross
Jane Ross
Becks Rossiter
P Rotterdam
Rowena Rouse
Carol Rowe
Rhona Rowland
Gail Rowlands

Sarah Royston
Lydia Ruffin
Judy Ruse
Alison Russell
Hilary Ruxton
Kate Ryan
Alison Rydings
Karen Rydings
Liška Ryška

Rae S
SA
Mark Sainsbury
Laura Salisbury
Emma Salmon
Ellen Sandberg
Susan L Sandenaw
Adrian Saunders and
    Minnie Birch
Carol-Anne Savage
Steven Savile
Dorothy Scanlan
Michael Scarman
Kati Schardl
Arthur Schiller
Alex Schlacher
Julia Schlotel
Jessica Schmidt
Kim Schnuelle
Kate Schockmel
Hildegard Schollaert
Janette Schubert
Lisa Schubert
Barbara Schwartzbach
Jenny Schwarz

SUPPORTERS

Devin Scobie
Anthony Scolamiero
Anne-Marie Scott
John A Scott
Matthew Scott
Elsie & Daisy Scrase
David, Regina, Paul & Emma Scrivens
Jonathan Seaman
Adelle Diggle Seaton
Silvia Secchi
Rose Secen-Hondros
Aurelia Sedlmair
Rosslynne Selous-Hodges
Dick Selwood
Frances Senneck
María Serrano
Helen Seward
Clare Seymour
Nikki Shabbo
Eric S. Shaffstall
Rhea Shami
Harriet Shannon
Cheryll Sharp
Faye Sharpe
Andrew Shaw
Eolanthe Shaw
Karen Shaw
Marnie Shaw
Tara Shaw
Lisa Shea
Patricia Sheath
Clare Sheffield
April Tuesday Shen
Ashley Shepard
Jacqueline and Francis Shepherd
Juliet Shepherd
Diana Sheridan
Alison Shore
Michelle Shore
Kate Shore & Beth Hopkins
Natalia Shoutova
Richard Shubrook
Sharon Shute
Carol Siddorn
Andrea Silverman
Clare Simmonds
Lyndsay Simmonds
Rob Simmons
Caroline Sincock
Sally Sines
Catherine Skowron
Caroline Slough
Paul Slydel
Michele Smalley
Fi Smart
Catherine Smillie
Maxine Smillie
Daria Smirnova
Alan C Smith
Alison Smith
Carolyn Smith
Cathy Smith
Jo Smith
Kate Betty Smith
Olvin Smith
Julie Smithies
Samantha Smithurst
Michael Soares
Murielle Solheim
Gaby Solly
Amanda Songer
Alison Souter
Rik Sowden
Dave Sox
Carrie Spacey
Kit Spahr
Mrs Sparkle
Glynis Spencer
Matthew W.B. Spencer
Lizzie Spikes
Kelda Sproston
Christopher Squire
Victoria Stahl
Alice Stauffer
Anna Stead
Oli 'Olikizuki' Steadman
Markus Steck
Lindsay Steel
Gabriela Steinke
Robin Stenham
Jonathan Stephen
Ruth Stephens
Michael Stephenson
Margit Sterring
Adam J Stevens
Linda Stevens
Penn Stevens
Ruth Stevens
Susan Stevens-Jenkins
Jan Stevenson
Paul Stewart
Terri M Stewart
Andrew DN Stocker, Cath Stocker-Jones
Lisa Stockley
Aurora Stone
Corinne Stone
Gwilym R Stone
Mags Phelan Stones
Pamela Strachman
Ailsa Stratton
Ellen Stratton
Kari Strebig
Debra Stringer
Jo Stroud
Yasmin Strube @ Old Chapel Gallery
Bridget Strugnell
Marisa Strutt
Merry Stuhr
Jet Stukey
Yve Sturgeon
Chris Styles
Lesley Styles
Rajeevi Subramanian
Jill Sullivan
Rachel Sullivan
Carrie & Andrew Sunaitis
Clare Surplice
Jo Suter
Meg Sutherland
Sara Sutherland, Marion Youngman
Suzanne
Megan Swain
Veronica Swain
Mary Swainson
Ruth Swann
Kaola Beth Swanson
Lauraine Sweeney
Jo Swift
Joseph Swift
Judith Swift
Christine Syers

SUPPORTERS

Rosie Sykes
Mary Symonds
Paula Symonds

Catherine Tagg, Ayla Atun
Mr & Mrs Tags
Liz Talbot
Liz Talbot
Pegi Talfryn
Stephanie Tanizar
Tank
Tara the Wild Swimming Woman
E Tarratt
Sabra Tarshes
Tash & Phillip
Virginia Tate
Alison Taylor
Claire Taylor
Emma Taylor
Georgette Taylor
Marion Taylor
Paul Taylor
Sally Taylor
Maddie Templeton
Stephanie ter Heide
Aiden terris
The Island Jeweller
The Mizon Family
The Warren Family
Cherry Thick
Emma Thimbleby
Pamela Thom-Rowe

Emma Thomas
Morgan Anwen Thomas
Shelley Kathleen Thomas
Trish Thomas
Andy Thompson
Brewer Thompson
Corinne Thompson
Helen Thompson
Jane Thompson
Liz Thompson
Marvelle Thompson
Pen Thompson
W J Thompson
Sarah Thomson
Gareth Thorne
Brigit Thurstan
Lesley Thurston-Brown
J & M Timberlake
Frances Timmermans
Joy Wassell Timms
Sarah Tinker
Kathryn Tinling
Anastasia Tiongson
Lucy Tipper
Katie To
To Healers Everywhere
Lucy Tobias
Mary Tofte
Helen Tolley
Juliet Tomlinson
Paul Tompsett
Hope Toogood
Angela Townsend
Ellie Tredwell

Lindsay Trevarthen
Leon Trice
April Tuesday
Hazel Tufton
Aria Tuki
Karen Turner
Shannon Turner
Jon Turney
Grace Tuttle
Zoë Twelvetrees
Jessica Twyman
Kate Tyrrell
Rebecca Tyson
Vangelis Tzanatos

Wendy Uchimura
Kirstin Uhlenbrock
Solveiga Unger
Kate Unwin
Annie Urry-Clark
Jennifer Uzzell

Jo Valentine
Fabio van den Ende
Lucy van Zwanenberg
Lies Vanhoucke
Wendy Varnham
Elizabeth Vavarella
Laura Veck
Jo Verity
Laura Vernon
Lucy Vernon

Rosemary Vernon
Adil Vezir
Philippa Vigano
Leonie Vingoe
Sharon Vivers
Marijke Vonck
Connor Voss
Sabine Voßkamp
Camille VW

Anna W
James Wade
Gillian Wagstaff
John Wainwright
Ruth J Wajsblum
Anne Waldon
Jen Walker
Liz Walker
Nessa Walker
Vicky Walker
Kirsty Wallace
Sue Wallace
R. J. Wallis
David Walsh
Steve Walsh
Sandy Walther
Carole-Ann Warburton
Arabella Ward
Claire Ward
John Ward
Elfrieda Waren
Georgina Warne
L Warner
Caroline Warnes
Abby Warren

SUPPORTERS

Dave Warren
Sarah Washko
Siu Ying Wat
Sandra Waterfield
Jeannette Waterman
Ellen Waters
Zoe Waters-Day
Jo Watson
Kathryn Watterson
Chris Watts
Christine Watts
Liz Waugh
Andy Way
Elizabeth Webb
Heidi Webster
Ange Weeks
Tina Weeks
Anne Weinhold
Julie Weir
Julie Weller
Gini Wells
Richard Wells
Leslie Wenzel
Kipp Wessel
Rebekah West
Sarah West, Kate Inglis
Crystal A. Weyers-Leuchtner
Orla Whalley
Katy Wheatley
Garth Wheeler
Richard Whitaker
Georgina White
Susan White
Jooles Whitehead
Sheila Whitehead
Vicki Whitehead
Christine Whitehouse
Paul Whitehouse
Ethel Lou Whitney
Jan Whittaker
Janet Whitworth-Robb
Jane Wickenden
Matt & Debby Wickham
Sarah Wicks
Mary Widdison
Bryan Wigmore
Rachel Wilder
Susan Wildhouse
Ella J Wilding
Lee Wileman
Denise Wilkin
Sallye Wilkinson
Victoria Wilkinson
Dawn Will
Jackie Willacy
Caroline Willby
Anamaria Williams
Kate Williams
Marietta Eshelman Williams
Moira Williams
Richard & Wendy Williams
Robert Williams
Sarah Williams
Paul Williamson
Sandra Williamson
Thom Willis
Hannah Willow
Melanie Willows
Andy Wilson
Jacqueline Wilson
Rebecca Wilson
Henriette Louise Wiltschut
Terri & Howard Windling-Gayton
Magi Winmill-Hermann
Rosie Winyard
Nastassja Wiseman
Vanessa Wiseman
Jane Wisewoman
Cheryl Witchell
Sharon Witt
Susan E Woerner
Marilyn Wolf
Richard Wolfströme
Women's Selkie Retreat 2023
Bethany Wood
Daisy Wood
Kate Wood
Lucy Wood
Matthew Wood
Rew Wood
Sally Wood
Techla Wood
Samuel Woolley
Sam Worby
Sara Wright
Marieke Wrigley
Holly Wunsch
Bridget Wyatt
Kaila Wyllys
Debbie Wythe

Naomi Xeros

Gayle Yeomans
Rene Yoakum
Angela Young
Anne Young
Jane Young
Martyn Young
Rick and Terri Young
Susan Young
Yvonne

Zala
Sally Zaranko
Donna Zillmann
Alaina Zipp

NOTES ON THE TYPE

The text of this book is set in JJannon and Albertus.

Created by graphic designer François Rappo, JJannon is a revival of the seventeenth-century French type of Jean Jannon. It reflects the sense of grandeur and elegance characteristic of the Baroque era. In 1641, Swiss-born Jean Jannon received a commission from Imprimerie Royale creating a project that came to be known as the *Caractères de l'Université*. The distinctive refinement and sharpness of his type was later attributed to Claude Garamond, an inaccuracy not rectified until the early twentieth century. Rappo reinvigorated the letters preserving the asymmetrical axis and the small inclined bowl of the 'a'.

Albertus was designed by Berthold Wolpe for Monotype during the period 1932 to 1940. Wolpe named the font after the thirteenth-century German philosopher and theologian, Albertus Magnus. Having studied as a metal engraver, Wolpe modelled his type to resemble letters carved into bronze. Initially only titling capitals were created. These were added to during the 1930s with releases of lower case lettering, italics and other characters. It remains a popular font and can be seen in wide use from book jackets and film and television credits to street name signs.

NOTES ON THE AUTHORS

JACKIE MORRIS is an author and illustrator. She studied illustration at Hereford College of Art and Bath Academy and has illustrated many books, and written some. *The Lost Words*, co-authored with Robert Macfarlane, won the Kate Greenaway Medal 2019.

TAMSIN ABBOTT has been creating painted stained-glass panels from her Herefordshire home for over twenty years. Her work is inspired by the British landscape, folklore and fairytale. Her pursuit of rural life began at Stirling University, where she studied Medieval Literature. *Wild Folk* is her first book as a stained-glass illustrator.

ACKNOWLEDGEMENTS

With thanks to all those who had faith in the book when it was embryonic. And thanks to Unbound, especially John Mitchinson. To Chris and Davina and Jan of Seven Fables, and the wonderful Northmoor House, where *Wild Folk* was born. To Robin Stenham and Mike Abbott, both much loved. To Sam Lee for inspiring the singer, and to the ghost of Yeats, much thanks.

*Let wild gods rise
land
sea &
skies
through turning year
of swallow flight
& blossom bright
while trout swim
in waters clear
& lichens map
the ancient's tomb
lark flies
curlew cries
at moon's rise
& raven speaks
and spirits rest
while seals sing
for soul's ease
land
sea &
skies
let old gods rise.*

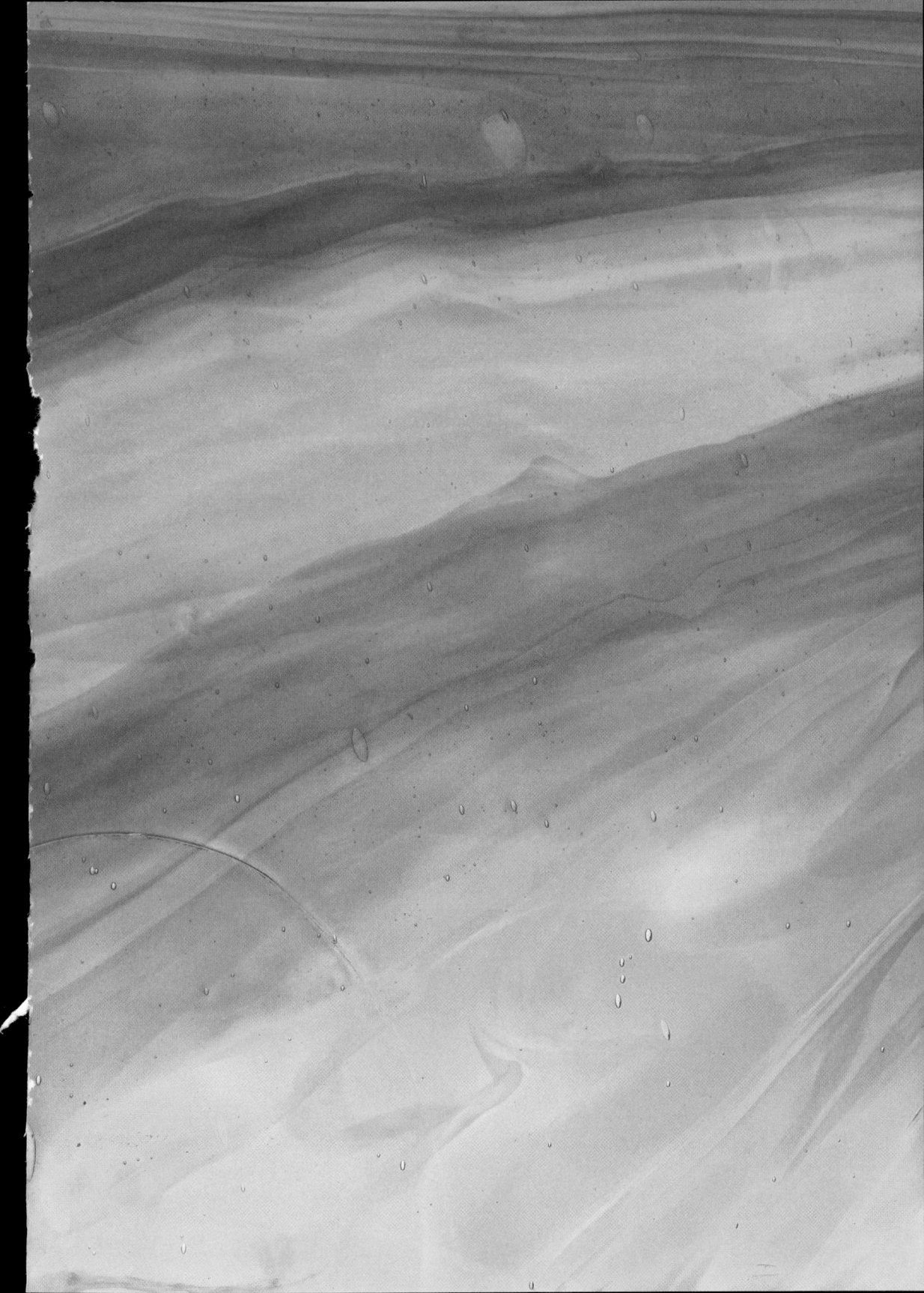

Wild Folk comprises seven richly illustrated fables of transformation and power, summoned from the ancient stones beneath our feet and hewn by word and image into portals between past and future. The tales are neither new nor old. They are full of 'wild folk', shapeshifting spirits that carry the energy that connects all things.

You will meet selkies and silver trout and the black fox, as big as a wolf and so fast and cunning she drives the lord of the manor to madness and oblivion; the woman of flowers who is happier living as an owl; the boy who learns to feel the songs and stories of trees through his skin; Wayland, the smith who can hammer metal to such airy thinness he makes his own wings; and the great white raven, a bird so rare it awakens the king who sleeps beneath the stones of the wild west cliffs of Wales.

This book brings together the words of Jackie Morris and the stained-glass paintings of Tamsin Abbott, but the stories come from both, a true collaboration born out of friendship and hope. These are tales to make you see, listen and most of all feel the wild magic that links stone, tree, fox and star.